To Sleep . . .
Perchance to Die

DONALD GRIPPO

PAGE TURNING BOOKS
an imprint of
Turn the Page Publishing LLC

Published by Page Turning Books

an imprint of

Turn the Page Publishing LLC
P. O. Box 3179
Upper Montclair, NJ 07043
www.turnthepagepublishing.com

ISBN-13: 978-1-938501-58-6

ISBN ebook-13: 978-1-938501-13-5

To Sleep ... Perchance to Die
Library of Congress Control Number 2012950541

PRINTED IN THE UNITED STATES OF AMERICA

Editor Ann Kolakowski
Cover and Interior Design by Robin McGeever, McB Design

ACKNOWLEDGEMENT

The transition from oral and maxillofacial surgeon to fiction writer was arduous and rewarding. My medical/technical background didn't provide the skill to write a novel. As with all professions, writing has to be learned.

Roseann Lentin and her team at Turn the Page Publishing provided invaluable assistance in the creation of *To Sleep … Perchance to Die*. They have lessened my weaknesses and increased my strengths. Their job is not finished.

Much of the credit for this novel goes to my greatest help in all things, Pauline. Her plot suggestions and countless hours of proofing make this book as much hers as mine.

DEDICATION

Connecticut: Unbounded beauty from sea to mountain.

Let me not to the marriage of true minds
Admit impediments...

———

*When in disgrace with fortune
and men's eyes,
I all alone beweep my outcast state . . .*

She's dead. Everything's changed. How could it have happened?

In a dark room, sunk in an overstuffed chair, the killer cried into his hands, silent sobs heard through intermittent squeaks of leather as his body jerked in rhythm with his sobs.

She's on a slab, cooling. I want to touch her and feel her warmth once more before it's lost forever.

He rubbed his face and smelled his hands. *Her scent.* Shaking his head, *they'll open her up and look for answers. Like peeling the lid from a can of sardines.*

He had turned off the lights and closed the blinds to isolate himself from the world. The room was as dark as his thoughts. Mechanical noise from the ventilation system remained, but it was white and helped him think. Leaning his head back, he stared into the darkness. "I've got questions too," he said to the empty room, his voice small.

My wife? My best friend? How can I tell them? He'll understand. She won't.

Another squeak of leather. *All I worked for. The life I earned and deserved. Lost.*

Looking to the ceiling, "I'm sorry. Forgive me for what I did." His words sent a shockwave that hit the walls and returned, a hurtling stone that took his breath. Trembling, he sank into the chair. His heart was being crushed.

Love's fire heats water,
water cools not love…

———

New York City: Three years earlier.

Summer, less than a week old, enveloped the Northeast in gentle heat. A cloud layer filtered the sun painting the sky rose-colored, like a canvas of one of the city's countless artists. Trees in the grass between street and sidewalk boasted new greenery. As he left the hospital, 28 year-old Dr. Bret Manley stood a moment enjoying the sun's rays on his face, and sighed. Too bad his jog through the park was going to be delayed on such a Goldilocks afternoon.

Jake Warden had called and asked to meet him at a local pub. Said he wanted to talk. No way could he skip it. Jake was about to become chief resident in the Department of Oral and Maxillofacial Surgery at Manhattan Memorial Hospital, and wanted a strategy meeting with his second-in-command.

Craving fresh air, Bret shunned his usual walk through the subbasement tunnel from the hospital to the upscale building across the street where he had an apartment on the sixth floor, two floors above Jake. The doorman, who was assisting a brunette with a knockout figure, saw him and waved. The air wasn't as clean as in his rural Connecticut hometown, but it was as good as you get in the city.

Waiting for the light, he yawned. The day started at three a.m. when he was called to the emergency department to see a drunk driver who had done a number on his face. He took the jerk to the O.R. and spent the morning and part of the afternoon fixing broken facial bones.

The light changed and Bret crossed. It was two blocks to the restaurant. In a way, he was glad of having the get-together. Jake had been moody. Seemed distracted. The meeting would give him an opportunity to discover what was bothering the man.

From a distance, he saw his friend waiting on the corner. Jake was a year older and at six-one, an inch taller than Bret. His swimmer's body and chiseled face made him an imposing figure. In addition, Jake was an exceptional surgeon with hands meant to hold a scalpel.

Bret had his fair share of admirers—women told him he was good looking in spite of his unruly hair and the slight irregularity of his nose. The latter was the result of a high school football injury. As with his prominent chin dimple, he thought it made him look rugged. Although solid, he was not in the same condition as Jake, who worked out several times a week in the hospital gym. Amazing, given the constraints of the residents' training program.

"Hey," he said when he reached Jake.

"Good timing," Jake said, pointing at his watch.

"Almost didn't make it. Been in the O.R. since early this morning."

"Oh? What was it?"

"Auto accident. A bag of broken bones, but the left eye was the challenge. Asshole was drunk. Police said it wasn't the first time he crashed his car after swimming in booze." Bret shook his head, "The muscles were entrapped, so I put in an implant." Balling his fists, "Damn, I hope they take his license away for a long time. Could have killed someone."

Jake shrugged his shoulders and turned to the pub's entrance. Opening the door, he asked, "Hey, did you see the news about your Uncle Hubie?" Hubie Santos was a famous litigator whose practice was in Hartford, Connecticut. "Seems he's got a high profile criminal case in Federal Court here."

"No, haven't heard, but he's in the news a lot. Argues most of his federal cases here. I don't get to see him much, but sometimes when he's in the city, he drops by. We do dinner or something."

Jake nodded, "Must be nice being related to a high-powered lawyer like Santos."

"Yeah, he's a great guy and was like a father to me when mine passed." Bret knocked his fist against the side of his head, "Hope I'll never need his services."

The Ale and Beef advertised itself as an authentic English pub, except it featured classic American food, French dishes, and about twenty micro-brewed regional beers. The lone English dish was fish and chips. A popular hangout for hospital personnel, they referred to it as the "A and B."

A mahogany bar with cushioned stools dominated the outer room. A bartender was busy drying glasses with a striped cloth towel. In a few hours he'd be facing a crowd of boisterous drinkers. For privacy, Bret and Jake walked past the bar and sat in the back at a table covered with brown paper.

A twenty-something blonde waitress approached. Bret did a double-take. *She could be Nicole Kidman's shorter sister.* Her name tag read "Liz." His gaze progressed from her tight fitting jeans to the clingy jersey that accentuated ample breasts.

"What can I get you boys?" A pleasant smile matched a pleasing voice.

Without looking at her, Jake said, "Double scotch, neat."

To Bret, "And you?"

"I'll have a Boston Homebrew, Liz," adding a few extra z's to her name in an attempt to appear cool. When she left to get their drinks, Bret looked at Jake, "Scotch? You're usually a beer or wine guy. And no vulgar comment about the waitress? Who, by the way, I'm thinking I need to know." Bret glanced toward the bar. Liz stood waiting for their drinks, and he admired the view.

Jake grunted.

Trance broken, Bret said, "Okay, what's going on? You haven't exactly been talkative lately."

Jake frowned. "We're always talking."

"I don't mean hospital stuff. I'm talking about you stuff. It's been a while since you've filled me in on Rachel and things going on at home."

Letting out a long breath with pursed lips, Jake said, "Okay, there is something … but let's take care of business first."

"If that's how you want it."

Jake glanced at a side wall, folded his hands on the table, and nodded.

Before he could speak, Bret said, "I know what you're worried about. Let me just say, you don't have to concern yourself about Tuttle. I'll keep the fire going under his butt." He was referring to Jim Tuttle, the current intern who was a year behind Bret. Tuttle was lazy and had to be monitored to ensure he did his job.

"You better. When Ed leaves next week, it'll be my chance to do the cases I've been waiting for, and I don't want anyone fucking it up." As an afterthought, Jake said, "I'll miss Ed. He's been a great chief resident. I hope I'm half as good."

Bret pointed a finger at Jake and said, "I told you. Don't worry about Tuttle." After a pause, he said, "Don't take this as ass kissing, but you're going make a terrific chief resident."

Jake smiled, "Sounds like ass kissing to me."

"Stick it. At least I got a smile out of you."

"Sorry for the attitude," Jake said. "Look, I appreciate how you've kept Tuttle under control, and I know you won't let him screw up." His hands drummed on the table, "God, I don't know what's going to happen to this program when he's chief resident."

Bret added, "Not to mention when you're out of here. I'll be the only one outranking him. Probably have to bypass him and work with the new intern who's arriving next week. A real crackerjack, by the way."

Jake stopped drumming and placed his elbows on the table and interlocked his fingers, "Yeah, I was impressed with Elaine when she interviewed."

"Likes to be called Lainey."

"Whatever. Hope she works out for you. We have to cover each other's backs like Navy Seals. When somebody doesn't do their job, makes it tough on the rest of us."

Thinking business was concluded and Jake satisfied with his promise to see things would run well, Bret saw an opening, "How are you and Rachel getting along?" Jake and his wife had a volatile relationship.

Jake shook his head. Bret sensed his friend was about to clam up.

Hospital gossip had it that Rachel agreed to a divorce. The couple's arguments were frequent and loud, and more than once neighbors called Bret and asked him to put a stop to the fighting. Most who knew Jake and Rachel were amazed they had remained together.

In truth, Bret was concerned about Jake's fiery and quick temper. He remembered the time he had to keep Jake from beating a homeless man. Not an easy feat for Bret. The man had been looking for a place to sleep on the sidewalk, and Jake didn't want him near his car. The look of fear on the homeless man's face as he fled for his life remained with Bret.

You're not going to give me the silent treatment this time. I'm going to fill you with drinks until you spill your guts.

As if beginning a serious conversation, Bret leaned across the table and said, "Word is the house specialty of escargot with garlic bread is responsible for half the heart attacks in the neighborhood."

Jake frowned and looked at Bret.

Hiding a smile, Bret continued, "Yeah, and you know what else? Their half-pound bacon-cheeseburgers with Cajun fries also claim a respectable number."

Jake leaned in, his shoulders a few inches from the table top, "What are you doing?"

Pretending to be surprised by the question, Bret said, "Trying to make conversation. Lighten things up a little."

Jake sat back. "Can't we just have a drink together?"

"Sure, but remember, you promised to talk about more than just what's happening at the hospital."

Liz brought their drinks. Jake took his from her hand and kicked it back in one gulp before she placed Bret's on the table. "Another double," he demanded.

Liz ignored him and turned to Bret. "Do you want something to eat?"

"I'll have a plain burger and Cajun fries," he answered.

To Jake, "And you?"

"Maybe later. Just bring another scotch for now."

Looks like he intends to get shit-faced. Good. After this beer, it's club soda for me. I'll tell him I've got emergency call. Pretty sure he doesn't know Tuttle is covering.

After Liz brought Jake's scotch, the men drank in a silence marred by inane comments from Bret.

"How about those Yamomami. You know, the primitive tribe in South America." Bret paused while Jake motioned to Liz for another. "They only have three numbers in their language, one, two, and more than two. Sure makes things easy. Would have come in handy in my calculus classes.'"

Jake raised an eyebrow but didn't smile. He poured the third scotch into his gullet while his drinking buddy nursed his beer. Bret was about to put a ketchup-laden fry in his mouth when Jake blurted, "Fu-uck!" It was loud enough to make Bret jump and to cause the couple several tables over to glare at them. The fry flew to the floor.

Leaning forward and with glistening eyes he looked at Bret. "I've fallen in love."

Bret understood in an instant why his friend had been acting weird. The outburst gave him the opening he was waiting for. He wiped his hands on a napkin and said, "So, tell me."

There was a silence during which Jake twirled his glass and looked down at the table. "We met on the Circle Line Ferry about six months ago. I've wanted to ride it since I came to New York and it was chilly and rainy so I figured there wouldn't be many people on it. I know it's touristy, but . . ."

Attempting to keep Jake focused, Bret said, "I've wanted to ride it myself. Go on." He took a big bite of his burger.

"She was leaning on the stern rail looking into the water. I saw her look left then right. There was no one near her. She leaned farther over, and it dawned on me. She was going to jump."

"No kidding. What happened?" Bret forgot about his food remembering when he pulled an old man out of the way of an oncoming truck.

"Well, I ran to her, of course. Got my arms around her and pulled her back. She fought, pounding her fists on my chest, but I held on. After a while she gave up and collapsed in my arms. I half-carried her to a bench, away from prying eyes." Jake's expression became vacant as if he was recreating the moment in his mind. "She had the most beautiful face I'd ever seen." He pointed and shook his index finger at Bret, "You know because of what we do that when I say that, I know what I'm talking about. The most beautiful face, exquisite bone structure, but a big bruise right here." Jake rubbed his fingertips on his cheek.

Bret waited for Jake to continue.

"I got her talking, and she began to cry, saying she wanted to drown herself because she couldn't deal with her abusive boyfriend anymore. She didn't know why he hit her. Said she did everything she could to please him, but it was never good enough. He criticized her all the time."

"What an asshole," Bret said, his cheeseburger growing cold.

"No shit. So this guy, that I didn't even know, began to really piss me off. I kept asking questions. She said she tried to end it three times, but he kept coming back saying he was sorry, he needed her, and would treat her right. She'd give in and take him back. It would be great for a while, then it would start all over again." Jake's voice cracked, "The bruise was the latest example. He has her so messed up, she figured killing herself was the only way out."

Jake picked up his scotch, but it had been drained. He raised his hand to Liz, and she started over, but he shook his head and waved a nevermind. Looking at Bret, "It took me a half hour to convince her there were other ways to solve her problem. I'd help her, I said. She stopped crying and started shivering. I wrapped my arms around her and placed her head on my chest. We remained that way for a long time. I told her the son of a bitch would never hit her again. I would see to that. She believes in Fate. Fate, she said, had sent me to her."

Jake picked up his empty glass and looked into it, but shook his head and put the glass down. "When the ferry docked, we went to a restaurant in Manhattan. She said her boyfriend's about to become a partner in an investment banking firm where she's an executive secretary. Because of office politics, he insisted they keep their relationship secret. At some point as she talked, I realized we were holding hands. Jeez, not only was she beautiful, but you could tell she was really smart."

Liz came to the table. "Something wrong with your burger?" she said. Bret looked down. He'd only taken a few bites.

"Uh, no . . . no. But thanks."

"Bring me another scotch," Jake said, sucking in his lips and glancing at Bret.

"No don't. He'll have one of these." Bret pointed to the burger.

Jake's eyes flashed a warning.

Liz left.

When she was out of earshot, Jake relaxed and said, "Thanks … I guess."

"No problem. Now, go on."

Jake complied. "Her friends at the office noticed the injuries and offered to help. They advised her to call the police." Jake's voice broke, "She wanted to confide in someone. To tell what she was going through, but didn't, afraid of worse beatings if she said anything. It wasn't fear of being killed. There were times she hoped he would kill her. It was the emotional pain she feared worse than the physical. Killing herself would stop it."

Bret took a bite of his hamburger. He understood Jake wanting to protect the woman.

Jake smiled, "All of a sudden she laughed and said she didn't want to talk about herself anymore and wanted to know about me. I told her I was married, but I'd help her. We walked to her apartment, and I went in. We settled on the couch and I held her in my arms until she fell asleep, then I covered her with a blanket and left. I was in love."

Bret finished the burger with a mouthful of beer and nodded.

"We've been seeing each other every chance we get. Three, maybe four, times a week.

Jake's burger arrived, and Liz put a Coke down with it. You'll need something to drink, so I took a chance with diet."

Jake's "Coke's fine" lacked sincerity.

"What's her name?"

Jake hesitated, seemed to think about the question. "I'm not ready to go there yet."

"Oh? Okay then, what are you going to do?"

"I don't know. Before, you asked about Rachel and me. Well, I told her I want a divorce."

Bret's eyebrows raised and chin dropped.

"Don't worry, she's fine with it. Saw the writing on the wall. Only thing is, she wants it to appear like her idea, especially to her la-di-da family. For reasons I don't want to get into, we're going to wait until I'm through." Even then, I'll still have problems."

"What kind?"

"Well, for one thing, the parents of the woman I've been telling you about hate Jews and would disown her if they found out she was seeing one. She's had to keep our relationship from them. It's one of the reasons I've been a bit down lately."

A bit?

"They were in business with a Jewish partner more than twenty some years ago. The business failed, and they blamed the partner." Jake grabbed his burger. "Same old story, blame the Jew for being underhanded."

"That's awful."

"What's awful? The business going under, Jews being blamed for it, or not letting her get involved with a Jew?"

"You know what I mean, wiseass. Not wanting her involved with a Jew." Bret was struck by the degree of clarity remaining in Jake's alcohol saturated brain.

"You're not kidding. Maybe they think if she gets involved with a Jew, poof, she'll turn into one." Becoming animated, "That's it! They're afraid she'll go poof." Shaking his head and in a somber voice Jake said, "You ever know me to be underhanded, Bret?"

"Not this week."

"I'm serious, man, you ever?"

"No. Never."

"See? If anyone would know, you would. You're my best friend."

Although he didn't show it, Bret was pleased at being called Jake's best friend. He was a good friend, sure, but best friend? That was a surprise. Bret always looked up to Jake. It called for a celebratory swallow of beer.

Jake took a bite of his burger and followed it with a slug of Coke. "Yeah, that's it. She might go poof and become a Jew," he burped and rubbed his stomach.

Looking through narrowed eyes at Bret, he said, "Hey, buddy, I think I'm drunk. I hope nothing complicated comes into the emergency department. Not that I'm on call or anything, but I won't be able to help. You're stuck with Tuttle." He laughed and took another bite of burger, wrinkled his nose, then covered his mouth with his napkin. "Not sitting right with the Scotch."

As Bret nursed his beer, Jake continued his story, "Not only her parents. My parents, too. Especially my mother." Imitating a Jewish accent, "Such grief she would give me if I came home with a shiksa." Dropping the accent, "She wouldn't disown me, but if you know Jewish mothers, you know the dozens of ways they can lay a guilt trip on you." Jake slapped his hand on the table, "Damn, where's Friar Laurence when you need him?"

"Friar Laurence? From Romeo and Juliet?"

"Never mind."

Jake pushed his plate aside and got up from the table. "Gotta go. Drank too much and talked too much."

Bret stood and put four twenties on the table. It would cover the food with a nice tip for Liz. Maybe she'd remember him.

"Let's get you home to bed. You'll feel better in the morning."

Jake burped before saying, "Too bad I can't sleep off my troubles." He swayed a little, faced Bret, and placed both hands on Bret's shoulders, "She's the best thing that ever happened to me, buddy. The really, really, really, best thing."

Bret hoped when the alcohol wore off, his macho friend wouldn't be embarrassed by his display of emotion. That is, if he remembered, which he doubted.

As they left, Liz raised an eyebrow. Bret looked at her and said, "Taking us home. Don't worry, we're walking. Money's on the table."

She tilted her chin toward Jake, "Okay, as long as he's not driving."

Bret smiled and gave her a two-fingered salute. *Another time, Liz.*

"I hear this is a terrific restaurant. Thanks for making time to visit with me," Bret said as he buttered his third roll. He and Hubie Santos were in *Peter's Off-Broadway* considered by many to serve the finest steaks and chops in the city.

"Don't mention it. I love to see you and catch up when I can," said Bret's uncle who sat across from him, shirt collar open and tie loosened. Hubie pointed to the roll, "Save room for the filet."

Stretching the waistband of his jeans with a thumb, Bret said, "Don't worry. At these prices, no way am I not finishing this meal."

"How are things going in the residents' program? Hard to believe you're just about halfway through. Only two more years left."

Bret answered, "Good, I guess, although I'm concerned about Jake Warden."

"The fellow ahead of you?"

"Yeah. He's got troubles at home and is about to add to them. It may sound selfish, but in our group, what affects one, affects all."

"It's the same as in my world," Hubie said. "What one lawyer in a firm does impacts all the lawyers in that firm." He made a circle motion with his index finger.

"Kind of like a family," Bret said.

"Yes, and if someone I worked with had problems similar to your friend, I'd give him or her all the help I could reasonably give. If they asked. Trying to do good when someone doesn't want you to can cause hard feelings, and, possibly, the loss of a friend."

Their food arrived and, not wanting to continue discussing

Jake, Bret changed the subject, "I'm going to buy a car."

"Oh?" Hubie said not looking up from peppering his food. He placed the shaker on the table and indicated to it with a hand gesture, "Don't use salt anymore, so I tend to overdo the pepper thing."

"You're a braver man than I am, Gunga Din," Bret quipped, his smile accentuating his chin dimple.

"What kind of car."

"A Firebird. It's seven-years-old and in pristine condition. Red with black trim. The owner pampered it."

"You've always liked muscle cars," Hubie said, "I remember the Camaro."

"She sure was a beauty." Bret took a bite of his steak, and after swallowing, asked, "So, what's happening back home in Connecticut?"

"Quite a lot," Hubie Santos said. "You won't believe how many new homes are going up in East Granby, and…"

And yet, by heaven,
I think my love as rare
As any she belied with false compare...

———

Lower Manhattan: Mai Faca's apartment. Lying nude on the sweat stained bed, Jake and Mai, the woman rescued on the ferry, enjoyed the sexual afterglow.

The venetian blind was raised to allow city light into the dark third-floor room. Street sounds penetrated the walls, and the rumble of the air conditioner, turned to its highest setting against the warm September evening, rattled the window.

Jake lifted himself on one elbow and stroked Mai's shoulder. "I love the feel of your skin. Wish I could be more poetic, but it's like silk. Smooth and soft."

Laughing, Mai said, "That's poetry. Keep going."

He rolled his eyes, "Give a girl a compliment, and she wants more. Well, let's see," his hand cupped his chin, "There's your aroma. It reminds me of gardenias. At first I thought it was perfume, maybe even soap, but it isn't. The scent is you . . . intoxicating."

Mai looked up into his eyes, "You're sweet."

"Well, it's the truth. And, that's not all." After giving Mai a gentle kiss on the lips, he said with an impish grin, "It's unbelievable how you do what you do so well,"

Unable to keep from smiling, Mai teased, "What are you talking about?"

"You know . . . sex. I've never been with anyone who was anywhere close to being in your league." A little laugh, "Not to mention being handcuffed to the headboard while someone had her way with me. Where'd you learn that?"

Propping herself to Jake's level, Mai blinked her pale blue eyes and shook soft curled brown hair from her face. She giggled, tilted her head, and said, "Well, sugar, I guess it comes, so to speak, naturally. Though any refinements I may have acquired along the way are none of your business." Tracing her finger along his jaw, she added, "Anyway, I'm glad you like it."

Jake smiled. "Well, keep it up, and you'll keep me up." He paused before mimicking, "So to speak."

Mai placed her head on the pillow and stared at the ceiling. After a while, she said, "I suspect my sexuality comes from my duel heritage. Both the Chinese and Portuguese are known for their sexual prowess, you know."

"I do now, and there's no doubt you're the best of both cultures in every way." Jake ran his finger down her slim body. "What do you think you inherited from your mother, and what came from your father?" Physically, Jake considered Mai the perfect melding of East and West. A razor-sharp mind and winning personality completed the package. He wasn't the first man or, in all probability, woman to think Mai was magnificent.

"I'd say my slender build and smile come from my mom, Jia. I don't know about my blue eyes, though. My guess is they're a genetic aberration. For sure, I get my height from my dad. He's over six feet with lots of muscles. Used to work on the docks before marrying mom and starting the water-taxi business. They're smart so I credit my intelligence to both." She qualified her words with, "Please don't think I'm bragging."

"What I think is you're absolutely unbelievable, and I'm lucky to have found you. You stir up something inside me. My inner animal." Without warning, he slammed the palm of his hand against the mattress. With steel in his words, he said, "I'll do anything to keep you."

Mai placed a reassuring hand on his shoulder. "You have me. I'm not going anywhere."

"Sometimes it's hard not to think of your old boyfriend." After a silence, he lightened the mood by saying, "Getting back to what we were talking about, I'm also glad you have Portuguese breasts."

Mai feigned disgust, "I should have guessed. You're a pig like most men."

Jake was quick to defend, "No, I mean it. Anyone can tell you have great genes. As my favorite aunt would say, 'God was having a good day when he made you.'"

Mai nudged him and teased, "I should tell my parents what you and your aunt said."

"You wouldn't?"

"No, silly. But I wish I could and have them love you like I do."

Jake kissed her neck and shoulders

Turning serious, Mai said, "Now that your wife has agreed to a divorce, is she going to leave soon?"

Jake shook his head, "Nah. Says she wants to stick around until May or June when I'm nearing the end of my training. That way she can finish her program at NYU. She'll tell everyone she left me because she didn't want to follow me to some hick town with no plum jobs in hotel management. In the meantime, everything has to appear normal." Shaking his head again, "As if what we have could ever have been called normal. In the meantime you and I have to be careful because if she finds out about us, she'll make a scene they'll hear in Nebraska."

Understanding the predicament, Mai nodded.

"Today she thinks I'm at a pathology conference at St. Luke's."

"She won't find out. If she does, we'll handle it together." Mai got off the bed and walked to the bathroom. Jake watched every graceful step of her taut body. Leaving the door open, she sat on the toilet. He heard her peeing and shook his head in mock disbelief.

Jake was dressing when Mai came out of the bathroom, wrapped her arms around his neck, and kissed him. "What did I do to deserve that?"

She smiled. "Since we were speaking of ancestry, I'm willing to testify that your Jewish heritage makes you a wonderful lover. You know how to create a symphony with that instrument of yours and get my strings vibrating with more intensity than a Jew's harp."

Jake expanded his chest and pounded it gorilla style, "I'm pleased to have pleased you." He buttoned his shirt. "Speaking of Jews, any chance your parent's feeling about them could change?"

"You could train a shark to stand on its tail easier then you could get my parents to change their minds once they're made up. Especially when it involves hating. They love to hate. I'm hoping we'll find some way to be together without them finding out and doing something like disowning me. Disowning is very Chinese, you know."

"Do you think they would? Would you be devastated?"

"Yes, and yes, to both questions. My mother would be honor bound to do so. As would my father, although his heart wouldn't be in it. I was brought up in the tradition of reverence for the family. Their rejection would tear me apart." Her eyes glistened, "It's . . . it's difficult for outsiders . . . don't take offense . . . to comprehend, but I could never be happy if they exiled me from the family."

Mai went to the bed and sat cross-legged on the edge, her expression solemn. Jake stopped dressing. She began, "I have two uncles who immigrated with us and live in Manhattan. They are members of the Shadow Dragons, a Chinese-American gang with connections to Hong Kong. They are the protectors of our family honor and take that responsibility seriously. If they find out I have dishonored my parents by consorting with a Jew, they would kill you and me for causing shame to fall upon the family."

Jake paled.

Mai warned, "You must believe me when I say they're dangerous, and so are my parents. I'm going to tell you something I've never told anyone. Something I feel you must know." She stopped to collect herself.

Jake started toward her. She waved him off and averted her head. "It happened when I was a little girl in Macao. I was four, maybe, five. We lived on our boat. One day Mom told me to go play on the dock. She didn't know it, but I didn't go outside and decided to stay in my room on the lower level."

Mai hesitated as if unable to go on. Jake waited, not sure what to do. She continued, "There was hollering and fighting on deck.

Frightened, I closed my door but peeked through the louvers. After a while my uncles dragged a man down there and hacked him to death with large knives. There was blood. It was awful. When they were through, one of my uncles whistled, and my father came running down. He lifted and carried the body to the deck. I heard the splash as my father threw the man overboard."

She looked at Jake with tearful eyes and said, "Floating bodies are not uncommon in Macao." The water in her eyes spilled onto her cheeks, "My mother cleaned up the mess."

Mai shivered and pulled the bedspread around her shoulders. "Throughout the ordeal I was too afraid to move and, later, too afraid to say anything. The memory lives in here," she held a fist to her heart. "It was the first time I realized members of my family could be monsters."

"Unbelievable," Jake said.

"You know what the worse thing was?"

"The whole story is the worst thing."

"As they were going upstairs, one of my uncles stopped and looked toward my room." She placed her face in her hands, "He saw me. His eyes met mine and he smiled. It was his way of warning me to keep my mouth shut." She paused, dropping her hands to her side and staring at the floor. "What if I inherited their personality traits, like I inherited my breasts, or hair, or any other part of me?"

"My God," Jake knelt on the floor in front of her. "Mai," he grabbed her arms and gave a quick shake. "Mai," he waited until her eyes met his. "No one is born with badness. You learn to do what they did."

Mai continued as if Jake hadn't spoken, "I didn't realize it until recently, but it was the Jew they murdered. The one I told you about. The one they think screwed them in their business. If you cross them, they kill you." She looked at Jake, "So you see, it's important they don't find out about us."

Jake sat next to her and shook his head saying, "You've seen some scary things in your life."

"Very scary, life and death scary," Mai replied.

Sitting side by side with their bodies touching, neither spoke.

After a while, Jake, in an animated voice, said, "What if we told your mom and dad I'm a Christian, or an Atheist, or something?" He smiled and looked into Mai's eyes.

"They'd find out. Sooner or later they'd learn the truth." Shaking her head, "And the fact that we lied would make their anger greater."

Jake nodded his disappointment and turned away. Both contemplated their unhappy situation until he broke the silence. "To tell the truth, I also have a family problem, although not as serious as yours." He swallowed before saying, "It's with my mother. She would do all she can to keep me from dating someone who's not Jewish. As for marrying a non-Jew, inconceivable. My father, like yours, would feel obligated to stand by her although I don't think his heart would be in it."

Mai put her arms around Jake's neck and looked into his eyes. "I don't know how, but we will find a way to be together. We may have to hide what we're doing for a while, but we will find a way." She slammed her open hand on the bed, "With all my heart I believe that."

"You're all I want," Jake said. He began to kiss her face and neck and breasts.

Mai unbuttoned his shirt as Jake's hands probed her body. For the moment, their problems were forgotten.

Jake was in his apartment sitting in a corduroy chair with shiny wear areas on the seat and arms. Eyes closed, he thought of when Rachel and he met. He had been attracted to the vamp in her. She had long black hair, wore loads of blue eye-shadow, and dressed in skin tight clothes. To Jake, she was the epitome of sexy. To his mother, she was Jewish.

Marriage was a mistake. The arguing began on the honeymoon and never stopped. They had abandoned lovemaking. Jake's sex life consisted of trysts with nurses, of which there were many anxious to offer themselves to a handsome young oral surgeon with marital problems. As for Rachel's sex life, he didn't know or care what she did.

Mai was that special person he had been looking for all his life. His One in a Million, Love at First Sight, Meant to Be woman. All clichés, all true. He leaned toward a cabinet and turned on the CD and put on headphones. Elvis Presley sang his upbeat Las Vegas version of *Can't Help Falling in Love*. The CD player was loaded with love songs, and an open can of Foster's rested on the coffee table. Until the music completed its cycle, he'd be listening and thinking of Mai.

Rachel stormed into the room and slammed a magazine on the table. Jake's head jerked and his body shot forward. Ripping off the earphones, he hissed, "Goddam."

With a smirk, she said, "Good, I have your attention." Jake fought to control himself. She continued, "You're going to have to do more to get the divorce you want."

This won't be good. "What are you talking about?"

"I increased the lump sum payment I want to five hundred thousand dollars." She eyeballed him and crossed her arms. "No arguing about it. I'm going to buy a condo outside of Boston. It's where I'm going when I'm finished here."

Although he had a source that Rachel didn't know of, he said, "Where the fuck am I going to come up with that kind of money?"

"Borrow it or steal it. I don't care how, just get it."

"What if I can't?"

Grinning, she said, "I'd get at least that much if we dragged this thing out in court. Remember, you're a doctor and going to be rich. My paycheck helped support us, and I deserve a return on my investment. That's what my lawyer says."

Jake stared in disbelief. The small amount Rachel made from her part-time job went to pay for her clothes, gym membership, and yoga classes. With the no-sex thing from early on, luckily they had no kids.

"If you don't give me what I want, I'll fight the divorce. That'll hinder your relationship with whoever it is you're seeing." She scowled, "Don't deny it. I know there's someone. I'm not stupid."

"I won't deny it."

"Bastard," she said, stamping a slippered foot, "I knew it." Saliva flew from her mouth. "What does she do for you? Kinky sex? The blow-jobs I won't give you?" Rachel made a face as if she had sucked on a lemon, "You'd like that."

"She makes me happy."

Rachel grabbed the magazine on the coffee table, threw it against the wall, and stormed toward the bedroom. Before reaching it she stopped and turned, "You're a no-good bastard, and you're sleeping on the couch from now on. Let's stop the charade. I don't want you near me." She entered the bedroom and slammed the door. A photo hanging on the wall fell, breaking the glass.

Jake ignored it. He extended his legs, clasped his hands behind his head, and thought about his friend, Carlton. It was a wise decision on his part not to tell Rachel the complete truth about him. All she knew was that Carlton was his wealthy college roommate, and they took yearly guy trips. She didn't know the extent of Carlton's wealth and that he owed Jake big. He'd be good for the money.

Jake was on the sofa in Mai's living room finishing his fourth beer and telling of Rachel's demand. Empties sat on a side table. Mai was at his side nursing a cup of tea.

"Her lawyer is drawing up the divorce papers. She promises to sign them when I turn over the money. Still insists on staying around until the end of my training, and I can't dispute her story of leaving me. Everyone has to think I'm an insensitive son of a bitch who wants to stifle her career tract by setting up a practice miles away from where she wants to work."

Mai asked, "Did she really say that she deserves the money because you're going to be rich someday?"

Jake nodded, "She did."

"Are you going to be rich?"

He nodded again, "Most likely. Doctors generally make good money."

She hid a smile and asked, "Where will you get five hundred thousand dollars? From a bank?"

"No. From my college roommate at Lehigh. Name is Carlton Benton, the Fourth. A real blueblood and filthy fucking rich. I did him a big favor once. Said he'd pay me back. Always saying it. Wants to clear his conscience, I guess."

"Try not to curse so much, darling. It's unbecoming. You're an educated man and know better. At least you should." Her squeeze of his arm said she loved him in spite of his rough language.

Jake's tone softened, "Sorry, I'll try to watch it."

Mai sipped her tea. "Do you think this Carlton person would be willing to give you half a million dollars?"

Jake said, "I'm sure he'll lend me the money. It's pocket change to him. He has millions if not billions. Since Rachel wants to delay the separation, I can wait until I see him in person. In January we're going ice fishing in Maine, and I'll ask him then."

"Can you two live in the same apartment for another eight or nine months?

"The fucking bitch . . . oops, sorry. Yeah, I can. She'll try to make my life miserable, it's just her nature, but we were married during my first year here, and it's been bad since the get-go. I've suffered for more than three years. Another few months won't kill me."

Mai extended her hand.

Jake held it as he said, "To paraphrase you a few days ago, nothing will come between us. Not Rachel, not your parents or uncles, not my parents. I promise you."

Jake let go of her hand and got up to take his empties to the trash. "Don't," she said, "We can clean up later. There are some things I want to talk about."

Jake sat.

"I've been thinking about our problem and have come up with a solution. I'm warning you, it requires great sacrifice from both of us, and we need the friend you're always talking about. Bret Manley."

Jake was against involving Bret in his personal affairs.

As Mai revealed her plan, his incredulity grew with each sentence. When finished, she said, "What do you think?"

After a period of silence, Jake said, "Are you fucking crazy? I don't know how you can ask me to do that. No man would do it. And what about Bret?" He didn't apologize for the profanity and Mai ignored it.

"Don't think about him. He's not important. What's best for us is what counts." Mai persisted, "Besides, it'll only be temporary until we come up with a permanent solution."

Jake straightened, sucked in a long breath and exhaled before he said, "I don't know. I can't even think about it at the moment."

Mai shook her head, "I wish we could simply go to some far off place where no one would find us, and we could live happily ever after. But we can't. My upbringing and my family prevent it." Placing a positive spin on her proposal, "What I'm suggesting allows us to be together. Out from under our parent's yokes and, more important, away from the scrutiny of my hoodlum uncles."

Jake looked into Mai's eyes. Shoulders slumping and voice solemn, he said, "You're not kidding, are you? You're willing to do this?"

Mai pulled him into her arms. "It's as big a sacrifice for me as for you."

He shut his eyes to block tears, and said, "I love you more than life."

Neither spoke as they held each other.

After a while, Jake said, "When you began, you said there were things you wanted to talk about. What else do you have?"

Mai shook her head and looked at the floor. "I don't remember. It must not have been important."

Jake put a finger under her chin and lifted. "Sure it is. After what you've told me, I'm prepared for anything."

"Promise you won't get upset."

His jaws clenched, "I promise."

Hesitating a long moment "Larry came over . . . my old boyfriend," she said and paused as if waiting for Jake to say or do something. He didn't move, though she saw his clenched jaws. Mai continued, "He pounded on the door and insisted I let him in. When I wouldn't open it, he threatened to break it down. Sound reverberates in the corridor, and the neighbor across the hall heard the commotion. He asked what the ruckus was. It quieted Larry in a heartbeat. He won't risk a public disturbance. Too much danger of word about us getting back to the office."

Jake felt heat radiating from his body. "Did he leave after that?"

"Not right away. He said he wanted me back and was going to do everything in his power to convince me he was a changed man. Promised he'd never hit me again and was sorr . . . "

"What'd you say? Jake demanded.

"I told him we were through. That there was someone else. My neighbor had closed his door, but I guess Larry still wouldn't risk a scene. He said he'd be there for me when I came to my senses, and left. I could tell he was seething. He's an angry man."

Rage rolled into Jake's chest, and his lips were a thin line. *He was an angry man.*

Mai put a hand on his arm. "I shouldn't have told you," she said. "Listen. Please. I'm not going to give him an excuse to come back into my life. Sooner or later he'll realize we're over, though sometimes, the thought of him scares me." She shook her head in frustration and said, "It's not right to say it, but I wish he were dead. Hit by a car or something. Then, he'd be out of our lives for good." Mai's look fixed on Jake's eyes.

Jake had gained control. "For the time being we'll forget about him, but if he comes back . . . "

Mai put a quick finger to his lips. "Shhh, he won't. He proved he was a coward when he hit and bullied me. Now that he knows you're in my life, he'll be afraid to come back."

A northeasterly wind blew leaves and chilled the air. Late Columbus Day revelers wandered the streets in all states of inebriation. Their shouts and singing mixed with the ever present noise of New York traffic.

With the collar of his windbreaker covering his face, Jake Warden hid among the shadows of an alley. He was surveilling a brownstone across the street. To pass time, he rehashed Mai's solution to their problem. It was what he had been doing since she proposed it, shocking him, and challenging every natural male impulse he had.

A loud muffler returned him to the task at hand. Larry Reid lived on the first floor of the building. It was a block from the Hudson River, and river odor permeated the atmosphere. Mai had given him Larry's address and photo when she told him about the beatings and humiliation she'd suffered. He figured knowing where the son of a bitch lived and what he looked like might come in handy one day. That day came when Larry went to Mai's apartment and banged on her door.

At nine-twenty, using a prepaid phone, he called Larry. When he answered, music, laughter, and boisterous conversation in the background told Jake the man was celebrating in a pub. Jake had said, "Sorry, wrong number," and hung up. He broke the phone and tossed it in a storm drain.

He was waiting for Mai's ex-boyfriend to return home from whatever merrymaking he'd been involved in. Mai had told him Larry liked to drink, but not to excess. Jake hoped he'd be lucid when confronted. He intended to convince Larry to stop harassing Mai. Larry was intelligent, and if Jake was clear, a verbal warning would make him see the light. He hoped to avoid a fight, but if one was required, that was okay with him. Jake fingered a switchblade in his jacket pocket. There were other ways to get him to stop, if reason or a scuffle failed. One thing was certain, after this night Larry would be out of her life.

To loosen the kinks in his back and shoulders, Jake shifted position and checked his watch for the umpteenth time. When he resumed his vigil of the building, he saw a man approaching on the opposite sidewalk. Dressed in slacks and a sports jacket, he wore a scarf wrapped in preppy fashion around his neck. An unsteady gait caused him to lean on a lamppost for support. When the man reached the stairs of the brownstone, he stopped and moved his head in several directions like a buoy bobbing in the ocean.

"He's had more than usual," Jake mumbled as he stepped from the shadows and walked toward the curb. Photo in hand, he confirmed Larry Reid was across the street.

Larry walked to the brownstone's steps and began to ascend them. Stout wrought iron railings were anchored in low stone walls on each side. He held the railing on the right with both hands as he climbed.

Jake crossed the street on sneakered feet and reached him on the landing. Larry fumbled for the key to the outer door, and Jake stayed back as if he were another tenant waiting to enter. Larry looked at Jake, a question on his face.

"Nice night, huh?" Jake said, smiling.

"Sure ish."

The reek of alcohol hit Jake.

Larry turned and opened the door and loosened his scarf as he entered. Jake followed and went to the bank of mailboxes on the far side of the main foyer. They were alone. Larry went to his apartment and placed his head close to his key as he inserted it into the lock. The door opened.

Forgetting diplomacy, Jake rushed Larry and pushed the thickly-built but shorter man into the flat causing him to sprawl on the Persian rug in the hall behind the door. The scarf flew from his neck as if thrown. Jake stepped back to see if anyone was in the building's foyer and looked to the outside entrance. No one. He slipped into the apartment, closed the heavy wooden door with a kick, and flicked a light switch.

On his hands and knees and straining to look over his shoulder, Larry blinked and shook his head, "What the . . . ?"

In a low, angry voice, Jake said, "Get up,"

"Okay, okay, motherfucker. My wallet's in my pocket. Take it and get out." Larry stood on wobbly legs facing Jake.

"Not why I'm here, asshole."

Larry's eyebrows raised. "Whatdaya want?"

"We're going to talk."

"Talk?" Larry's arms motioned left and right, "You come in here pushin' and shovin' and you just want to talk?"

"Yes. About a woman you're never going to see again."

Larry's eyes widened then sharpened. "You're the one," he said. "I'm gonna kill you." Spittle flying from his mouth, Larry took a wild roundhouse swing that Jake side-stepped causing him to miss by a foot. Unable to stop his momentum, Larry spun around and fell to the floor. For the second time in a minute, he was on his hands and knees. He began to fast-crawl from the anteroom, mumbling, "My gun, got to get the gun. Kill him."

Adrenaline burst inside Jake, and he sprang and slammed Larry onto his back. He took the switchblade from his jacket. Straddling Larry with his knees, Jake pressed his left hand on Larry's mouth, while his right laid the knife's blade against his neck. Face contorted in rage, he growled, "Forget about your gun. Just shut your fuckin' mouth and listen."

There was fear in Larry's eyes.

Jake's anger rose to a fury that threatened his breathing and his reason. In order not to hyperventilate, he forced himself to hold his breath.

Larry moaned and lost control of his bladder, soiling himself and Jake's pant leg. His tears flowed onto the Persian rug.

Jake's exhale came out ragged, and he leaned to within six inches of Larry's face. "You ever contact Mai Faca, I'll kill you. You got that?"

In spite of the pressure from the hand over his mouth, Larry nodded. His breathing was labored and his eyes bulged.

A picture of Mai under this man, at the mercy of his abusive ministrations, brought an uncontrollable rage from the pit of Jake's stomach to his strong arms and hands. He wanted to tear Larry apart. Jake plunged the knife into Larry's neck slashing to the ear. Blood gushed as if from a fire hose. Larry went into a spasm that ended with his open, unblinking eyes fixed upon Jake.

As if in a dream, Jake removed the knife from the neck and stared at the crimson blade. A lifetime passed before he blinked. Drenched in blood, he ran a forearm across the wet on his face, and stained his sleeve red. With both arms he pushed off Larry's body and stood keeping his feet in place. It occurred to him to check for a pulse, so he leaned and pressed a finger on the neck. A glop of dark blood oozed from the wound.

Grabbing the dead man's collar and shaking it, he said, "Shit. I didn't mean . . ." but couldn't finish.

What do I do? Call the police, say it was an accident. No. No one would believe me.

Mai's words came to him. She had wished Larry dead. Had it been his intention from the beginning to follow her command?

He forced the thought from his mind and panic rushed to fill the void. Instinct urged he bolt for the door. *Think before you run . . . think.* He considered his predicament and formed a plan. Lifting his right foot, the puddle of blood covering the sneaker made a sucking sound. Bringing his right leg over the body, he put it behind his left leg. Bending without moving his feet, he searched the body and found a Rolex, phone, wallet, and keys. Jake put them in his jacket pocket. He took off his left sneaker, leaving it in place, and stepped onto a clean area of the carpet. He did the same with the right. Both stockings were free of blood.

Got to wash. He picked up his sneakers and went into the kitchen where he removed his bloody clothes at the sink. He ran the sneakers, clothes, knife, and the things he took from Larry under cold water. A crimson swirl flowed into the drain. When traces of red were gone, he dried everything with paper towels and left them on the counter.

Jake needed to cover his hands. He looked under the sink and found plastic garbage bags. *They'll work.*

After covering his hands and feet, he went into the bedroom and searched the closet. The pants were short and big at the waist, but wearing them low on the hip with a belt solved the problem. A shirt fit although his wrists protruded beyond the sleeves. Keeping his hands in his pockets would take care of the same problem with the trench coat he confiscated. No one would notice, assuming anyone he met was sober.

Returning to the kitchen, he put on his sneakers before stuffing his wet clothes in a plastic bag. Although the sink looked clean, he let the water run for a few minutes before towel drying the basin. After wiping down the light switches, the used paper towels were placed in another plastic bag. The bags were flattened and hidden under the trench coat. The knife and effects taken from Larry went in the left coat pocket, and his own wallet and keys went into the right. He saw no one when he exited the building.

Public transportation was risky so Jake decided to walk the four or five miles to his apartment. He threw the wallet and its contents into several garbage cans. The rest went into a dumpster. He was tempted to keep the Rolex, realized it would be unwise, and chucked it with the other items.

Two and a half hours later Jake stood before the open incinerator chute in his apartment building. He pushed the plastic bags and his sneakers into it. After changing into fresh clothes, he did the same with what he had been wearing. They went down in plastic grocery bags Rachel had saved. *Good thing she sleeps with the door closed.*

Jake was satisfied no evidence of his involvement in Larry's death would be found. He felt euphoria that might be termed a murderer's high. He had done what needed to be done. What in her heart Mai wanted him to do.

In the living room, Jake danced a quick jig. He went to the window and opened it, wanting to shout to the world that Mai was his. He didn't. Rachel might hear and come to see what the commotion was.

The guiltless elation had evaporated by the time Jake arrived for surgical rounds the following morning. Sweat covered his forehead and his hands were shaking.

"You okay?" Bret asked.

"No big deal. Haven't been feeling a hundred percent last day or so."

Lainey and Tuttle became interested in their smart phones.

Bret said, "I tried to get you last night. Kept going to voice mail. I thought about stopping by, but Rachel . . . well, you know how it is with her and me."

Jake's reply was curt. "Turned the phone off. Wanted to sleep." After a moment he added, "What did you want me for, anyway?"

"Fellow jumped from three stories. Too much Columbus Day celebrating. Friends said he told them he could fly. Seems he couldn't. Lainey pitched in with the repairs."

Tuttle turned his back to the group.

"Didn't need you after all. Hope you're feeling better." Bret said. There was a hint of sarcasm.

It was a violation of On-Call protocol not to be available when summoned. Jake had risked he wouldn't be needed since he was on second call, and Bret was on first. It was rare for Bret to require help. He asked, "How'd it go?"

"There were four of us working on him, orthopod, general surgeon, Lainey, and me. Died on the table."

Lainey nodded.

Jake apologized, "Sorry. Won't let it happen again."

"You were sick," Bret said with false sympathy, "Couldn't be helped. Just sorry I wasted my time trying to get hold of you."

The tone angered Jake. "Like I said, won't happen again."

Bret assumed Jake's not being available had something to do with the new woman in his life.

That afternoon Jake waited in Mai's apartment for her to return from her new job as executive secretary at a Lower Manhattan law firm. It was critical to tell her what he did before she learned of it from the media. In a few days, the principals at Larry Reid's investment firm would wonder why he wasn't showing up for work and attempt to contact him. When that failed, the police would be sent to his brownstone. If not, odor emanating from his apartment would alert neighbors something bad had happened. The media would spread the news. Although informing Mai of

Larry's murder carried risk, he had no choice and was counting on her to protect him. He gambled she would not call the authorities.

When Mai opened the door and saw Jake on the couch, she said, "Hi, angel. Didn't expect you. Have you eaten?"

"No, but that's not why I came." Patting the couch, "Come. Sit."

Jake's somber expression caused Mai to hesitate before approaching. Her eyes fixed on his face as she lowered herself to the couch.

"Tell me," she said.

He put an arm around her shoulder and turned to her. Heart beating fast, he thought it best to get to the point. "I killed him."

"Killed? ... What? Who?"

"Larry Reid."

Mai's hands flew to her face covering her eyes.

Jake noticed that as she raised her hands, the corners of her mouth betrayed a fleeting smile.

"Why?" she asked.

Jake wanted to say, "Because you wanted me to." Instead, in a stern but calm voice, he said, "Let me tell you what happened."

Mai left the couch and began to pace.

Jake knew she had to digest what he told her. Hell, he was still trying to digest it.

After taking a deep breath, Mai returned to his side, composed and prepared to listen to what he had to say.

Minimizing gore and exaggerating Larry's anger, he related the details of her ex-lover's death. His hope was Mai would conclude he had killed in self-defense, a misconception he cultivated.

Her emotions were under control as she responded, "Sounds like you did all you could to reason with him. I'm surprised he tried to strike you. Other than hitting me, he avoided physical confrontations. I remember some guy cut in front of us when we were on-line for a movie. Larry asked him to go to the back. The guy said he wouldn't and wanted to know if Larry was going to make something of it. Larry took my arm and we walked away. He never gave the impression of being the macho type who would get into a fight. Especially, with a man like you."

Mai sat tall, "From what you told me, he deserved what he got." She looked into Jake's eyes, "I have to admit in some small way, I'm happy. Now he's out of my life . . . our lives . . . for good."

Jake exhaled a breath of relief. By siding with him, Mai made herself an accomplice to the murder. He hoped she wouldn't change her mind. At that moment he decided to agree to the scheme she had proposed. He didn't want to, but it would keep her on his side.

"The investigation will be unbelievable. Is there any way they can connect you to him?" he asked.

"No, I don't think so. He was adamant to the point of obsession that we be secretive. No one in the office knew about us. It would have ruined his career, and his career was the most important thing in his life."

"Well, that's good," Jake replied. "The commotion surrounding his death will eventually blow over. It looks like we've gotten rid of what I thought of as our minor problem." He paused before saying, "If you're up to it, we can get to work on the major one. The one we talked about?"

"I'm ready if you are." Mai leaned into Jake and put her arms around his neck. Soft breasts pressed against him. "There's something smoldering inside you. It's a turn-on. Even more than your good looks. With you, I sense danger and feel alive." She let go one arm from his neck and slid her hand low. She felt his response. "Care to get started on something else first?"

When to the sessions of sweet silent thought
I summon up remembrance
of things past ...

—————

Lower Manhattan: Mai sat on a park bench a block from her apartment. She was thinking about her encounter with a police detective who had called and asked if he could discuss the murder of Larry Reid. He said he was interviewing everyone who worked at Larry's firm, including ex-employees. She agreed to be interviewed, as it was best to appear helpful.

Detective Abdow was older than his phone voice, and his shaved head didn't hide the stubble of male pattern baldness. Purplish cheeks and a large nose cluttered with veins betrayed a fondness for a nip.

While she poured coffee, he said as if making conversation, "The murder appears to be the consequence of a robbery." He took a sip, "Good coffee."

Mai noted his scrutiny of her apartment. Nothing remained to connect her to Larry.

"Probably committed by someone who followed Mr. Reid home," the detective offered. "Judging by the injuries, we've determined the assailant was larger and stronger than Mr. Reid." Giving Mai a close look followed by a smile, "Much bigger than you, I'd say."

He took another sip of coffee, "A neighbor across the street may have noticed a suspicious character in the area at about the time of the crime, but can't be sure it wasn't her imagination." He shook his head in disappointment, "In any event, she couldn't give an accurate description of what or who she saw. It's hard to distinguish things on the streets if a light or two isn't working."

From his pocket, the detective removed a crumpled envelope with a list of questions written on it and began his interrogation. Mai was sure Abdow's unsophisticated manner was a purposeful deception.

Jake had prepared her for the expected questions. Answers such as, "Yes, I knew who Mr. Reid was when I worked at his firm, but I've had no contact with or knowledge of him since leaving the organization," were given in an honest and forthright manner. The absolute secrecy of their relationship that Larry insisted upon meant no one at the office was aware they were dating. Fellow employees knew she was in an abusive relationship, but would not have suspected the office poster boy.

When the interview concluded, Detective Abdow handed her his card, "Call me if you remember anything. Even if you think it's unimportant."

"I will," she said with what appeared the utmost sincerity.

"Thanks for your help." He brought his coffee cup to the sink and placed it in the basin.

Mai followed, "I hope I was of service, but I can't imagine my answers have been terribly helpful."

He faced her, "You never know. Something that seems trivial may turn out to be important when all the evidence is put together." He lowered his voice and spoke as if she were a colleague, "Between you and me, we'll be lucky to solve this one."

When she closed the door, she breathed a sigh of relief and shook off the nerves she had kept hidden. The process wasn't as difficult as anticipated, and she doubted the detective would return. Grabbing her coat, Mai decided on a walk to the park to get some fresh air to clear her head.

A light breeze crisped the sunny autumn day. She pulled her collar around her ears then stuffed her hands in the pockets. The park was full of children with their mothers or their nannies. Happy voices contrasted with the impatient honking of vehicles.

Mai smiled as she recalled the childhood joy of playing in a park. She had played in them in Macao and the U.S. It had been sixteen years since she, her parents, and two uncles emigrated from Macao via San Francisco to Staten Island. Although six-years-old at the time she left, she retained memories of life in her native land.

Mai had been told that Lam Jia, her mom, was considered rebellious for wanting to marry Pablo Faca, who was Portuguese and a foreigner by Chinese standards. Jia's parents, with the approval of her two older brothers, threatened to banish her from the family if she married outside her culture. Although the familial discord carved deep scars in her psyche, Jia stood her ground and married Pablo. The Lam patriarchs didn't ostracize her, but it was years before they gave their reluctant approval of the union between their stubborn daughter and the outsider.

Pablo and his pregnant wife started a water taxi business ferrying passengers from Macao to Hong Kong. It was a mom-and-pop affair that struggled to stay competitive with the large ferry companies. They managed by offering cheap fares and surviving on small margins.

On the day of Mai's birth, her parents had returned with a fare from Hong Kong when Jia's water broke. To people of meager means, summoning a doctor for anything but critical medical conditions was unthinkable. Boat women delivered each other's babies, and they brought her into the world. Because of the circumstances of her birth and the significance of the South China Sea to the young family's existence, she was given the name Mai, meaning Ocean. In spite of the uproar her parent's marriage had caused, Mai was welcomed into the Lam fold and raised to respect Chinese cultural customs and principles.

After Jake became her lover, she visited her parents to tell them about her new beau. The three were drinking tea in the main room of their Staten Island apartment. As she was speaking, her mother's face displayed uncharacteristic anger. Jia looked at Pablo, who nodded.

"There is something we have to tell you," Jia said. "It is time for you to learn the full story of our taxi business."

In some way it involved her relationship with Jake, and Mai began to fidget.

Jia slipped into her native dialect. She spoke excellent English, but her habit was to revert to Chinese when discussing important matters. "As you remember, we had one boat. It had many hours on its engine and was owned by our so-called partner, an old Jew." Jia spit into the glass she was holding. "I get angry thinking of him," she said as an apology for her uncouth act.

Jia's words poured from her mouth, "We've never told you about the man. He demanded fifty percent of our income for the use of his boat. For that, he promised to maintain it. He did nothing." Jia's voice cracked, "Your father did the maintenance that kept the boat afloat. For five years we worked seven days a week to build a business that could support us." Hatred filled Jia's eyes. "Then, without warning, the Jew told us he was selling our boat . . . our livelihood . . . to one of the large taxi companies. For health reasons, he said. We knew better. He saw a way to make a profit. He didn't care about what happened to us. Only about his money."

Jia caught a sob, "We couldn't afford another boat." Pointing to Pablo, "That man, that wonderful man, spent the next year going from one menial job to another with little help from the family because he was not Chinese. That's why we decided to come to the U.S."

"So you can see what a Jew did to us, and what marrying an outsider can do to you." Jia's anger threatened to overwhelm her, "That's why you are forbidden to consort with this Jake Warden. He will hurt you and, through you, us. You can no longer be part of this family if you refuse to let him go."

Mai tried to reason with her mother saying that this was America, not Macao, and that Jake was a good man. But in the Chinese custom, her mother's words had the strength of law. There was no challenging them without consequences.

A cloud hid the sun and the breeze freshened, scattering leaves about the brown grass. Mai turned her head from the wind.

It wasn't until her mother told her the story of the Jewish partner that she realized he was the person murdered by her uncles and thrown overboard by her father that day on the boat. A smile appeared on her face, *The old Jew and Larry . . . They got what they deserved.* Mai wondered what her mother would think if she knew Mai witnessed the killing of the Jew.

What about Jake? I saw him sitting alone that day on the ferry and pretended I was going to jump. Had a feeling he was the type that would rescue a lady in distress. Not proud of beginning a relationship on lies, but they were necessary. Told him it wasn't the first time I'd tried to end my life. Someone had to save me from that beast, Larry. Glad I found Jake, but he's a man. Like Larry, and my uncles, and my father. He's also a Jew. Mom says I can't trust him-that he'll turn on me. Despite what she says, I hope she's wrong. I'm beginning to love him.

Mai's growing feeling of love for Jake was mixed with other emotions including ambivalence toward the men in her family and hatred for Larry. She couldn't unravel the emotional twine wrapped around her.

Mai's two uncles accompanied them to America with the Lam clan's admonition to protect Lam Jia and her family in their new environment. As important, they were to see that family honor was maintained. Mai's uncles had their goal of creating business ties between the Hong Kong tong with which they were associated, and local Chinese underworld figures. Upon reaching San Francisco, the brothers urged continuing to New York City. For them, there were better business opportunities, and the Chinese settlement rivaled that of San Francisco.

For a time the group lived in a two room apartment in New

York's Chinatown. When Mai's father landed a job teaching Spanish and Portuguese at a Catholic high school on Staten Island, she and her parents moved to the borough. Her uncles remained in Manhattan, glad to have more privacy for their business dealings. They would not shirk their duty to family honor, and Mai had seen what they were capable of.

Life on Staten Island proved idyllic for Mai. In her senior year of high school, she was a cheerleader, president of the student council, and prom queen while maintaining a high honors class ranking. The future was hers to grab.

Upon graduation, she received a scholarship to NYU. Fate intervened. Jia became ill forcing Mai to forgo college and get a job to help support the family. She found an apartment in lower Manhattan and employment as a secretary at a Wall Street investment firm, the one where Larry Reid was on a fast track to becoming a partner.

Larry walked by her desk one morning and introduced himself. Mai returned a demure hello, but pretended to be busy and ignored him. Shyness enticed men. She liked Larry's looks, and he was going to be a wealthy man. After that first greeting, he disappeared from her life.

One evening he phoned her at home. He'd been thinking of her, but had to be discreet regarding office relationships. There was rigid enforcement of the office non-fraternization policy. It was the reason he had avoided her at work. He asked for a date, and she accepted. It was the beginning of their love affair.

Larry was exciting, a whirlwind, and she was caught in it. It was he who introduced her to the S&M side of lovemaking. She liked and encouraged it.

Without warning, Larry began to exhibit a "Jekyll and Hyde" personality. He alternated from loving and caring to mean and demanding with the latter traits dominating. The sex degenerated. Larry insisted she be submissive. To insure she was, he slapped, punched, and hit her with a large buckled belt. Mean and degrading, it was not the S&M she enjoyed. The episodes ended in rough, painful intercourse. Bruises, lacerations, and swellings covered her body. Ashamed, as if it were her fault, she tried to hide her injuries with cosmetics and clothes and wouldn't think of telling anyone what she was forced to endure.

When Mai had attempted to break up with Larry, he threatened more violence. Although she had considered suicide, she didn't have the courage. Had she been serious and jumped from the Circle Line ferry, there would have been poetic justice to being born on a boat and dying on one.

Jake was the savior who turned her life around, and she was rewarding him by making him do something that violated every masculine value ingrained in him. It had to be done if they were to remain together. Jake loved her and would do what she wished.

*Two loves I have
of comfort and despair ...*

Friday afternoon, four hours before the end of the work week and the beginning of an off-duty weekend, Bret Manley was sitting at a table in a breakroom drinking coffee. Mentally, he was down and was trying to figure out why.

For him, November in the Northeast was gloomy. Thanksgiving cheered him, but it wasn't for another three weeks. He hadn't been able to get home for the holidays since beginning training, and this year wouldn't be different.

Another problem was a lack of exercise that caused him to gain a few pounds. He played squash with Jake in the hospital courts two or three times a week, but his friend had been unavailable for a while. Bret didn't like playing with anyone but Jake, so he opted to do nothing.

The condition of the breakroom added to his woes. A wealthy hospital like Manhattan Memorial shouldn't have ratty lounges filled with cheap furniture. Resident doctors and nurses deserved real utensils and ceramic cups instead of plastic and Styrofoam. Microwaves that worked. Coffee makers instead of containers of hot water and packets of instant coffee.

Although he wouldn't admit it, the underlying cause of his complaints was the lack of a date for the weekend. All his usual ladies were busy. *Sorry state of affairs when you have no one who will change their plans for you. It may be time to stop in at the A and B and get to know Liz better.*

While Bret was holding an empty coffee cup and contemplating if he should expend the energy to get another, Jake Warden rushed into the room.

"Hey, Bret. Been looking for you."

"Well, you found me. Good for you." Sarcasm dripped from each word.

Jake pulled the chair out across from Bret and chuckled, "Take it easy, boy. I've got something you'll want to hear."

"Shoot," was the curt reply as Bret tossed the cup into a bin. It missed and fell on the floor. He didn't retrieve it.

"You seem edgy. Bet you're not getting enough sleep. It happens to all of us, you know. Part of the job. Ignore it." Jake leaned on the table.

"No, smart guy, I'm getting enough sleep. Just a little pissed, that's all."

"Okay, okay, I believe you but won't ask why." Jake scanned the room. No one but Bret. "Listen up. Some of the actors are throwing a party tomorrow night, and they want us to come. It's not far, the East 90's."

Manhattan Memorial was frequented by a contingent of aspiring actors. The hospital had the reputation of catering to high society, and the actors wanted to be part of the ambiance. Both Jake and Bret treated many in the clinic and became friends with several.

"Are you taking Rachel?"

"Matter of fact, no. She's in Boston for a few weeks visiting family. Preparing them for what's to come, I guess. Anyway, I'm going, but alone."

Bret was hesitant, but asked, "Ahh, what about your new love that you told me about? Why don't you take her?"

Jake seemed at a loss for words. Replied, "Oh that? Been over for a while. Didn't work out."

Bret was sorry. Jake had loved the woman he met on the ferry. That was obvious. He gave a sympathetic nod.

"So," Jake said, "What about you coming to the party?"

"It's only a day away. I wouldn't go without a date, and not sure

I can find someone for tomorrow."

Jake teased, "What happened to the famous Bret Manley fleet of women? I've been led to believe that the problem was choosing between a beautiful blond, brunette, or redhead."

Attempting to save face, "Don't you worry, I can find someone if I really need to. In fact, before you came I was thinking of looking up the waitress at the A and B. The one that waited on us when we went there for a drink? You probably don't remember her."

"How could I forget? The sexy one with the boobs."

"I guess you weren't as drunk as I thought. In any event, I'd be lucky to wrangle her into going to the party with me. Probably swamped with dates when she's not working. Guys gotta be hitting on her all the time."

Smiling, Jake said, "That's what I wanted to tell you. A girl from back home recently moved here and looked me up. I've set you up with her for the party. When you see her, I promise, you'll be happy I did."

Bret put both hands on the table, and looked at Jake. "No way you're going to fix me up with some dog from back home."

Jake's shrug of his shoulders and showing of his palms proclaimed he was not guilty of what Bret suggested. "You're being ridiculous. Believe me. I'm telling the truth when I say she's a beauty, an exotic beauty, and intelligent."

Since he had no one and nothing to do on Saturday, Bret agreed to Jake's offer. He was curious . . . anxious . . . to meet the so-called exotic beauty.

"Great," Jake said, "Be at my place at seven. We'll be waiting."

The woman opened the door and extended her hand in greeting. Bret took it and gave a gentle squeeze. She smiled, "Hi, you're Dr. Bret Manley. I'm Mai Faca." Holding onto his hand, she said, "I've been looking forward to meeting you. Jake has said many nice things about you."

Bret couldn't speak. The woman was exquisite. He had an

instant mental image of himself as the Big Bad Wolf, jaw dropping to the floor, tongue unrolling about four feet, with more saliva flowing than from twelve rabid dogs. Jake's reference to Mai as an exotic beauty was a bold understatement. She was the most exotic and most beautiful woman he had ever seen.

When his voice returned, Bret squeaked, "Hi, it's nice to meet you." After another pause, he said in a macho voice, "Please, call me Bret."

"Okay, Bret, I will. Call me Mai."

Bret's eyes were feasting on the tall, shapely woman . . . and those breasts. If Jake had asked about Liz of the "A and B", he would have answered, "Liz, who?"

Mai was wearing a black silk skirt with embroidered black flowers and a pale orange jersey that might have been painted on her. A dainty curl accented her brown hair, and it, in turn, accented her rosy skin. Her nose was small, her lips pouty, and her teeth perfect. All blended into a face and body that came as close to perfection as possible this side of Heaven.

Reigning over all were light blue eyes under long lashes. They appeared otherworldly, and gave the impression of penetrating your skin like painless surgical lasers. While exchanging pleasantries, Bret tried to determine if Mai was wearing colored contacts. She wasn't. Her eyes were a delightful surprise that added to her breathtaking beauty. It reminded him of a line in a poem, *If I could write the beauty of your eyes . . .* He thanked the quantum randomness of the universe for allowing him to be with this woman.

Jake approached and handed Bret a glass of wine. To Mai, he said, "Would you excuse us a moment?"

"Of course," she replied. Indicating her glass, "I could use a refill of this excellent wine." She went to the kitchen.

Bret couldn't help gawking.

Jake said, "Did I lie?"

"No. No you didn't. And get that shit-eating grin off your face."

Intending to drink at the party, they took a cab. Bret bombarded Mai with questions. She answered providing enough detail to satisfy his curiosity, yet not appear as if her responses were prepared. Jake listened without interrupting.

"When I was a child," she said, "my parents emigrated from Macao to Kent, Connecticut ... I'm sure you know that's where Jake's from. They wanted to come to America, and dad was able to get a job teaching Spanish and Portuguese at the prep school there."

Attempting to keep his eyes from fixating on Mai's body, Bret paid close attention to every word she spoke and concentrated on looking at her face.

"I loved growing up in the Kent area. After graduating from the school where my father taught, I decided not to go to a traditional college. My mother had been diagnosed with severe fibromyalgia, and I wanted to remain close to home. Her illness was a financial strain on the family, and you know how expensive college is."

Mai glanced at Jake, then to Bret and continued her fabricated story. "I enrolled in a nearby community college and earned an associate's degree in legal assisting. After graduation, I took a position in a small law firm in town and planned on staying there until I saved enough money to continue my education and get a degree in business. Assuming mother was feeling better, of course."

Every detail fascinated Bret.

"I had been working for only a few months when my parents decided to return to Macao and spend their remaining years with family. Their decision had to do with my mom's declining health. The fibromyalgia was getting worse, and she wanted to see her family before anything happened. Prior to leaving the country, they gave me a small inheritance. It was what they were able to afford."

As they transited Manhattan's Upper 80's, Bret pointed out that they were in one of the fun parts of the city. Referred to as Germantown, it was safe and clean. Heavy German influence ensured a plethora of bakeries and biergartens. "I'd like to show you the area, sometime."

"I'd love that," Mai said.

The trio reached their destination and conversation was put

on hold. The address was a three-story brick building without an elevator. Irregular vertical cracks in the exterior gave it an out of kilter appearance. Creaky stairs led to the top floor.

As expected, the event was a blast. There was a wall-to-wall crowd with most of the guests holding glasses in one hand, and various types of cigarettes in the other. Loud music made for loud talking. A generalized din similar to traffic on a busy highway permeated the apartment.

Classic posters of Katherine Hepburn, Cary Grant, Marilyn Monroe, and others papered every wall. Most in attendance considered themselves actors. Few could be credited with more than a bit part in movies or theater, yet they partied like academy award winners.

In spite of the conversational difficulties because of the noise, Bret was driven to learn as much as possible about his date.

Mai doled out snippets of information, each planned to fit into a complete Mai Faca history as pieces of a puzzle contribute to the whole. "I wanted to expand my admittedly limited life experience and decided to move to New York City. Friends suggested I look up Dr. Warden who was in New York completing his dental surgery training. I had never met him . . . he was seven years older than me . . . but I was familiar with his reputation as a stellar athlete in high school. Kent people still speak of his achievements."

"I'm not surprised," Bret said. He didn't like her talking about Jake.

"Before leaving, I found out where he was training and called him. I introduced myself and said I very much wanted to come to New York. I had no place to live and only a little money. Jake said he would help with finding an apartment, but his wife mustn't know about it. They're having marital problems, as you're aware, and she wouldn't understand his intentions were honorable. We found a place in lower Manhattan. The rent was doable if I found a job. Otherwise, I could live there until my money ran out."

"What would you do if that happened?" Bret asked.

"I don't know. Maybe go back to my old job in Kent. On the other hand, I might find my Prince Charming here in the City.

One thing is sure, because of his dicey marital situation, I can't ask much more of Jake."

Bret saw himself as that Prince Charming. He had difficulty trusting Jake's motives. How would he have reacted if in the midst of a bad marriage, a beautiful and vulnerable woman arrived in the city and asked for his help? Would his intentions have been honorable? He doubted his own altruism, but gave Jake the benefit of the doubt regarding his.

At 1 a.m. the party was going strong. Mai said she was tired and wanted to leave. Bret agreed, but Jake decided to remain saying there was nothing he had to rush home to. Bret assumed he would escort Mai to her place in lower Manhattan. If he was lucky, she would invite him in for coffee.

In the cab, Bret was about to ask Mai where she lived when she turned to the driver and said, "York and East 56th, please."

Bret's penis realized before his brain she had given the driver his address. *She's planning to spend the night at my place.*

With an impish grin, she turned to him, "Is that okay with you?"

Trying to sound as if it was normal for a woman to return to his apartment after a date, he heard himself saying, "Of course. No problem." Like a man at a funeral service when he discovers all his Powerball numbers match, it took great effort to keep from jumping up and down in the seat.

In bed, Mai was a sexual dominatrix. Supple as a cat and graceful as a gymnast, she was able to contort her body into positions he would have sworn impossible. She brought him to and kept him at the height of ecstasy until he could stand no more and exploded in her. For a man who would have settled for being in her company, the sex proved an unimaginable bonus. Exhausted from the after-party activities, Bret fell into a deep and restful sleep. When he awoke, Mai was gone. A note on the nightstand read, *I'll call you.*

With note in hand and at warp speed, he ran barefooted down the two flights to Jake's apartment. He put his ear to the door and listened. Hearing noise, he knocked with force that hurt his knuckles. No response. He knocked a second time.

The door opened a few inches. Jake had a glare on his face. "What the hell do you want?"

Suspecting someone was with Jake, Bret tried to look into the apartment.

Jake blocked his view, saying, "This really isn't a good time."

Since Rachel was out of town, Bret figured Jake had hooked up with a woman from the party. Given the noises, there was a good chance he interrupted their lovemaking. Shoving his bare foot between the door and the jamb, he handed the note to Jake. "Here."

Bret gambled Jake wouldn't close the door on him. If his foot was injured, he couldn't do his job, and it would mean extra work for Jake. After Jake took the note and read it, Bret removed his foot. The door closed followed by the sound of the lock.

Bret waited. It was five minutes before Jake returned and tossed the crumbled note to him. "Nothing to worry about. If she didn't like you, she wouldn't have left this. She'll call you."

Bret said, "Let me have her cell number. I'll call her."

"I can't give it to you. She doesn't want it given to anyone."

Enraged, it was Bret's turn to glare, "Look, I'm not anyone, I'm the one she fucked all last night."

Jake flinched but said nothing.

Embarrassed by his outburst, Bret looked left and right. Other than his friend, no one appeared to have heard him.

Jake said, "Don't worry. As I said, I'm sure she'll call." He closed and locked the door.

Some of Bret's anger was ameliorated. Turning and stomping to the stairs, he muttered, "I hope I gave him a temporary case of ED."

"Hi, it's Mai."

It was 5 p.m. Bret had been waiting for her call since leaving Jake's apartment. No doubt Jake informed her about their encounter.

"Well, hello." He stretched the hello to make it sound inviting, "You had me concerned. Leaving without waking me. I thought something was wrong."

"Not at all," she purred, "You were masterful and needed your sleep after all the energy you expended."

Confidence restored, Bret launched into an animated conversation. Within a half hour he had her cell number and a date for dinner the following weekend at an Italian restaurant called Bella Vista. She didn't give him her address, and he understood. In today's world it was prudent for a woman not to reveal such things until a significant relationship was established. After the call, in an attempt to give Jake a jab, he sent him an email: I've got her cell number, and we're having dinner next Saturday at the Bella Vista.

A great deal is going on in my life. I never imagined being with a woman like her, and I sense my life is about to undergo a profound change.

Jake was glum the following week while Bret's spirits soared as Saturday approached. On Friday, the doctors were in the operating room attempting to drain an infection in the neck of a patient in danger of dying. Bret was the surgeon in charge and Jake acting as his assistant.

Bret kept his eyes on the surgical field as he spoke to Jake who was on the other side of the operating table. "His tongue's swollen and pushing back into his throat. The airway's blocked."

With a slight turn of his head toward the anesthesiologist, Bret said, "Did you have a hard time putting the endotracheal tube in his throat?"

The anesthesiologist looked from her instruments and said, "Yeah. It was tough. There was so much swelling I had to use the fiberoptic scope. Lucky to get the tube in."

Attempting to put her at ease, Bret said, "If we don't get good drainage, we'll do a trach. No sense risking his inability to breathe after you remove the tube."

Separated from the surgeons by sterile surgical drapes attached to poles, the anesthesiologist said, "On my pre-op evaluation, I learned the reason he waited so long before seeking treatment was lack of insurance. Didn't think he could afford to come to the Emergency Department. Wonder if he thought dying was cheaper?"

The two surgeons shook their heads.

"The regulars know the hospital never turns anyone away because they can't pay," Jake said. "Apparently, this guy didn't. Poor bastard almost died from ignorance."

The surgery was successful, and a tracheotomy was averted. In the recovery room Bret and a nurse were at the patient's side monitoring instruments, while Jake was sitting at a long counter writing post-operative orders. When Bret was confident the man was stable, he took a seat at the counter.

Jake put his pen down and said to him, "Have you thought about setting up a practice when you get out of this place?"

Surprised by the question, Bret answered, "Of course. You know all residents think about where they'll practice."

Jake pressed on, "I've been thinking. Since we're both from Connecticut, it might be nice to go back there and open an office together. Not in one of the larger cities, but in a place like the ones we grew up in."

It was the offer of a lifetime. Under normal circumstances Bret would have jumped at it. Both men came from small Connecticut towns, he from East Granby and Jake from Kent. Practicing in a similar place would be satisfying. He respected Jake as a surgeon. They had a good working rapport, and, no doubt, would continue that relationship in private practice. His developing situation with Mai made him hesitate. He didn't want to do anything that might jeopardize what he had with her. She left a small town in Connecticut and might not want to return to one.

Being truthful, he said, "I really appreciate the offer, but it's Mai I'm thinking of. I'd like to wait until I know if there's a future for us before I give you an answer. If there is, she'll have a say in where I practice."

"Trust me," Jake said, "If she wants to be with you, she'll

follow. I'm not asking for a decision now. Think it over, and we'll talk again." He resumed writing post-operative orders.

Bret returned to the mobile surgical stretcher that held his patient. The head of the stretcher was against a wall loaded with monitoring instruments. Several were attached to the sleeping man. While checking the patient's oxygen level on the pulse oximeter, he thought about telling Mai about Jake's proposition. He'd have the opportunity at the Bella Vista.

With the hum of the instruments in the background, Bret returned to his home in Connecticut.

The village of East Granby was situated in the Connecticut River Valley. Blessed with the proper soil and climate, a great deal of its history revolved around the growing and processing of broadleaf tobacco. East Granby was populated with millionaire tobacco farmers when a million dollars meant something. In the latter part of the twentieth century, the tobacco growing industry died, and, with it, much of the wealth of the town. Before Bret was born, the district had transformed itself into a bedroom community for several of the surrounding cities.

He enjoyed living in East Granby. The death of his father from an auto accident was his worst memory. While devastated by the loss, his mother and Uncle Hubie provided the emotional support he required. A favorite pastime was watching the large jets that flew into Hartford's International Airport. Town residents complained about "the dammed airplane noise," but it kindled in Bret the desire to become a commercial pilot.

In college he concentrated on science and engineering courses. During the summer between his junior and senior years, he took the test given by Florida Airways and failed because of a benign heart condition. "Washed out," the flight surgeon had pronounced. "Today's result will be entered into a permanent file all air carriers have access to. No one will hire you."

"Go fuck yourself," Bret had said.

A tap on his shoulder yanked Bret out of his daydream. "Excuse me, but Doctor Warden forgot to sign the post-op orders, and he's gone." A nurse was holding the order sheet on a clipboard. "Would you sign them?"

"Sure, Melissa." He took the board and signed the orders.

She gave him a husky "Thank you" and returned to her duty station. Walking accentuated her exceptional ass.

Bret stared at it until she turned and gave him a wink of mission accomplished. She was his favorite of the Recovery Room group. Young and cute, they had dated a few times. He couldn't remember why they stopped seeing each other.

Glad I decided on dentistry when they threw me out of aviation. As someone said, way leads on to way, and here I am at Manhattan Memorial in love with Mai Faca.

Mai and Bret were at the Bella Vista, an Italian eatery located in midtown Manhattan. The restaurant was classic Italian with checkered tablecloths, singing waiters, and colorful scenes of Tuscany displayed on the walls. The best part was the wonderful smell of food—a savory perfume of tomatoes, basil, and garlic that greeted you upon entering.

"Do you like Italian food?" Bret asked as the waiter brought Mai's linguini and clams and his lasagna.

"Love it," she answered. "My father taught me to appreciate pasta and other dishes made with tomato sauce. Italians and Portuguese share many culinary similarities." She wrapped strands of linguine around a fork and took a bite. Wiping sauce from her lips with a cloth napkin, she added, "I also love Chinese food. By the way, did you know the Chinese probably invented pasta? They say Marco Polo brought it to Europe."

He pleaded ignorance, "No kidding?"

"That's what I heard." She took a sip of Chianti. "Do you know what they call Chinese food in China?"

Bret had heard the silly joke many times, but pretended he hadn't. "No, what do they call it?"

"Food. Get it?" Mai belly-laughed thinking she had gotten him.

Bret laughed as if it were the world's funniest joke.

While eating, they engaged in small talk. The usual What do you think of this? Did you see that? banter. It revealed they had similar likes and dislikes. Not until Bret had drunk several glasses of Chianti was he able to summon the courage to talk about his future plans.

"I've been thinking about going back to Connecticut when I leave Manhattan Memorial. What's your feeling about my practicing there?"

Mai, who had been smiling and laughing throughout the meal, became serious. As with Bret, she had finished a few glasses of Chianti, and was feeling the alcohol. Not to the point that she couldn't respond to the anticipated question with her prepared answer.

"Me? Well, as a disinterested observer, I would say you should practice wherever you think it best. After all, you're the one who knows what it takes to be successful." She pointed her fork at him, "Then again, if I were more than a disinterested observer . . . a serious girlfriend, for example . . . I would say exactly the same thing and be by my man's side."

As in their first encounter, Mai's sexual prowess proved magical. She was a living Kama Sutra. Bret was addicted to her body and couldn't imagine sex with another woman. Although she had given him great physical pleasure, it was her response to his question about returning to Connecticut that he considered the best part of the evening.

He called Jake the next morning to tell him of Mai's answer.

"Why don't you come to my apartment this afternoon? I'm planning to watch an early season Knicks game on my new flat screen TV."

" A new one? How big?"

Sixty eight inch Samsung. Real narrow. Had it installed on the wall last week. Since Rachel's gone a lot, and we don't associate with each other when she's here, I need it for entertainment."

"Wow."

"If you drop by, we can continue our discussion about setting up a practice together."

"And Rachel won't be there?"

"Naw. Not for another week. Still in Boston. We'll have the place all to ourselves. Be here around two."

Jake opened the door holding a bottle of Foster's in his hand. "Glad you could make it."

"Thanks for the invite." Bret went to the kitchen, and plucked a Coor's Light from the refrigerator. "See you still keep a supply of my favorite on hand."

"Of course, nothing but the best for you." Jake emptied half the bottle of his Foster's in one swallow. He followed with a loud burp and a forearm wipe of his mouth.

The television was on. "Game's already started. Have a seat," Jake said.

After watching for a few minutes, Jake turned to Bret and without preamble said, "Windham, Connecticut."

Caught off guard and not sure what Jake was referring to, Bret's expression revealed his confusion. "What?"

Jake grabbed the remote, muted the TV, and adjusted his chair to better face his guest. "The Windham area of Connecticut. That's where I suggest we practice. It's in the northeast corner of the State. They call it the Quiet Corner."

"I've heard of it, but that's about all."

"Let me fill you in. It's really Windham and Mansfield and several small surrounding towns I'm referring to. A great place to live and work." With a wink, "And raise children."

Jake grabbed a map from the coffee table and opened it as he began a dissertation about the advantages of settling in northeast

Connecticut. By the time he finished, Bret felt he had lived in the area. In addition, any worries about not taking part in the selection of a place to practice were allayed by the in-depth research Jake had done.

Hours had passed and day was fading into night. Lights showed in windows of the apartment complex across the way, and pole lamps threw circular yellow flares on sidewalks and streets. Shadows were crawling up buildings.

"Any more questions?" Jake asked.

Bret couldn't think of anything that hadn't been answered.

Jake got up from his chair. "That's all I have for now, but I'll continue my research and keep you posted."

Bret stood and stretched.

Jake went to the kitchen, retrieved another Foster's. "Now, all we have to do is go there, and scope out the place. Really get to know it." He chugged the bottle.

Bret was anxious to explore the area, "Tell me when. I'm with you."

"How about going after the first week of January?" Jake said, "We'll take a few days ... maybe a long weekend." Tossing the empty into the trash, he said, "The first weekend I'm committed to an ice-fishing trip in Maine with my college roommate. It's been planned for a while, and because of his schedule, can't be changed. It was the only time we both could get together.

"If it's okay with you, let's make it the one after that. I'll arrange for our hospital coverage. I assume Rachel's not part of the equation."

Jake chuckled. "No ... no she's not. He paused, "But I have an idea. Mai might be interested in seeing Windham. Why don't you ask her to come with us?"

"You bet." Bret found it difficult to keep from filling the apartment with joyous laughter.

Some glory in their birth . . .

———

Moosehead Lake, Maine: "Those global warming assholes should be here measuring the ice covering this lake. The locals haven't seen it this thick at the beginning of the season in seventy-five years. By the way, I think you've got a bite," Carlton Benton IV peered at Jake Warden from the upper bunk of the two bunk cabin. His legs dangled over the side as he talked and watched Jake fish from a chair.

Carlton was Jake's age but looked older. Below average height, he had developed a paunch. His wire rimmed glasses held thick lenses that magnified his eyes, making them owlish, and he parted his thinning hair low on the left. Carlton looked and dressed like a kindly college professor, although in business he was cold, calculating, and gave no quarter. Associates at his family's investment banking firm nicknamed him, "The Assassin," a moniker he was proud of and did his utmost to preserve. Although wearing a thick down parka, for additional warmth he was drinking from an initialed silver flask filled with rare brandy.

The men were in an aluminum-sided portable cabin a hundred yards off the shore of Moosehead Lake in northwest Maine. The structure was the equivalent of a deluxe double-wide mobile home with bathroom, sleeping, and cooking facilities. Electrical power was supplied by a protected cable that ran from the shore. A four wheel drive pickup for their use was parked in an onshore lot. The cabin contained limited foodstuffs and the bare essentials required to survive three days of wilderness ice-fishing. The only supply in abundance was alcohol. In addition to Carlton's flask, there was the equivalent of a two week stock of all types of alcoholic beverages from beer and wine to hard liquor. If that wasn't enough to sustain two men for three days, Carlton had brought several bottles of aperitifs to complement meals.

Access to the lake was through two rectangular openings in the floor. It was recommended they be covered when not fishing, as fishermen had been known to fall through the holes and drown. Having a high blood alcohol level while peeing into the water was the usual cause of accidents.

Accumulating slush in the openings was kept at bay with shovels and rakes. Serious icing was handled with the axe, pick, and chainsaw stowed in the pickup. Fishing equipment stored in the cabin was meant to satisfy the novice to expert ice fisherman.

"I hooked one," roared Jake as he pulled on his pole, excited by the possibility of catching a fish on his first day. The fishing line with a mass of dark debris clinging to the hook flew out of the water. He looked at Carlton, "Damn. Just seaweed and grass." Cleaning the junk from his line and tossing it on the floor, he said, "If we don't catch something pretty soon, it's going to be burgers for dinner."

"I would rather like that," Carlton said as he descended the ladder attached to his bunk. He sat in the chair by the fishing hole designated as his. "I so rarely get to eat them. Do we have potato chips and pickles to go with the hamburgers?"

"We sure do, but don't tell me rich people get sick of pheasant under glass and caviar?" Jake teased.

"Of course. Most people don't know it, but we rich have a constant craving for chips and dip."

With his boot Carlton slid the seaweed and grass Jake had thrown on the floor into the water. Smiling, he said, "And our mouths drool when we're around rib-eye steaks and Cold Duck. Just like the common folk."

Jake was familiar with Carlton's wry sense of humor. They had known each other since their undergraduate days at Lehigh when they were roommates. The proverbial odd couple, Waspish Carlton hailed from a family of fabulous investment banking wealth and political power while Jake was the product of a middle class Jewish family. Despite their social differences they became inseparable friends at college, and their friendship lasted to the present. After college the men went different ways, but every year they spent time together doing something they both enjoyed. They had gone white water rafting, skiing, bow hunting, and, this year, ice-fishing.

After the dinner of the hamburgers, pickles, and potato chips that Carlton had craved, the men relaxed in padded wooden chairs and watched the unsettled movement of the water in the fishing holes. Neither spoke.

Carlton blew a cloud of smoke from his cigar into the stuffy air. "When we're together like this, I can't help thinking about the time you saved my ass in college. I laugh about it now, but it wasn't funny when it happened."

Jake, who smoked when he was with Carlton, was puffing on a cigarette. Both had smoked in college, and it seemed the natural thing to do on their get-togethers. He said, "We were kids and did stupid things without thinking. I was glad to help." With light sarcasm, "You would have done the same for me, of course."

"Of course."

The combined cigarette and cigar smoke filled the room like a Maine fog. Carlton continued, "Why I decided to steal a valuable painting from the library, I don't know. And to add to my problem, I jimmied a door, so it made it breaking and entering. I could have gone to prison and become someone's bitch."

"You loved that painting. I can't count the times you said that."

"Yes, I did. An original Axeldon." Carlton exhaled smoke as Jake flicked his cigarette on the floor and crushed it before kicking it into the water. "It was a Friday night. I had been drinking but not that much when the whim struck me."

"An example of the famous Carlton mantra, resist everything but temptation." Jake chuckled.

Carlton grunted, "That's funny. But if I got caught . . . well, you know my family. They'd never forgive or forget my smearing the family name. Even my closest friends would have ostracized me."

"You were in a jam." Jake leaned in his chair and balanced

on the two back legs. "I figured that if the painting was returned without damage, the university would drop the matter. They didn't want the negative publicity associated with the theft of one of their most valuable works of art. I simply left it on the library steps at three a.m. on a Sunday morning and called the campus police to let them know it was there. Luckily, I was right and we never heard another thing about it."

Carlton patted Jake on the shoulder. "And you were willing to take the blame, if the plan backfired. You're a true friend and that's why I've always told you if there's anything I can do to pay you back, let me know."

Jake returned the front legs of his chair to the floor and took another cigarette from his pack. It was filled with marijuana. He lit it, inhaled deep, and held it before exhaling. "Yes, you're always reminding me." Nodding to Carlton, "Every time you get a new cell number, you give it to me." He continued in a joking manner, "Which, in my opinion, you change them way too much."

"I have to. It doesn't take long for the numbers to get out. If I didn't change them, I'd be hounded by charities and other organizations wanting a piece of my hard-earned fortune."

Jake stared into the fishing hole. Shaking his head, "Problems of the rich, I guess."

They sat smoking in silence for several minutes. Jake took a last drag from his joint and flicked it into the fishing hole. "We should close these things before one of us falls in."

"Yeah, we should," Carlton agreed.

Jake stood, stretched, and walked to the corner to retrieve the two hole covers leaning against the wall. After placing them over the openings, he stepped on each to ensure they were in place.

Returning to his chair, he waited a bit before saying. "I need that favor now."

Carlton removed his cigar from his mouth and appeared to contemplate Jake's words. "What is it? I'll do all I can to help. Knowing you, I assume it's legal." Carlton laughed.

Jake's confidence was boosted. "It is, and I might as well get to the point. I need five hundred thousand dollars to give to Rachel so she'll give me an uncontested divorce. You're my only source of such a large amount of money until I begin private practice."

Carlton took a long drag on his cigar and blew a cloud of gray smoke. "Goddammit, she's asking for a lot. I'll give it to you, but it's important to make sure a money transfer of this size passes IRS, SEC, and Banking Commission smell tests. Bastards would love another reason to investigate me. Carlton shook his head and pursed his lips in a gesture of disgust.

He continued, "I'll have my people draw up a loan agreement with a fair interest rate. It'll say you're personally on the hook for repaying the loan. That should satisfy the government."

Carlton stood and began to pace, "I'll be back in Pittsburgh on Tuesday. You'll have the papers no later than the end of next week. Sign and overnight them to me. The money will be deposited to your account within forty-eight hours. Soon enough?"

"Absolutely. You're more than generous, and I really appreciate what you're doing. You've made it possible for me to start a new life."

"You did me a favor once."

"Thanks."

"For the record, there's no time limit on the money. You can repay it whenever and however you prefer. And I don't want any interest although it has to be included in the agreement."

Carlton tossed the cigar on the floor and with his heel ground it to a black gunk. Reaching into his pants pocket, he removed a small leather bag. After loosening two strings, he removed a wad of marijuana and proceeded to make two, as he was fond of calling them, doobies. With a grin, he handed one to Jake. "By the way, what's her name?"

Jake lit the proffered cigarette and took a drag. He exhaled, "Her name is Mai . . .

What potions have I drunk
of Siren tears . . .

———

Windham, Connecticut: Bret suspected Jake had chosen the Windham area as an ideal location to practice because of its proximity to the University of Connecticut in the Storrs district of Mansfield. In other words, its proximity to the men's and women's basketball teams. Jake's friends knew he was a rabid basketball fan, and the university produced many of the finest college teams in the game's history. Had basketball been the major reason for choosing northeast Connecticut, Bret would have quashed such foolishness. It was not the case. Prior to the visit, an internet search revealed the Windham area had the qualities they were seeking in a place in which to set up a practice.

Mai, Bret, and Jake arrived in Windham on a Friday morning and spent the day exploring. Although patchy snow covered the ground, the trio had entered a region filled with vistas seen in paintings and on postcards. Willimantic and Mansfield, the two major towns, and their hinterland of villages and hamlets encompassed a large and picturesque geographic area.

They shared a pizza and drank beer in one of Windham's many pizza restaurants before procuring rooms at a motel. Mai and Bret took a room, Jake another. On Saturday they explored, and at the end of the day, were convinced of wanting to live and work there.

To get maximum exposure to the residents, a practice building advantage, Jake and Bret decided to live in different towns. No one was surprised when Jake volunteered to settle in Mansfield. Bret chose Windham. Since Mai had accompanied Bret and all signs pointed a return with him, he asked for her opinion. She agreed Windham would be delightful.

Before returning to the motel, the group decided to have dinner at a well known historic restaurant on Route 195 between Windham and Mansfield. In colonial times it had been a busy inn frequented by horse drawn coaches filled with passengers who were traveling between Hartford and Albany.

At the entrance of the establishment, Mai clapped her hands with delight and pointed to a poster. "Look, they're having a wine tasting." Turning to her friends and sounding like a child begging to open Christmas gifts, "Can we give it a try . . . can we?"

"Sure, it'll be fun," Bret said.

"Fine by me," was Jake's response. Mai glanced at him and gave a slight nod.

The hostess explained the event as she escorted them to their table. The wine tasting dinner would consist of several gourmet courses from appetizers to dessert, each accompanied by an appropriate wine. She assured them they would not be disappointed.

The main course ended, and Bret signaled the wine steward to pour him another pinot noir. As he and the steward chatted, his attention was drawn from the table. Mai scanned the room to ensure no diners were watching and winked at Jake who slipped a liquid in Bret's wine. The steward left.

Bret stood and held his glass to his friends. "I'd like to propose a toast." The others raised their glasses. "I want to thank Mai for suggesting the wine tasting. It was a great choice." Three glasses clinked in unison.

Dessert was cherry pie. Before taking a bite, Bret placed his arms on the table and laid his head in them, "Man, the wine really hit me. I feel like sleeping." He yawned, and his eyelids fluttered before closing.

His friends watched. Jake reached across the table and put a finger on the pulse of the unconscious man. He mouthed to Mai, "He's out."

One of the diners at the table to their left noticed. "Is your friend okay?"

Jake said, "Nothing serious. Too much wine. This isn't the first time it's happened."

Mai turned to Jake and said, "It's time for us to go. He's sleeping like a baby."

Jake left his chair and went to his future partner. He hefted Bret from the table, put the unconscious man's arm over his shoulder, and carry-walked him through the dining area. Mai summoned the waiter. "He's overdone a good thing," she said as she paid the check.

Bret slept in the back seat on the drive to the motel. Mai, not sure of the effects of the valium in the wine, leaned into Jake and said, "How long will he be out?"

With his index finger to his lips in a hushing manner, Jake whispered, "He drank a lot. Wine and valium is a potent mixture. Especially, liquid valium. It gets into the system quick. He'll be dead to the world for eight, maybe ten hours. I wish we had more time, but we have to be satisfied with what we get."

Mai kissed Jake's ear and murmured, "Let's make satisfied the operative word."

Bret woke with a pounding head. It took a while to focus on the clock atop the nightstand. Eleven thirty. Tired and lethargic, he managed to dress. His traveling companions were in the coffee shop attached to the motel. Mai beckoned with a pat of her hand on the seat.

Jake's voice screeched in his brain. "Welcome to the land of the living, old buddy."

Bret could taste bile and wasn't in the mood to be teased. "Very funny, but I'm not laughing. If you want to help me, get me aspirin. I need aspirin. And be quick about it."

Mai opened her bag, rummaged, and found a container of Tylenol. She handed it to him. "Will this do?"

He opened the container poured four capsules into his hand. Grabbing Mai's coffee he swallowed them in one gulp, emptying the cup.

She refilled from the pot on the table and said, "You were the life of the party at dinner."

Bret raised his sore eyebrows.

Mai told him about his drunken shenanigans at the restaurant. She ended with, "As for the other patrons, most couldn't stop laughing although a few wanted you escorted out. One guy even threatened to call the police."

Shaking his head, Bret said, "I hope I didn't embarrass us too much."

"You didn't. It was all in good fun," Mai said. Changing the subject, "I did an Internet search on Windham this morning and found some interesting facts."

Jake and Bret looked at her.

"For example, it was the origin of the Boom Box Parade. A very popular local disk-jockey came up with the idea one Fourth of July. Now, tons of towns and cities across the country have them."

"No kidding?" Jake said.

"That's not all. You know the bridge with the frog statues we liked. People from all over the world come to see it. Those are just a few of the things I found. Not bad for a place tucked away in a sleepy corner of the State."

Seeing that Bret's eyes were glazed and he was about to fall asleep, Jake stood and said, "Time to go."

On the trip to New York, Bret resolved to control his drinking. He didn't want Mai to think he was an alcoholic.

"Hope my drinking isn't worrying you," Bret said. He and Mai were in his bed. "Even though I binged, I don't think I'm in danger of becoming an alcoholic." Nodding, "I haven't had a drink since we left Windham."

Mai leaned on an elbow and faced him, "No, I'm not worried," she said. "Don't even think about it."

He faced her. "It's difficult not to. Alcoholism and drug addiction are real problems for doctors. You know, stress, access to drugs, and all that."

She put a hand on his shoulder, "Believe me, you don't have a drinking problem. Just blowing off steam when you get a chance. It's only natural."

"That's about what Seth Stevens said. He's a psychiatry resident. Asked if it interfered with my work. I told him no, it only happened when I was with you guys. He's happy to talk to me about it ... you and Jake too, if you want. He said to get in touch with him right away if things get worse."

"That's great," Mai said. "He can monitor your work and I'll monitor your play." She smiled, "You had no problem in my playground a few minutes ago."

There was a time when Bret would have blushed upon hearing such words. "If I ever do, I'll be pounding on Seth's door."

Mai pulled him on top of her. "Now, let me show you my wildest ride."

The following two months Jake made day and weekend trips to Connecticut and found an office to rent on the outskirts of Windham. Patients from all parts of the region would have easy access to it.

"Your hands can't be tied by my reviewing everything you do," Bret told Jake. "You have *carte blanche* on all decisions." Bret wanted the renovation and equipping of the office to go without a hitch. Their goal was to have the office open for business by the time Jake completed his training at the end of June.

Using the money borrowed from Carlton, Jake finalized his uncontested divorce from Rachel. Their last words fit with everything that had gone before. "I never want to see you again. May you die and rot in Hell," was Rachel's comment. Jake's return was, "Likewise, bitch."

Jake rented a two bedroom condo in the Storrs section of Mansfield. His boast was, "It's only a ten minute walk to the university where most of the home basketball games are played."

He hired three employees, a receptionist, Brittney LaFreniere, a dental assistant, Sue Palmer, and an office manager, Corrie Hunter.

Corrie was a forty-one year old registered nurse. She had the bronzed skin and discolored fingers of a heavy smoker, and there wasn't an ounce of extra flesh on her bones. During the interview, she kept her hands moving in an attempt to hide their shaking. Jake suspected a drug habit.

Reviewing her resume as he spoke, "It says on your application you worked at the Fenton Convalescent Home for two years."

"Yes, that's correct." Corrie shifted in her chair.

"Why did you leave?" Jake was aware of misuse of narcotics by employees of convalescent homes. It involved stealing narcotics intended for patients and using them to satisfy a drug habit. Water would be substituted for the narcotic and injected into the patient. Because of a facility's fear of bad publicity, an employee who was caught might not be prosecuted but discharged without mention of wrongdoing in the record. In many cases the offender got a job at a similar institution where an opportunity to handle narcotics existed.

"Umm, I wanted to try something different, and, ahh, find a place where I could really use my nursing skills."

Her answer convinced Jake she used illegal drugs, but it didn't mean he wouldn't hire her. He was a schemer and planner and had dealt with addicts throughout training. Should the need arise, people like her could be manipulated and coerced into doing anything he wanted. Making her a good employee would be child's play.

"Please answer honestly. Do you take drugs?" His manner was polite but blunt.

Without a word, Corrie stood and walked to the door.

"Wait, don't go," Jake half-shouted as he got up from his chair.

Keeping her back to him, Corrie stopped and let a few seconds pass. Radiating defiance, she turned. "I guess you must be very proud of yourself. You caught me. Now let me get out of here with what little dignity I have left."

Jake raised a calming hand. "Take it easy, you don't know what I was going to say. I had to confirm my suspicion."

Corrie grimaced.

Jake continued, "Your drug habit shouldn't be a problem. We can deal with it." He sat. In a soothing voice he said, "Come back and have a seat."

Corrie did as he wished clutching her hands in her lap as if in prayer. "I'm willing to listen to what you have to say."

Jake dangled a carrot, "Look, it can be arranged so you don't have to scrounge for drugs."

Corrie betrayed no emotion.

He smiled as if they were fellow conspirators. "It's only a matter of creative record keeping. You know what I mean?"

A slight movement of Corrie's head.

"You have enough experience working in health care facilities for me to make you my office manager. It'll give you access to what you need."

Jake looked at her, "What I'm about to say is critical to our working relationship." He paused for emphasis, "You're never to be high here, or I'll fire you on the spot. You won't be able to prove a thing against me. On the other hand, what you do out of the office is your business. In addition, you'll be my personal confidant. Know what I mean by that?"

Corrie shrugged her shoulders. "I think it means you expect sex." She lowered her voice although they were alone, "I can give you oral sex. I'm told I'm good at it."

The words caught Jake by surprise. He was between falling on the floor laughing and vomiting into his wastebasket. Shaking his head, "No, that's not it. That's not what I meant at all. What it means is I want you to be there when I'd like to talk to someone. Or," he added, "If I need a favor."

Corrie retreated from her faux pas, "Oh. Sure. For a moment I thought you were like someone else I used to work for." Seeming sincere, "Of course, I'm grateful for what you're willing to do for me, and you can count on me. I won't disappoint you." Looking at Jake's handsome face, she said with a wink, "If you ever want the favor I mentioned, don't hesitate to ask."

*When my love swears that
she is made of truth
I do believe her, though I know she lies ...*

———

New York City/Windham, Connecticut: Jake was practicing in Connecticut and Bret had become chief resident in the training program. His relationship with Mai was getting better. She spent nights at his apartment, and he stayed a few times at her place in lower Manhattan. When he asked her, Mai refused to move into his apartment claiming she wasn't ready to take that step. Bret was in love and thinking of marriage.

When they had sex, he was able to, as the expression went, light her fire. Typical of men his age, he believed several women would sign affidavits attesting to his superior talent in that regard.

Mai's law firm had begun work on a hush-hush project for an important client. The venture was slated to take several months to complete and required working most weekends. Although Bret accepted her new schedule, he didn't like it. Weekends were lonely.

One Thursday afternoon in November, Mai came to his apartment from her office. She was bubbling with joy. "I'm free for the next few days. Let's visit Jake. We can have a pre-Thanksgiving celebration."

"I don't see why not. I'll get Lainey to take my call."

Clapping her hands as she did when excited, "Let's call him now." Mai dialed and turned on the phone's speaker.

Jake was in the office completing charts when they reached him and told him of their plan to visit. "I can hardly wait," he responded. To Bret, who hadn't seen the office since the open house party in July, he said, "You're going to like what I've done here. I've set it up so we'll be able to work and not get in each other's way."

"Can't wait to see it and you," he said.

Mai chimed, "Until tomorrow."

The next day they packed the Firebird and before noon began the drive to Connecticut. Traffic, a stop for a quick lunch, and a wrong turn got them to the office a little after four. They called when they reached Coventry. Jake said he cleared his schedule and was waiting. He and Corrie Hunter were in the parking lot when they arrived.

Mai ran to Jake and gave him a bear hug. It was followed by Mai reaching out and grasping Corrie's hands. Both remarked that the other looked terrific.

Bret and Jake embraced.

Pointing to his assistant, Jake said to Bret, "You remember Corrie Hunter, don't you?"

"Of course I do." Bret said, "We met at the grand opening party."

"Yes, we did," Corrie agreed. "That was fun, especially getting to meet so many of the local dentists who stopped by. Although, as I remember, you left a little early. You weren't feeling well."

"Ahh, right about that." Before Corrie could ask another question, Bret said, "So, how do you like working here? I gather from Jake you've adjusted nicely to the new job."

Jake answered for her, "She's doing a bang-up job as my combination anesthesia nurse and office manager. Couldn't get along without her." He winked at Corrie, "She's a regular Gal Friday."

Shaking her head in an 'ah shucks, you mean little ole me' fashion, Corrie said, "Doctor Warden, you're exaggerating."

Corrie checked her watch, "Look at how the time flies. I've got to run. Nice seeing you both again."

Jake couldn't hide his excitement as he asked Bret and Mai to follow him for a tour of the office. As promised, Bret was impressed with the improvements meant to make it user friendly. It excited him to know that in a matter of months he would become part of the practice.

After finishing the tour, Jake said, "Now that you've seen the nuts and bolts of the business, let's go to my place and have a drink? The drive must have made you thirsty."

Mai agreed, "You took the words out of my mouth."

Bret said nothing.

"You two follow me," Jake said, "We'll drive through the university so you can see how active it is."

The campus walkways and streets were jammed. Bret followed Jake's Subaru. "The students look so young, don't they?" he said to Mai. "Hard to believe that just a little more than seven years ago, I was walking a campus like this. So much has happened since, meeting you being the best part."

Engrossed in the activity around them, Mai didn't respond.

At the condo Jake served martinis.

"Just one for me." Bret said accepting the drink. "I haven't forgotten what happened on my last visit here." Although he hadn't had a reaction to alcohol since that time, Bret was determined to have one martini. He refused when offered a second.

Jake mentioned his new interest in cooking. "I've signed up for a class at the university. The next time you visit you'll have gourmet food, but today it's spaghetti and meatballs with a green salad and bottled dressing."

With an encouraging smile, Mai said, "My favorites."

Bret was hungry and ate every morsel on his plate. He finished first, and while waiting for the others, said, "It won't be long before I have to find a place to live here." Eschewing subtlety, he indicated Mai with a movement of his head, "I hope to have someone help me look for one."

Mai saw his gesture and responded, "You're right. And, you're going to have to do it soon. I'd like to help if it's okay with you."

Bret was wearing his happy face, "That'd be great."

The condo bedrooms were situated off halls at opposite ends of the living space, an arrangement that pleased Bret. It afforded the privacy he wanted. He was planning on having sex, and didn't want carnal noises emanating from his bedroom to reach Jake.

That evening, while they were making love, Bret whispered, "I love you, Mai."

Without skipping a beat of the fierce rhythm of her hips, Mai responded, "I love you too, Jake."

It took a few seconds for Bret to realize she had said Jake's name. When it hit him, he flew from her body as if it was charged with a thousand volts of electricity.

Startled, Mai exclaimed, "What are you doing? What happened?"

"You said Jake . . . you said you loved Jake." The words had to squeeze through tightened lips.

"No I didn't. You must have misheard me." She wrapped her arms about him and held tight.

A tug of war raged—he certain of what he heard, and she denying it. As they argued, Bret became confused and gave Mai the benefit of the doubt. He had misheard. There was no reason she would say Jake's name when they were making love.

In the morning neither mentioned the incident, although Mai was clingy and paid extra attention to him. The remainder of the weekend went without a hitch. They made love that night. Bret overcame a cautious beginning and finished in grand style. He was glad they resolved the issue and continued to have sex. Like Jake, he had an inner animal, and Mai unleashed it. She made him feel like a man.

In three months, Bret was slated to begin the next chapter of his life, and he hoped Mai would be with him when he went to Windham. During their visit with Jake, Mai implied she would accompany him to Connecticut, but seemed to have let the matter drop. He didn't want to apply pressure for fear of panicking her. The hope was within a short time she would make up her mind. In the interim, his plans were on hold.

Although working weekends, Mai spent the major portion of weekday nights at his apartment. She continued to maintain hers, and Bret thought she was using it as a psychological sanctuary to which she could run if the need arose.

In May, she spent a rare weekend at Bret's apartment. On Monday morning as Mai was leaving for work, she turned to him, "We should free up a few days and go to Windham to look for a place for us to live."

Bret was dumbstruck by the suddenness of the proposal. He wasn't sure if she was saying they should reside in Windham as a married couple, or they should live together. He hoped the former, but would settle for the latter. "You're right, and soon," he said.

"Yes. And if it's okay, I'd like to give up my apartment and stay here."

His pulse racing, "That would be terrific," he added, "Does this mean marriage?"

Her pale blue eyes fixed on him, "No. For the time being it means living together, although as a matter of decorum we'll tell most people we're married."

"What about Jake, what do we tell him?"

"The truth, of course."

Mai returned at eight that evening. Bret was watching television in the living room.

"I've done it," she announced.

"Done what?"

She related the details of her busy day. "Instead of going to work, I called my boss and told him I wouldn't be at work for several days. After that, I contacted a bunch of moving companies until I found one willing to come to my apartment today and give me an estimate."

"You did all that?"

"Yes, and more. I want to make the move on Thursday, and they can do it. I agreed to their fee. It's expensive but worth it."

Mai continued, "Then, I informed the manager of my building I'll be leaving by the end of the week. The downside is I'm going to lose my deposit. I spent the rest of the day getting boxes from local businesses and packing things I want to keep. The packing should be finished tomorrow."

While Bret had been unprepared for Mai's quick action, he was obligated to encourage her. He didn't want to risk her thinking him wishy-washy after he'd spent a huge amount of energy to convince her to do what she was doing.

"Where will we put your furniture? I don't have much room. Should we store it?"

"I'm giving away a lot of it. The movers are going to take most of my stuff to the Salvation Army. We should be able to fit what's left in here, although we'll be crowded. It saves the expense of storing it. Besides, it won't be for long."

Mai turned the topic to Connecticut. "I want to live in a real country home. Out in the sticks. It's one of the benefits of a place like Windham."

Bret agreed. "It's your choice where we live. While I'm working, you'll be home, and you've got to be happy."

"Let's tell Jake what we're doing. He can hook us up with a realtor."

They were having martinis at Jake's condo. Mai, her customary exuberant self, was in the kitchen with Jake while Bret was on the couch in the living room feeling the effects of a sinus condition. As a precaution, he had taken a half dose of NyQuil. Being a big guy, he didn't think the alcohol and NyQuil would make him drowsy.

Jake wore the apron he used in his cooking class at the university while preparing Coq au Vin. In addition to sports events, his television viewing included cooking programs. *Cook's Country*, a PBS program, was his favorite because it took a scientific approach to food preparation.

Between sips of her martini, Mai said to Jake in a voice meant for Bret to hear, "So you're seeing a pharmacology grad student, huh?"

"Yeah," Jake said, "Her name's Grace Putman. We've been

spending a lot of time together." With a wooden spoon, he stirred the brown liquid simmering in a pot on the stove. "I even get to go to her research lab some evenings and watch her work. I'm there for hours."

"I see," Mai said, "Is it just the two of you? I mean, alone in the lab."

"Usually. She picks times other students generally don't like."

Another, "I see," followed by, "Ummm."

It's nice being with her, but I don't think the relationship is going anywhere." Jake gave her a playful wink, "There are so many beautiful and lusty women at the university that there's always someone catching my eye."

"Pig." Mai raised her knee as if about to hit Jake in the groin. He dropped his hands to protect himself. "I didn't think you were such a misogynist," she said, "You're lucky I didn't follow through with my kick."

Turning sideways for better protection, he said, "I'm not. Those are just the facts of life at a university." He was quick to add, "Although I haven't seen anyone half as intelligent or as beautiful as you."

Mai pantomimed licking his face with her tongue and gave him a big smile.

Bret was listening to the banter and was pleased by Jake's compliment. From the living room he said, "You'd be hard put to find anyone with Mai's looks and intellect, Jake. By the way, what time tomorrow morning are we meeting this realtor of yours?"

"He'll be here at ten with a list of places to see. I told him you said you wanted a home with lots of privacy."

From their separate areas of the condo, both guests nodded agreement.

The discussion of house hunting continued during the meal. The Coq Au Vin in a large crock displayed the newfound skills of the neophyte cook. Beaujolais at the proper temperature was an excellent accompaniment.

Bret began to feel the effects of the medicine. "NyQuil's hit me. Think I'll take a little nap." As he walked to the bedroom, he turned and said, "Wake me in an hour, okay."

Jake and Mai assured him they would.

While Bret was in a drug induced sleep, the woman he loved and the man he thought of as his close friend were on a couch in the living room. Mai sat lotus-like facing Jake and leaned into him for conversational privacy. She looked toward the bedroom door, "I checked in on him and heard loud snoring. I assume you spiked his drink?"

"Yeah. I gave him the usual twenty of Valium. We don't have anything to worry about."

"Are you sure you didn't overdose him? I always worry about that. We could get into trouble if he dies."

"Pretty sure. If he did die, though, all we'd say is he had a drug habit. He told us he was getting help, and we thought he kicked it. Fooled us." Shaking his head, "Naw, we wouldn't get in any trouble."

Mai said, "But we'd have to start all over and find someone else to take his place. Is there another candidate available?"

Jake gave a weary, "At the moment, no," and sighed.

Mai looked into his eyes. "What's bothering you? You're not going to purposely overdose him, are you?"

He clasped his hands. "Don't worry about that. It's just that I agreed to go along with this charade, but I don't like it."

Mai swallowed. "Don't think I like what we're doing. Because of my parents and uncles, I've got to pretend to be married to him." She paused before saying, "I told them about him and they didn't object." She could hear Jake's teeth grinding. "If they ever found out about our cover-up, I shudder to think of how they would react."

"What did you tell them? Your parents."

"That we were married by a J.P. in a simple ceremony witnessed by the J.P.'s wife. Said he had been raised as an orphan. Had no family ties and didn't want to create any. They were not to expect him to visit, ever. It's just the way he is. They gave me their blessings. They want me to be happy. Made me promise to visit once in a while."

"And his family?"

"Although he has a bunch of relatives, he hardly ever sees them. He's only close to his mother and one uncle. Refers to him as Uncle Hubie. Big time lawyer, I guess. The only contact I've had with his family is talking to his mother on the phone."

"He doesn't say much about her," Jake said, "But he really looks up to his uncle. Name is Hubie Santos. And you're right. He's one hell of a lawyer."

His family knows we're living together," Mai said. She turned her head from Jake. "Damn. I'm getting sick of the lies and machinations.

Jake took and squeezed her hand.

Mai's anger had built. "It's tougher than I thought it would be. My skin crawls when he touches me. And when he fucks me . . . that's what it is, you know, because I won't call it making love . . . I have to pretend to like it. "I'm constantly faking orgasms." She began to sob.

Jake winced. That another man was having sex with Mai drove him wild. During a man-to-man discussion they had, Bret let slip that he "loved the taste of Mai's pussy." The words nailed images into Jake's brain, and he hated Bret for saying it.

In spite of his negative feelings toward Bret, he had to buoy Mai's spirits before everything came unraveled, "Think of him as our instrument," he said. "To be used for our purposes until we don't need him anymore. We'll discard him like rotting meat."

Mai dried her eyes with a tissue and shook her head. "I know you're right. As long as we love each other it doesn't matter what we do."

Jake saw an opening, "I hesitate to bring it up, but I've been thinking. You and Bret should tie the knot."

Mai's eyes widened. "Oh? Why marry him and not just keep pretending we are?"

"Because of your uncles. If they decide to make sure you're really married, it wouldn't be hard for them to learn the truth. Marriages are part of the public record. A trip to city hall is all it would take."

Mai agreed, "You're right. In spite of what you and he said earlier, I'm not so smart, after all. I should have thought of that."

"Well, it's easy to take care of. Contact a J.P. when you get back to the city, and get married. There's no blood or other tests required, only paperwork. I looked into it when I was hoping to marry you. It would solve a potential problem with your uncles, and our situation won't change."

"I'll tell him when we are back in the city," Mai replied. "Bret will jump at the chance to make our cohabitation legal." She leaned forward and gave Jake a kiss, "There's no doubt about it. You're the smart one."

Jake was pleased Mai was feeling better. "Remember, we're a team."

"We sure are."

"By the way, I hope you're not concerned about Grace and me . . . or any other woman."

She smiled and with a tilt of her head indicated the bedroom where Bret was sleeping. "Of course not. My reaction was for his benefit. All the same, because of the way Larry treated me, I'm sensitive about anyone talking of women in a degrading manner. I know you're aware of my feelings and would never say anything to intentionally hurt me."

Jake cupped her face with his hands. He leaned and kissed her forehead.

She took his hands and held them in hers.

Neither spoke.

After some moments, Mai kidded, "You were smart to mention the favorable comparison between me and them. I might not have held back with my knee, and your voice would be a few octaves higher."

"I see, sorta like cutting off your nose to spite your face. It was the truth. No one comes close to you."

Mai mimicked a clown face before saying, "I know for appearances you have to date local girls, and Corrie is helping you find them. In fact, she refers to the honeys as *bimbos du jour*. She likes playing Cupid." Mai leaned in as if telling a secret. "When

I'm here permanently, I'll take her out once in a while to keep her close. As you've said, who knows when we'll need her."

Jake hadn't told Mai that for her help in procuring women he was providing Corrie with narcotics. He wanted to change the subject. "Listen, I have a few ideas I've been meaning to run by you."

She straightened, "Okay, so tell me."

"There's a home the real estate agent told me about. It sounds perfect for what we have planned. The house is on a road called Lover's Lane, and ..."

Interrupting, Mai said, "You're kidding? They named a street Lover's Lane?"

"Yeah, Google Earth it and see for yourself."

In a southern drawl, "Isn't that precious."

"If you'll let me finish ... ,"

Rolling her eyes, Mai sang, "I'm listening."

He continued, "There aren't any close neighbors, so no one will notice who comes and goes." He did an exaggerated clearing of his throat, "If it appeals to you and you wouldn't mind living there in spite of the hokey name, tell Bret it's where you want to be. He's so gaga over you he'll do anything."

"Well, he's not my cup of tea," she said as she checked her nails.

Jake pressed on, "Once Bret comes into the practice, I'm going to set a schedule allowing each of us a day off during the week. For me, I'm thinking Wednesday. For him, say, Thursday. When I'm not working, you and I can be together knowing he'll be in the office."

Mai's tone was tentative, "Sounds like that'll work, but what if he comes home unexpectedly?"

"I'll arrange for Corrie to call us. I'm pretty sure I can get her to do just about anything for us.

"Handy person to have on our side," Mai said.

"Sure is. In fact, she may be useful if something comes up that will change our situation." Jake raised his face to the ceiling as if looking toward heaven. "One opportunity is all I'm praying for."

Mai said, "Amen to that."

In contrast to her emotional state at the beginning of their conversation, Mai's mood had improved. She turned and began tickling Jake's ear, "I'm impressed. You seem to know just what to do." Kissing his cheek, "I didn't know you could be so devious." Sitting back, she said, "Although in my heart I knew we'd find a way out of our predicament, I wasn't sure it would work. Now, with your plan, we can do this." Her eyes held a touch of worry, "As the expression goes, we've begun the first day of the rest of our lives."

Jake caressed her cheek, "Glad you're feeling better."

She leaned in and they embraced.

Standing and pulling her to him in one motion, Jake led her to the bedroom, leaving a trail of clothes behind them.

In the throes of passion, Jake mumbled into her neck, "I love you so much."

Grabbing his head and holding his eyes with hers, Mai said, "I love you too, Jake."

The morning sun filtered through sheer curtains and woke Bret. He was greeted by a hangover headache similar to others he had when visiting Jake. He reasoned the headache wasn't from alcohol as he only had one drink the previous evening. He might be sensitive to a local allergen, perhaps pollen or a pollutant, and should see an allergist when he moved to the area. The good thing about his lost evening was his sinuses had cleared.

Mai was sprawled on her side of the bed. Bret gave her a kiss on the forehead before going to the bathroom. When finished, he decided to let Mai sleep and headed to the kitchen. Jake was watching the coffee machine complete its brewing cycle.

With an index finger Jake pointed at the pot. "Won't be more than a minute."

"Great, I need it." As Bret was speaking, he heard movement and turned toward his bedroom. In the last vestiges of sleep, Mai was walking and yawning her way down the hallway clad in a skimpy bra and lacy panties. A dark triangular patch showed under the panties.

"Whoa ..." Bret said, glancing at Jake.

In mid yawn, Mai stopped and looked at the men. She looked at herself. Eyes widening, she turned and ran to the bedroom. Within a few moments, she reappeared wrapped in a terry bathrobe. "If either of you say a word, I'll strangle you both."

The men, who hadn't moved since seeing her, looked at one another and began to chuckle. Male nervousness turned the chuckles into jokes and belly laughs.

An "Ahem!" from Mai put an end to the frivolity.

Bret attempted to allay Mai's embarrassment. "Don't be upset. It's not like Jake hasn't seen a woman in her underwear."

Mai and Jake glanced at each other and to Bret.

Jake took the baton, "Sure. We're men of the world, and we always have beautiful half-naked women around us.

"Always," Bret seconded, "That is, until you came along."

"Nice save," Mai said.

Seeing Mai relax as a result of the lighthearted camaraderie, Bret smiled. Looking at Jake, "Yeah, and anyway, I consider you like a brother to me."

Lover's Lane was a narrow curvy street bounded by Brick Top Road and Plains Road. The latter run from Willimantic, the main commercial area of Windham, to the historic and picturesque village of Windham Center. It was easy to imagine an earlier century when travel was by horse and buggy. They were at the house that Jake had mentioned.

After touring the house, Mai, Bret, and their realtor walked to their cars. Mai turned to Bret and said, "It's perfect. The moment I saw it I knew it was perfect." Sporting a big grin, she poked Bret's arm, "Even the name, Lover's Lane. Don't you think?"

"Yes, it's exactly what you're looking for. No doubt about it, it's a real country home away from noise and congestion."

The house, built in the 1800's, was a two-story white colonial with black shuttered windows. Full length brick chimneys ran up the exterior of the left and right sides and a third protruded from mid-roof. Both levels of the home consisted of wide-boarded hardwood floors. Despite its age, the house was in excellent condition.

It was set fifty yards from the road on fifteen acres of land. A dense wooded area of pine, maple, and oak surrounded the house on three sides. Across the street were acres of protected wetlands. A cinder driveway ran along the right side of the property before curving left to a free standing two car garage behind the main structure.

Mai insisted, "I really want to live here." Pouting, "Can we buy it?"

"You mean instead of renting?"

"Yes, then it would truly be ours."

"It's got four bedrooms and five fireplaces. It'd be difficult to manage," Bret cautioned.

Mai responded, "You forget, I won't be working. I'll be a full-time housewife. It shouldn't be too much for me to keep it in shape."

Bret ran the numbers in his head. Shrugging his shoulders, "I don't think we can afford it. For one thing, we'd have to come up with a thirty thousand dollar down payment. Where would we get that kind of money?"

Her voice was filled with excitement as she said, "What about the line of credit you got for opening the practice? It's more than enough to cover the down payment, and once you begin working, your salary should easily take care of the mortgage payments."

Acting as the devil's advocate, Bret said, "But it would put us at the limits of our budget. We'd have to forgo doing some of the things we were planning on, like a new car for you."

"I don't care about a new car," Mai insisted, "A cheap used one would be fine. As long as it runs."

Mai persisted, and that afternoon Bret arranged for a local lawyer to be their proxy at the closing. The next morning he and

Mai left Storrs to visit his mother and uncle before returning to New York.

"I'm really happy for you," Hubie Santos said. He and Bret were barbequing steaks in the backyard of Bret's mother's home in East Granby. "And I've got to tell you, she's a real looker."

"I know," Bret said. "Sometimes I wonder how I got so lucky. She could have anyone she wants, but she picked me. I'm just glad my buddy Jake didn't decide to hit on her. He's got it all over me."

"Don't sell yourself short," Hubie said. He rearranged the steaks cooking on the barbeque. "So what's the deal? You're going to be living together but tell everyone you're married?"

"Yeah, well, we're taking one step at a time. She agreed to go to Windham with me. Marriage can't be far behind."

Bret's uncle shook his head, "I guess I've been a lawyer too long, but my instinct tells me something isn't right. Why would she not want to marry you, but say she is? It doesn't make sense." Hubie looked into his nephew's eyes, "Don't take this wrong or get angry, but if you want, I can have my investigator check her background. I'm only saying this because I don't want to see you get hurt."

Bret was hurt, "Look, I know your intentions are good, but I could never do that. Please don't mention it again."

"Sorry." Hubie gave Bret a pat on the back before turning his attention to the steaks.

So shall I live, supposing thou art true,
Like a deceived husband...

———

Windham, Connecticut: In New York City Mai surprised Bret. "I've been thinking. When we go to Connecticut, it would be better if we're really married rather than just saying we are."

Bret's "There is a God" was unintelligible.

"Let's get married," she said.

The proposal was the answer to Bret's prayer. It proved his uncle was wrong about Mai. Controlling his excitement, he said, "I think so, too." His mind was swirling with questions about the ceremony. How lavish? Who to invite? What facility? And a million other details that had to be resolved.

Bret wanted Mai to have the major say in what they did. He asked, "How should we arrange it? Your family isn't around, but mine is. My people can come here, or we can hold the ceremony and reception in Connecticut. Whatever you want."

Mai seemed to consider Bret's questions and suggestions, "It would be nice to get together with your relatives, but please, try to understand my feelings. Since my family back in Macao won't be able to attend, I'd rather not do anything elaborate. It wouldn't feel right if we did. Let's just get married by a JP and keep it to ourselves for now."

After further discussion and encouragement by Mai and her delicious body, Bret acquiesced, and they were married by a local justice of the peace. The JP's wife acted as a combination witness, maid of honor, and giver of the bride. In his past, the JP had been a professional singer, and as a welcome perk, he serenaded the newlyweds for the better part of an hour with a repertoire of 1960's songs. The bride couldn't wait to leave, but the groom loved it.

On a sunny June afternoon, Mai and Bret were at Penn Station waiting for a train to take her to New Haven. That morning their possessions were loaded on a van bound for Windham. Bret had asked Jake to meet Mai at the station and drive her to the Lover's Lane home. Bret was left with what was needed to survive a few weeks in the city.

As she boarded the train, Mai said, "Don't worry about me. I'm going to fix up the house, so it'll be ready for you. You'll only have to concentrate on beginning your new practice."

Bret was going to be on a tight schedule. His plan was to leave New York on a Thursday and start practicing in Windham the following Monday. He hugged her and spoke into her ear. "That's great. I'm going to have a lot to do as it is. Having the house squared away will allow me to give all my attention to the office." His eyes glistened, "I've said it many times, and it's always true, you're wonderful. I love you for what you're doing." Bret's final piece of advice was, "Remember, any problems, call Jake. Damn good thing he's available while I'm not there."

"Yes," she agreed, "damn good thing."

Two weeks after Mai left, Bret loaded his suitcases in the Firebird and departed the city. He anticipated a special and personal greeting in Windham.

When he arrived, Bret found that Mai had kept her word about taking care of the place. It was in pristine condition. She greeted him with a glass of iced tea. He didn't want tea. He was horny and wanted her. Glass in hand, he followed her from room to room as she reviewed what had been done in his absence. He couldn't take his eyes from her body or stop thinking about sex.

Since Mai seemed disinterested, he tried to redirect his thoughts. "You've really done a terrific job of turning an old house into a terrific home," he said. Eyeing his suitcases, "I guess I should get started on unpacking."

"Leave them," Mai was quick to say. "I'll take care of everything later. Right now, I want to introduce you to a neighbor."

Aware he wasn't getting anyplace with Mai, he said, "Say no more. Let's go visiting." He headed to the front door. "Tell me about this neighbor."

Before answering, she said, "Not that way. Follow me."

Mai led him to the kitchen in the rear of the house and opened the back door. "Her name is Frankie Grimaldi. A wonderful person. A few generations ago, she would have been called a flower child. You're going to like her."

They walked onto a large back porch bordered by a small patch of grass. The vista was dominated by thick woods on three sides. Mai walked to the tree line on the left. With Bret in tow, she found and followed a winding and overgrown footpath for fifty yards. Walking it was not a problem if you were willing to duck under branches and hop an occasional log. It opened onto the rear of the Grimaldi property.

Bret marveled at Mai's courage. He was certain spiders and ticks were seeking every aperture in his clothing trying to take a bite of his juicy pink flesh or a drink of his high octane blood. Not to mention snakes. "Aren't you worried about getting bitten by something?"

"Who, me? Of course not. Don't forget, I was a country girl before I met you."

Breaking from the woods, they came upon Frankie Grimaldi's manicured lawn. Flowers and other plantings were proof Frankie spent a good deal of time working in her yard. Bret was sure that endeared her to Mai, who talked of the flower and herb gardens she was planning for her country paradise.

Instead of going to Frankie Grimaldi's Cape Cod style home, they milled about the property as Mai pointed out the features of the yard. "Look at her roses. I count at least five varieties. They're floribundas."

With a confused expression, Bret replied, "Flora-what?"

Before Mai answered, a slim, red-headed woman wearing bib overalls came sprinting out of the screened back door. It would be a crass understatement to say the overalls were baggy. Someone twice Frankie's size could have fit into them. With a broad smile and a cigarette in her hand, she approached Bret with her right arm outstretched in the female fashion of no bend at the elbow when shaking hands. "You must be Bret," she said as she grabbed his hand and pumped it with vigor.

His feeble attempt at a glib reply was, "Yes . . . I must be Bret."

"Frankie . . . Frankie Grimaldi . . . sooo good to finally meet you. Welcome to my home." She continued pumping. Anyone observing them from a distance would think they were having an arm wrestling contest. "Is it okay to call you Bret, or is it more proper to call you Dr. Manley?"

"Bret. By all means, call me Bret."

Frankie let go of his hand. "Some of my friends call me F.G. You can call me that if you want. I just know in no time we'll be great friends."

"I'll stick to Frankie, if it's all right with you."

"Sure is," Frankie said, as she turned to Mai to give her a kiss on the cheek and a prolonged bear hug. Mai hugged back with equal force. Bret saw the women had become great friends and was pleased. He liked Frankie. It was hard not to. As Frankie predicted, Bret knew he would become a great friend.

"Why don't you guys come in for a cup of coffee?"

"You don't have to ask twice," Mai said.

They sat at an antique coffee table in the family room drinking strong coffee from an espresso machine. Frankie chain smoked and didn't apologize for it. What followed was a pleasant afternoon during which Frankie gave an unabbreviated history of the Windham region spoken from the viewpoint of a native. Her verbosity was part of a charming quirkiness radiating from her like rays from an exploding sun. Her love of the area gave a welcome affirmation to Mai and Bret's decision to come to Windham.

Her personal history followed. "Frankie, that's what is says on my birth certificate. Most people think its short for Francis or something, but it isn't." She turned to Mai, "Didn't you?"

Mai nodded.

Bret wondered if she was being polite.

"Yeah, mom and dad wanted the name, even if they had a girl. It was the name of my grandfather." Frankie continued, "Let me tell you a little about myself."

Without taking a breath, "I'm an artist. My father's a businessman. Owns a plumbing supply store downtown. Mom manages the books and helps out in the place. I'm not ashamed to say their financial backing allows me to pursue art as a career."

About five-foot-four, Frankie looked to be in her mid-twenties. She had a boyish body and natural red hair. "I got my hair from my mother. She's pure Irish and, as they say, has the map of Ireland on her face."

Bret guessed her emerald green eyes, small upturned nose, and pale mini-freckles that illuminated her skin like fairy dust were also bequeathed from the same source. If she received features from what he assumed was her Italian father, they were hidden by clothes.

Most of the rooms in the lower level were cluttered with the paraphernalia of an artist. Paintings and canvases were strewn everywhere. Multicolored dried paint was seen in copious amounts on furniture and floors, although most of the paint spatters and brush wipes were on Frankie's bib overalls. The overalls, Bret was to find, were an all-purpose outfit she wore and may have slept in. The acrid odor of cigarette smoke clung to everything in the house. It was the one thing that could be considered offensive, and he was sure Mai would wash their clothes the moment they returned to their house.

Throughout the home were several photographs of a woman who looked younger than Frankie. Dark haired and sultry, the mysterious lady seemed as serious and contemplative as Frankie was lighthearted and carefree. Judging from pictures of her with Frankie and other family members, she was adored. Bret assumed she was a sister who resembled their dad.

In contrast to her demeanor in the photos, a portrait of the young lady hung over the mantle. She was wearing a red dress and smiling as if she had heard a hilarious joke and was about to laugh. The portrait was signed by Frankie. As Bret was examining it, Frankie came to him, put a gentle hand on his shoulder, and said, "That's Sara Cunningham. She was my partner before she died two years ago from ovarian cancer." Shaking her head, "She's left a big void in my life."

"I'm sorry," was his automatic response as he glanced at Mai.

In a positive tone, Frankie replied, "Don't be. I miss her very much . . . more than I could have thought possible ... but the happiness we shared was enough to last two lifetimes. For that, I'm grateful. From what I've seen, most people never experience the kind of love we shared." Her eyes reflected the sincerity of her words, "I truly hope you and Mai have what we had."

Bret felt a tightening in his throat and looked toward Mai. "We do," he said.

Although Mai had been a guest in Frankie's house several times and familiar with the photographs and portrait, she appeared affected by the genuine display of love for Sara. Going from photo to photo, she gazed at them as if trying to memorize every detail and concluded with a study of the portrait. Wiping tears with the side of her hand, Mai turned and made a beeline for Frankie and embraced her.

These rare views of Mai's inner feelings were welcomed by Bret. He was eager to glean as much about her as possible, and moments like this exposed facets of her personality hidden by an aura of sophistication. The more he learned, the more impressed he was by the depth of her emotions. Early in their relationship he came to realize that within her was heartfelt compassion for the suffering of others. He remembered walking into her New York apartment and catching her weeping as she listened to Bob Dylan's *Boots of Spanish Leather*, a ballad about a woman who sails away and out of the life of the man who loves her.

While Mai grieved, Bret couldn't keep from pondering the sexual relationship between Frankie and Sara. Although physically feminine, Frankie had an outgoing and assertive personality he considered masculine. Bib overalls added to her masculinity. On the other hand, both in portrait and photographs Sara seemed feminine and submissive. *Those have to be the roles they played in their daily lives and in the bedroom.* Images of the two women in the throes of lesbian sex flashed in his brain. Aroused, he went to Mai and put a hand on her shoulder, "Don't you think we should be getting back?"

That evening Bret got the welcome he craved. Lying in bed with arms behind his head, he looked to Mai whose back was to him. "I've been thinking," he said, "It's very likely we've come to the community where we will die. Hopefully, of very old age." He propped himself on one elbow and pressed against her back to determine if she was awake. She was sleeping. He continued talking as if Mai was listening. "This is where almost all our good and bad memories are destined to be made. Where our kids, if we have any, will be born." Another nudge garnered no response. "And less than two years ago, I was no more familiar with this place than the dark side of the moon." In the answering silence, he turned, arranged his pillows, and went to sleep.

Morning brought a gust front that promised rain, and the wind played a dissonant tune through the trees. Bret performed a final review of applications for his 10 a.m. interviews. His plan was to spend about a half-hour with each candidate, but he would be flexible if circumstances warranted.

By noon and the start of a torrential rainstorm, he had chosen two assistants: Juanita Perez, called Pearlie, was a graduate of the local dental assisting school, and Ronald Franks, a combination licensed practical nurse and emergency medical technician, was a recent discharge from the military.

Pearlie was twenty-years-old and possessed the enthusiasm characteristic of her age. Tall with full lips accented by dark eyes and jet black hair worn in a ponytail, Pearlie was fluent in English and Spanish, skills useful in a dental office. She wore a necklace holding one large black pearl around her neck.

"I've never met a Pearlie before, is it a family name?"

"No. As you can see from my application, my birth name was Juanita. When I was a child, my father found this black pearl while clamming at the shore." She held the pearl from her neck with her thumb and index finger to give Bret a better look. "His habit was to eat the clams on the spot as he dug them up. Always had Tabasco and lemons with him. Just as he was about to swallow one, dad felt something hard. It turned out to be this pearl. Good thing he didn't swallow." She let go of the pearl, "Working with jewelry is his hobby, so he set it in a necklace for me. I've worn it ever since. My friends started calling me Pearlie, and the name stuck. Now, everyone knows me as Pearlie. I like it better than Juanita."

In his early thirties, Ron Franks was of average height with a trim athletic build and buzz-cut brown hair. He was ex-Special Forces, having been a member of the elite U.S.A.F. Pararescue unit until an injury resulted in a permanent limp and ended his military career.

Upon discharge from the Air Force, he earned LPN and EMT certificates and worked at several jobs including a hospital emergency room and an ambulance service. Bret was happy to have him on board, although the interview led him to suspect Ron had a bit of wanderlust and would seek a more exciting job when the opportunity presented. Until that time, Ron would be a good man to have working with him.

On the glass door of the reception room, *Bret Manley, D.M.D.* and *Jacob Warden, D.D.S.* were stenciled in black paint. In smaller lettering was *Oral and Maxillofacial Surgery.* An unmarked staff entrance was available, but pride and excitement caused Bret to use the main entrance on his first day in private practice.

The physical set-up was typical of two-doctor dental offices with three operatories, laboratories, a reception room, and business area. Jake and Bret had separate offices for privacy. Paintings and prints adorned the pastel colored walls and satellite radio supplied music.

His most interesting patient that day was Giovanni Rossi, an elderly Italian man brought in by his wife. He was frail and anemic looking and unable to stand without assistance. Bret recognized his condition was grave.

Taken to an examining room and interviewed, Mr. Rossi's heavily accented words revealed that English was not his first language. "I tella you I hava no much money. I pay you with vegetable from my garden. If that'sa all right with you."

"It would be wonderful, Mr. Rossi, we would love fresh vegetables. But, at the moment, I need to know what's bothering you."

The old man pointed to his gums with a finger, "This'sa. They bleed."

Bret suspected a form of leukemia. Bleeding gums were a common symptom of the disease. "I have to take a blood test. Is that okay with you?"

"Schuu."

A stat blood confirmed Bret's suspicion, and he referred Giovanni to a hematological oncologist.

When his last patient of the day had been discharged, Bret poked his head into Jake's office. Jake was sitting at his desk completing records. "Thanks for booking patients for me and filling my first day's schedule."

"No problem. I wanted you to be busy, although you'll find it's a lot less stressful here than in the clinic at Manhattan Memorial."

"I found that out by lunch. Pearlie and Ron were great. I set the bar high, and they exceeded my expectations. I can say my debut into the practice of oral surgery in Windham has been a resounding success."

"Glad to hear that. Having good people to assist is important."

"By the way," Bret said, "I was going to consult with you about a patient I saw, an old Italian gentleman by the name of Giovanni Rossi. He told me he was from, as he quaintly put it, the old country. Talked with a heavy accent."

Jake's interest was piqued, "What about him?"

He came in complaining of bleeding gums. I did a stat workup. His white cells were off the chart. I was going to ask who to refer him to, but you were in the middle of a case, and I didn't want to disturb you. I remembered Jerry Pringle. Met him at our opening party. He agreed to see my guy. Said he'd keep me posted on the man's progress. Thinks it's one of the curable leukemias. I hope so."

Jake nodded, "Jerry's who I would have told you to send him to. If anyone can cure him, he can."

Bret looked at his watch, "Well, I'm going home. See you tomorrow."

Jake said, "Till then," and continued doing his paperwork.

Entering the house through the back door, Bret headed to the kitchen counter he used as a bar and celebrated his first day of work with a Hendrick's gin and tonic with a slice of cucumber.

Mai came from the living room and saw the glass. "I don't know how you can drink that with cucumber in it."

"Well, at first, I didn't think I'd like it. But the packet that came with the bottle suggested a cucumber slice, and believe it or not, it tastes really good. No one objects to drinking a Bloody Mary with celery."

"Well, if you like it." She went to the pantry, "I've got to organize this room better. I can't find some spices I need for dinner."

Bret heard rummaging.

"Ah, good. Here they are."

Bret continued the discussion of his liquor preferences. "It must be my Scottish blood. I like everything from Scotland. You know I think Glenrothes is the nectar of the gods. *Glad that reaction to alcohol I was having seems to have disappeared.*

"Uh-huh," Mai said from the pantry, "I've heard that plenty of times."

Mai had ironed the tablecloth and set the table as if company were coming. Dinner was a pork loin marinated in red wine and cooked with prunes.

"This is great," Bret said as he placed another piece of pork on his plate. "You obviously put a lot of effort in tonight's meal."

"Thank you." Mai smiled, "You know how terrible my cooking

skills were. In spite of all the good Chinese and Portuguese dishes I grew up on, I didn't learn a thing other than how to eat them. But, I've been reading up on culinary techniques. That's how I was able to make this loin." With a knife Mai pointed at the leftover pork. "I want to be even better. I'm going to take the same cooking class at the university Jake took." She added, "If you have no objections."

"Certainly not. It'll benefit me, too."

"Ohh!" was Mai's involuntary reaction when startled by the unexpected rapping at her back door. She had been watching for the approach of Jake's car. His habit was to enter the driveway and continue to the garage in the back of the house. It was part of their usual Wednesday routine. Braless under a pink sleeveless jersey and wearing denim Daisy Duke shorts, she approached the kitchen door and looked through the window of its upper half. Jake was standing there with a grin on his face.

Gazing past him to confirm no hiker or nature lover was walking the forested area behind her house, she opened the door. "Quick, come in before someone sees you."

Jake entered, and Mai closed the door. It was a gorgeous late summer day and the windows of the kitchen provided a rustic view of tall grass and woods.

"I didn't see your car come up the driveway."

He removed his royal blue New York Yankees baseball cap and hung it on the pointy back of one of the kitchen table chairs. "I didn't drive here. My car's on Plains Road in the recreation area lot. I jogged."

Mai took a close look at him, "So that's why you're all sweaty." Jake's gray shorts and blue tee with the Eastern Connecticut State University logo on it were darkened with sweat stains. She asked, "Why did you do that? More than for exercise, I assume."

"It's safer. At least during those times when people expect to see joggers around. No strange car driving in and out of your yard." Jake went to a window facing the side yard and pointed in the general direction of the Plains Road ball field. "I pretended to be just another exercise fanatic. It's less than a mile, but by the sweat on me, you can tell I'm not used to running." He grabbed a dishtowel hanging from the stove and wiped his forehead. "To make it seem legit to some kids who were playing there, I did some stretching before I started out."

Mai shook her head, although her smile revealed she was impressed.

Jake continued, "This way, if something unexpected happens, like Bret showing up in spite of our precautions, I can slip out any door and take the path to the Grimaldi property. From there it's just a matter of sneaking through the woods to get to the road. Then, I simply jog back to my car." Jake went to Mai, took her hands, and held them. "Pretty good, huh?"

Being the devil's advocate, Mai said, "And when it's cold or there's snow on the ground and people aren't jogging?"

Jake feigned exasperation and let go her hands. "No plan is perfect. I'll drive into the garage as usual, or you can come to my place."

Mai seemed to consider Jake's words. Her face lit up, "You dog," she said "You're absolutely right. And, who would suspect? I haven't heard of any neighborhood watches in this area, so I guess what you're doing is safe."

Jake gave her an *I told you so* look.

It was Mai's turn. "I'm doing my part, too, by enrolling in the same cooking class at UConn that you took. It will give me an excuse to come to your condo on Monday nights. All you have to do is give me a few pointers." Batting her eyes and mimicking a Southern belle, "If y'all know what I mean, Rhett?"

Jake chuckled at the double entendre. It was a good sign Mai was active in arranging for them to be together. He reached out and wrapped his muscular arms around her and pulled her to him. "Why yes, ma'am. I rightly know what you mean, and I intend to give you some, as you say, pointers." He brought his lips to hers. The familiar and exotic taste aroused him. He wanted her.

Mai enjoyed their stolen moments of intimacy as much as he, but wasn't ready for lovemaking. There were issues to be addressed.

"Hold on, we need to talk first."

"What?" Jake groaned as his arousal subsided.

Mai said, "I've been thinking. Maybe, I can use Frankie as an excuse to stop having sex with him."

"What are you talking about?"

She walked to the kitchen window and looked at the distant trees before turning and leaning against the counter next to the sink. "Look, I don't' want to give you the wrong impression. Frankie hasn't made the slightest sexual overture toward me. But, what if I told Bret she had?" She paused as if thinking. "What if I said I was receptive to and even welcomed her advances? I've come to realize I'm a lesbian. I didn't know it until her prodding uncovered what I really am."

Jake wanted Mai to understand her idea wouldn't work as she envisioned. He knew Bret. The man would become angry, charge Frankie with something she hadn't done, and want to divorce Mai. Instead of being a solution, her plan would create a Pandora's Box of problems. He had enough of a problem coping with her last scheme. She was acting in desperation. He had to convince her it was a poor idea without causing an uproar. He asked, "Have you thought it out completely?"

Mai showed her hurt over Jake's implied rejection, and retorted, "At least it would keep him off me."

Although the words stung, he had to settle her. "Bret would confront Frankie and accuse her of sexual harassment. She'd have no idea what he was talking about and, naturally, would deny it. With accusations and counter-accusations, it would escalate into a real shitstorm." He apologized, "Excuse my language. You hate it when I swear."

Mai nodded and said, "That's another subject, but, yes, I do. It reminds me of my father, always cursing, and mother tolerating it. He thought I was too young to understand, but I wasn't."

She took a breath, "But I see your point."

Seeing Mai accepted his argument, Jake tempered her letdown by suggesting, "Let's keep your idea on the back burner. Why don't you develop a close friendship with Frankie, not sexual of course, and make sure Bret is aware of it? We may be able to use your relationship with her to our advantage if an opportunity presents." Jake turned serious. "Remember, everything between you and Bret has to seem normal for the scheme to work. I hate what we're doing even more than you, but we've committed, and that's how it's got to be. We're in this thing too deep and can't afford to take chances."

Mai put her arms around his neck. "Not only do I love you, I trust you. You're my lighthouse in a storm, guiding me to a safe harbor. I'll do what you say." She kissed him long and deep. It was the signal he was waiting for. She began to rhythmically grind her pelvis into him, and he became hard.

Jake couldn't resist saying, "So, you're thinking of becoming a lesbian?"

Caught off guard, Mai said, "No . . . Never . . . I was only . . ." before she realized he was teasing. Taking his cue, "I mean . . . why, yes. I thought I would give it a try . . . see what it's all about."

In his most sexy voice, "Would you be a Frankie or a Sara?"

She answered in a murmuring, breathless voice, "Sara. I'd be a submissive Sara . . . very submissive."

"Then, I'll be Frankie."

Pressing with all her strength against his body, she whispered, "Yes, you be Frankie. I'll call you Frankie."

He turned her, placed a guiding arm around her back, and escorted her to the couch in the adjacent family room. "And I'll call you Sara."

He unzipped and removed Mai's shorts, and, to his pleasant surprise, she wore nothing under them. True to her word, Mai in the role of Sara was obedient and submissive. Jake's rough beard rubbed against soft inner thighs. He felt the sweet shivering sensations that roamed her body.

"Do you like this, Sara?"

"Oh, Frankie, I like it very . . . very . . . much."

Jake continued his Wednesday jogs to Mai's house. On this

particular Wednesday, they were in an upstairs bedroom, and Mai was riding him like a bareback bronco rider. It was her favorite position. She relished the control.

The bells attached to a leather strap nailed to the kitchen door chimed signaling the door was being opened.

"Hi, hon," Bret called, "I'm home."

"Oh my God," Jake grabbed her hips, lifted her off, and was out of bed in a flash. "He must have left the office early and that fucking Corrie didn't phone. He's going to catch us." Jake snatched his clothes from the floor and began to dress in a fumbling hurry. "I'm going to kill her."

Mai scooted off the bed and took her clothes from the chair they were on. "He won't catch us," she said in a calm voice. "I'll go downstairs and keep him busy in the living room. In the meantime, hide in my closet and wait. When the coast is clear, come down and sneak out the back."

Jake was nervous, "Okay, but make sure he stays in the living room so he won't see me."

Mai whispered, "I'll handle it. Be careful, Frankie may be working in her yard. I'll call when I can." She kissed him on the cheek and went to the stairway. "Be right down," she called.

It wasn't until the weekend that Mai got in touch with Jake. She said, "When he came in the door, he heard noise coming from upstairs and asked what I was doing, I told him I was exercising. Doing squats to tone my legs. He believed it. In a way, it wasn't a lie." They both chuckled.

"How come Corrie didn't call?" she said.

Jake's hangdog expression said it all. "My fault. I was at a hospital meeting that morning, and had put my phone on vibrate. She called several times, but it was in my pants pocket."

Mai teased, "Doofus."

"I know, I know," Jake said. "We lucked out. If he caught us, it would have been the end of our so called well-laid plans.

Mai was as relieved as Jake that Bret hadn't discovered them. Thinking about their close call had put her in a giddy mood. "Well . . . they were almost well-laid. About as close as you can get."

"Very Funny," he said, and added, "How come we didn't hear him? The Firebird's loud enough."

"Didn't pull all the way into the driveway. Most of his afternoon patients cancelled, so he rescheduled the rest and left the office early. He had set-up a tennis match at the club and was just stopping by to change into his tennis clothes and get his racket. The front door was locked, and he didn't have the key with him. Doesn't like to carry a lot of keys. Walked around to the back door. After a moment, "By the way, were you in the closet when he was changing?

"No, I ended up going out one of the windows onto the porch roof and shimmied down a pole. The bushes hid me." Jake added, "My plan of jogging to your house saved us."

The first months of private practice proved to be a learning experience for Bret. Seeing patients who were not the property of a hospital required both technical prowess and a pleasant bedside manner. Ron Franks left for more exciting days. He accepted a position with an agency rescuing Thai children from cruel and perverted masters. Bret wished him luck in his new endeavor and hoped Ron would find the fulfillment he was seeking.

Sandy Lizee, an LPN, replaced him. She had been employed by Windham Hospital and was looking for less stress and a work schedule that didn't include weekends. She was competent in the skills needed for the office and was accepted by Pearlie and the gang.

Giovanni Rossi's leukemia was in remission, and he made an unannounced visit to the office. Handing Bret a bag with vegetables, he said, "You sava my life. I always remember. Feel bad I no pay."

Bret tried to dispel Giovanni's feeling of indebtedness.

"Making people well is my job. That's reward enough for me. Besides, these vegetables are better than money."

The old man smiled.

Giovanni made several unannounced visits to the office. They were welcome respites in Bret's day. The staff, who handled the interruptions in the schedule, had a different opinion.

The two men chatted in Bret's private office. The eighty-one-year-old man was born and raised in Italy and came to America when in his thirties. Giovanni spoke of his youth in Umbria and of his reputation as the best mushroom picker in the region. He knew everything about mushrooms and at a glance could determine if one was poisonous.

He enjoyed having his wife drive him to a favorite rural area to pick them. Giovanni would disappear into the solitude of the forest and go to a secret place he discovered. When Bret asked why he didn't tell his wife about the spot, Giovanni said, "She lika to talk and tella her friends."

Bret stifled a laugh.

Summer flew as Mai adjusted to life in Windham Center. A favorite pastime was tending to the vegetable, herb, and flower gardens she planted.

On a Saturday morning in August Mai was weeding in the garden while Bret was on the porch sitting in a rocker and skimming a medical journal. He placed the journal on a wicker table and looked at his wife, "You're unbearably cute when you put your hair in pigtails and wear old jeans."

Mai stopped working and straightened herself. Leaning on her hoe, she said, "I'm becoming an expert in handling gardening tools. Look at these plants. They're huge with not a weed among them."

"I noticed. And I believe you've set a record for growing tomatoes and squash."

We can't possibly eat all of them."

"Fortunately, being a good neighbor and friend, Frankie takes the overflow of vegetables although she has more than enough from her own garden."

"Yeah, I'm glad you and she have become such good friends."

Mai walked to the flower beds and worked with the hoe as she spoke, "Did you notice how well the herbs and flowers are doing? With my new interest in cooking, the ability to pick fresh herbs is nothing short of thrilling. And cuttings of my irises and roses look beautiful and perfume the house."

"Not enough to cover remnants of cigarette smoke. When I come home, I can tell if Frankie has been here by the odor. She seems to be a frequent visitor."

Mai stopped hoeing and challenged, "You're not bothered by her visits, are you? You know, because she's a lesbian?"

"Not at all. I look forward to seeing her and listening to her unconventional thoughts on any subject that pops into her mind. Most people have a filter that limits what comes out of their mouths. Frankie doesn't have one, or if she does, it's broken. She marches to a different drummer."

Mai laughed, "You said a mouthful."

In September, Mai announced she had enrolled in a culinary class at the University of Connecticut. It gave her the excuse to spend Monday nights with Jake. She left her house minutes after Bret got home. There was time for a quick kiss goodbye as she rushed to her car.

Autumn foliage painted the landscape in bright reds, oranges, and yellows. Cooler days required sweaters and jackets, and evenings were warmed by heat from furnaces. The community anticipated the first snow.

Mai decided to display the cooking skills Jake had taught her by inviting Frankie and Jake to Thanksgiving dinner. Jake brought Molly Robinson, his current girlfriend. Having close friends present for her first attempt at preparing a major holiday meal lessened the pressure of the event. If she wasn't ready for prime time, no one was going to be disappointed.

"Not seeing Grace Putnam anymore?" Bret asked Jake when

they were alone. Jake had not mentioned a breakup.

The reply was vague, "Naw, it just didn't work out. Corrie introduced me to Molly. She's a substitute first grade teacher."

Molly Robinson looked about five years younger than Jake. Tall and skinny, she tried to hide her height by slouching. Molly was not a user of cosmetics, and her eyeglasses were kept from falling by a chain attached to the earpieces. She was the type you might see every day, but couldn't describe. To say she was unremarkable was to be kind. Bret was surprised Jake settled for someone as plain as she.

It was conversing with Molly that brought you to the pinnacle of disappointment. Her most poignant opinions were agreements with whatever was being said put in the form of what sounded like "A-haw." The most intellectual assessment she gave of anyone was, "He's (she's) so funny."

Boasting he had completed the university culinary class the prior year, Jake played the role of master chef. He hovered about Mai in the kitchen offering various cooking tips. "Remember, sausage and cheese have salt in them, so don't add more to the stuffing mix."

Mai didn't order him from her domain as some temperamental chefs would have. She thanked him for his advice and suggested he and Molly watch the Macy's Parade on TV.

During dinner, Frankie said to Mai, "I used to teach art, and a few of my friends have asked me to give them some pointers. I'm putting together a beginner's group with a flexible schedule. Sort of a come when you can type of thing. Have you considered taking up painting?"

Mai turned to her with a surprised look. The tongue in cheek response was, "I take it you're not impressed with my cooking."

A blush covered Frankie's light complexioned face that hid her freckles and accented her green eyes. She verbally retreated, "Oh, no. Gosh, you're a fine cook. Today's dinner proves it. I was only suggesting another outlet for your considerable talent.

Mai chuckled. "Good comeback, Frankie." Responding to the question. "I have to admit seeing what you've done has made me think about it." After a moment of thought, "Sure, I'd love to join your class."

"Wonderful. It should be fun," Frankie said.

The next day Frankie and Mai visited a downtown Willimantic art supply shop. They returned with a variety of brushes, paints, canvases, palettes, an easel, cleaning supplies, and *How To* books.

When he saw the cost of what were considered basic art supplies, Bret remarked, "No wonder they're called starving artists."

Canvases in various stages of completion began to fill the family room. Several were covered with cloth. "Until I complete a painting, I don't want anyone to see it," Mai warned.

One afternoon after work, Bret peeked under the cloth covering the largest of the paintings. Although incomplete, it was a painting of Mai lying naked on the living room couch. "What's this?" he called to Mai who was in the kitchen, "Is Frankie painting a nude of you?"

Mai came into the room and replaced the cloth. The chill in her voice was evident as she said, "Please don't remove this again."

Bret stared at the covered painting as she returned to the kitchen.

Knew curiosity would get the better of you. That's why I painted it. Are you wondering why a lesbian is painting a nude of your woman? Sorry, Jake, had to do it.

Mai rang in the New Year by losing interest in sex. Within weeks the condition progressed to a complete lack of desire for physical intimacy.

"Why don't you see Dr. Ross? She says she may be able to help us with our problem," Bret said. Mai and he were sitting at the kitchen table after dinner. Bret was referring to Dr. Elaine Ross, a psychologist who specialized in treating sexual disorders. She had an office in Mansfield and was associated with a local psychiatric hospital.

Mai looked at him with anger plastered on her face. "Don't tell me you talked about me without my permission?"

Bret backtracked. "No. I only spoke in general terms when we were sitting next to each other at a hospital staff meeting. I want you to feel better before we go to Las Vegas. Even though I'll be tied up at the meeting a good deal of the time, it should be a fun getaway."

Mai calmed and said, "About the Vegas meeting," she paused to insure Bret's attention, "I'm not going with you. You should be spending all your time concentrating on passing your board certification examinations. I don't want to distract you."

Bret spent a half hour trying to convince her to accompany him to Las Vegas. She wouldn't budge, but promised to make an appointment to see Dr. Ross.

Bret told her, "At the staff meeting she recommended I masturbate . . . you too . . . until we solve the problem of your loss of libido. Psychologists recommend it when couples are having problems."

"Oh, God."

"Don't worry. I don't intend to follow her advice, either."

Bret arrived in Las Vegas on a clear, crisp February day. Although the city is located in a desert, it is a high desert, and winters are cold. He had never been to Vegas and based on its geographical location assumed it would be warm if not hot. He had packed light summer clothes and had to visit to a local clothing store to get warmer things. The challenge was to avoid looking like a cowboy from Montana.

A bellman named Sal escorted Bret to his room. After reviewing the room's features, Sal said with a raspy accent, "Not for nothing, but there ain't nobody here wich you. I'm right, no?"

Bret wondered why the leer and the question. He nodded.

"You need or want anything . . . anything . . . give me a shout." To make certain Bret got his unsubtle meaning, the second anything was spoken as if it was a piece of taffy being pulled to its limits. He handed Bret a hotel card on which Sal and a telephone number were handwritten. With one hand cupping the side of his mouth, he repeated, "All's it takes is a call." and slinked out of the room.

Bret rolled the card between his thumb and fingers and wondered if the management knew Sal, the bellman, had a side business at the hotel. He assumed they did but turned a blind eye. Sal was giving the customer what he wanted. The card deserved to be thrown in the trash or flushed. He placed it in the top drawer of one of the nightstands next to the bed.

The first day of the conference proved long and boring and resulted in an eyestrain headache. Eight hundred milligrams of ibuprofen and a double shot of scotch was his preferred method of treatment. The hotel bar didn't carry Glenrothes so he ordered Johnny Walker Black, the designated and capable pinch hitter. He downed the ibuprofen with the Black before returning to his room. A room service dinner was on his agenda.

After finishing his meal, he called Mai. The phone rang several times.

"Hi, it's me," he said, trying to sound upbeat.

There was a pause, "Oh, I didn't recognize your voice." After another moment of silence, "How's the conference?"

"Agony. I feel like coming home."

"Don't do that," she advised. "The course is only for a few days. You'd feel guilty if you left before it was over."

"Ahh, did you make an appointment with Dr. Ross?" he said.

"Not yet, I haven't gotten around to it." Mai yawned into the phone.

"Tired?"

"A little. Remember, its three hours later here. It's after eleven, and I was set to go to bed."

They spoke for another five minutes. The coolness in her voice chilled him. He reflected on their conversation and became angry. *She should have encouraged me to come home. We could spend a few days together before I have to go back to work. Take a sort of mini-vacation. Maybe even go to New York and see a show. Pisses me off that she doesn't want me home, and that she didn't schedule an appointment with Ross.*

Had Mai stopped loving him? He feared the answer. He

had been doing all he could to help Mai with her depression, but it'd been close to a month without sex. *I'm not going to waste my time jerking-off while she's done nothing to help herself.* He made a decision. Opening the night table drawer, he found the bellman's card. After calling room service for a double shot of Mr. Black, Bret dialed Sal's number.

Nervous sweat covered him. He had never needed the services of a prostitute and hadn't the faintest idea about dealing with one. He'd give it three rings.

Before the second ring, he heard, "This is Sal."

Caught off guard by the prompt and abrupt answer, Bret hesitated.

"I said, this is Sal," louder and less friendly.

"Uh, hi . . . um . . . this is Bret Manley . . . in room 510. You gave me your card yesterday when I checked in."

"What's it you want?"

Has he forgotten giving me the card? "Well, as I said, you . . ."

Interrupting, "Look, what I got to know is what kind of broad you want? Or if you want more than one? White, Black, Asian, I've got them all. What's your kink?"

Words failed Bret.

"Ahh, now, I remember you. You're into the kinky stuff, right? Man, have I got someone you'll like. She'll handcuff you to the bed and use whips and sticks like you ain't never gonna forget. Whatever you need, I got it. Long as you're willing to pay."

"No," Bret shouted into the phone. "I want one woman. No whips or other gadgets. Just one" . . . it was uncomfortable for him to say . . . "Gorgeous woman."

"Any color preference, or to be more p.c., ethnic group?" He made p.c. sound like profanity.

The question raised disturbing possibilities he hadn't thought of. He didn't want anyone who would remind him of Mai.

"C'mon, I ain't got all night."

Bret chose plain vanilla, "White." He corrected, "Caucasian," as if proper English was required when negotiating with a pimp.

"You're going to thank me after you see the one I'm sending.

Beautiful … twenty-one … but, it's gonna cost you."

To his surprise, Bret felt himself becoming erect. "How much?"

"Five C-notes for an hour. In cash."

Horrified, Bret repeated, "Five hundred dollars?"

"Yeah, and in cash. You give it to her first thing, see. And don't force her to do nuthin she doesn't want, capisce? Remember, we know where you live, and I'm not talking Vegas."

Bret became nervous. Sal's words implied he had dangerous associates and access to hotel records. *Am I involved with the infamous Las Vegas Mafia and getting in over my head? Was it an empty threat meant to intimidate me or a serious warning about what would happen if I cross them?* In spite of his misgivings, Bret answered, "Five hundred … okay, I'll give it to her up front."

"Your room bout an hour." The call was terminated before Bret had time to reply.

As he closed the cover of his phone, there was a knock on the door. *She can't be here this quick unless I've entered the Twilight Zone.* He had forgotten about his scotch order.

There was an ATM in the hotel lobby. Bret withdrew a thousand. It was another example of the difference between Las Vegas and the rest of the country. At home the most he could get in one day from an ATM was five hundred dollars.

He'd tell Mai the withdrawal was to cover gambling losses. She would be angry, but he could deal with that. If she discovered the true reason for the withdrawal, Mai wouldn't accept his excuse of being horny because she wasn't giving him sex. His marriage would be in jeopardy.

Under the category of wishful thinking, he purchased half a dozen condoms from the vending machine in the men's room. In the bar he was overcharged for a bottle of Johnny Walker Black. He needed the courage.

Bret was in his room thirty minutes before the anticipated arrival of his companion. He sat on the couch and poured himself a scotch. Guilt pangs poked at him. He would have preferred to be waiting for his wife instead of some low-life stranger who was, in all likelihood, carrying a suitcase full of diseases. He had the condoms for protection. The last thing he wanted was to bring Mai a surprise gift from Las Vegas.

Time slowed as if he was in a spaceship approaching the speed of light. He made another drink, turned the TV on and off several times, and had a thousand second thoughts about what he was planning to do.

The knock was soft. He went to the door intent on cancelling the deal. He'd have to pay her, but his record of never having been with a prostitute would remain intact. Bret froze when he saw her. Instead of the vamp with wig and painted lips he was expecting, in the doorway was daddy's little girl returning from church choir practice.

"Hi, I'm Lila." Breezing by him, she went to the bed and plunked on it. The woman, who looked younger than the twenty-one Sal had advertised, was pretty and radiated wholesomeness. Her ski slope nose and lips not pumped with silicone were pleasing as was her ponytailed auburn hair tied with a green ribbon. She wore a short Scottish plaid skirt with a beige-colored sweater and mid-calf boots. No tattoos, decorative rings, dumbbells, or pins adorned her. Bret had heard some college girls pay their tuition by taking the profitable path of prostitution and assumed she was one.

"What's your name?" she said.

"Bret . . . Name's Bret." He closed the door.

"So come and sit, Bret." She patted a hand on the bed. "I won't bite you." With an impish grin, "At least I don't think I will." Lila had a friendly laugh.

Bret sat. It was easy to forget that she and Sal the bellman were being paid for sexual services. "Glad to meet you," he said, as if they were at a Young Republicans social.

Appearing bashful about broaching the subject, she said, "I hate to bring it up, but I'm supposed to ask for the money now." Giving a cute wiggle of her nose, "And I should tell you I get my tips in advance." She shrugged her shoulders, "You know how it is."

Bret didn't know how it was, but he had cash. For the services and tip, he handed her seven C-notes, as Sal called them. The financial transaction completed, he relaxed and waited for Lila to lead in their dance.

"Well, Bret, thank you for your generous tip. What is it you want me to do? I'm all yours for, say, an hour and a half. I'm adding a little extra for the tip." She looked at her watch, "Starting about now." She winked, "That is, as long as you're not too perverted." Lila began to remove her clothes in a natural and unselfconscious manner. No different than if she was at home and decided to take a bath.

Lila's body was a work of art. Her combination of feigned innocence tempered by a modicum of sophistication inflamed Bret's desire for her. It took all his willpower to keep from diving on her and carrying out his side of the bargain. Lila reclined on the bed and arranged her legs allowing him a partial view of her primary site of business.

He was Superman. Buttons from his shirt became missiles flying across the room. His belt was a whip cracking the air as it flew from his waist. There was a pounding in his neck and a throbbing at his temples. He was on the cusp of a full-blown frenzy when sanity intervened.

"What am I doing?" he said. Lila gave him a quizzical stare. Thoughts raged, *Sure, we're going through a rough patch. We'll resolve our problems. I'm not going to sacrifice my marriage for the proverbial romp in the hay. Mai would never find out, but I would know and couldn't live with the deception.*

His arousal passed, and he looked at the woman in his bed. "I can't do this." He began to put on his clothes, less a few buttons.

The sweet choir girl soured. She spit words at him. "What the fuck are you doing? No way are you getting your money back."

He took a deep breath. "Keep it, Lila. Just get out of here."

She grabbed her clothes and in a fury began to dress. The antithesis of her undressing. Muttering expletives, she hopped about the room on one foot putting her boots on. As she stormed into the hall, her parting shot was, "So long, asshole, don't call me again." The door slammed.

He was perplexed, and didn't understand why Lila was upset.

She got her money without having to work for it. Was being rejected a blow to her pride?

Bret endured the remaining two days of the meeting. A few times while passing through the lobby, he noticed Sal shaking his head. Bret ignored him.

He left Vegas the afternoon the meeting ended and arrived in Windham Center at four in the morning. Having slept on the plane and anxious to see if Mai's depression had lessened, he decided to stay awake. When Mai walked into the kitchen that morning, he was sitting at the table drinking coffee.

"I was expecting you, but wasn't sure when you'd get here," she said as she filled a cup and sat across from him.

"I got in at about four. Looked in on you but didn't want to wake you."

Before asking about Las Vegas or his course, she said without emotion, "Jake's mother died. Happened the day you left."

The news shocked Bret. Sophie Warden was in her fifties and healthy. "She was so young. What did she die of?"

"The flu. Can you imagine that? She had been sick for a few days, but seemed to be recovering. Then, to everybody's surprise, including her doctor, she died. When Mr. Warden found her unresponsive in bed, he attempted CPR. It was too late. She had been gone for a while."

"Why didn't you let me know?" Bret asked, upset he hadn't been told. "I would have come back to be with Jake? He must be devastated. They were close."

Mai's lower lip began to quiver. "Your coming back wouldn't have made any difference. You couldn't have gotten here in time anyway. In the Jewish custom, she was buried the same day. Jake and his dad didn't want to follow the traditional sitting of Shiva. She was buried and that was the end of it."

Mai explained, "As I said, no one thought she was going to die. Her doctor feels it was probably the result of years of smoking and not getting a flu shot this year. There was no autopsy. We'll never know for sure what happened." As if it justified Mrs. Warden's death, "Thousands of people in the U.S. die of the flu each year."

"Yeah, they do," Bret said shaking his head." He slammed a fist on the table, "I've got to talk to Jake, go see him." He grabbed his phone.

"Don't bother," Mai said, "He's not around. Left yesterday afternoon to spend time with his family in Kent and doesn't want to be disturbed."

Bret put the phone in his pocket.

"He got Jack Sweeney over in Manchester to cover for him until you returned. He wants you to keep the office running. Doesn't know when he'll be back." Mai went to him and kissed him on the cheek, "Welcome back."

The welcome wasn't enthusiastic, but under the circumstances, it was enough. "Thank you," he said, "It's good to be back."

It was cooking class night and Mai was at Jake's condo.

She said, "Weatherman says we might get a storm this evening. Bret tried to discourage me from going to class. He said if there was a problem driving, I should call you and ask to stay here tonight. Of course, we both assumed you would say yes." Rooting like a cheerleader, "Come on, snow."

"Yeah," Jake said, "I hope we get covered by six feet of it."

Mai shivered, "Don't wish for that. Sounds too much like a grave."

Jake responded, "I forgot how superstitious you are. Okay, make it five feet, eleven inches."

"Sorry. Blame my Chinese upbringing," Mai said. Changing the subject, "By the way, I'm going to join a fitness center in Storrs, not far from here. I like to work out, and it'll give us an excuse to spend more time together."

"What'd Bret say about it?"

"He wanted me join the one where he plays tennis. We could

go together, he said. I told him I picked the one in Storrs because it was for women. I didn't want men watching me. He agreed."

Jake smiled, "Well, you seem to be feeling better and have adjusted to your parents going back to Macao."

"Yes, finally. Even though I didn't visit them often, I could have if I wanted. Now, I wonder if I'll ever see them again. It had me down for a while, but I realized it was for the best. They'd been vacillating about going back. The super-storm was the last straw. As you know, it didn't do much damage here, but devastated Staten Island. They had prepared and came through it fine with little damage to their building, but it really scared my mom. That's when they made the decision to go."

She snickered, "I have to say I felt a little sorry for Bret. He did everything he could to get me out of my depression. Even tried to get me to see a psychologist. Of course, it was for his selfish reasons. He wanted sex, and I wasn't giving him any. He sure was ecstatic when I got back to being myself again."

"Good for him," was Jake's sarcastic reply.

Mai said, "Don't be upset. He doesn't matter a bit."

Giving a long exhale, Jake said, "Sometimes, easier said than done."

Mai mused, "Strange how things work out. Part of our original cover story was that I went to New York after my parents had returned to Macao.

"Yeah, I remember," Jake said.

Mai gave a 'life's funny like that' shrug of her shoulders.

She continued, "My uncles are the only problems left on my side. I hope now that my parents are gone, they'll pay less attention to what I'm doing. Problem is, we can't count on it. They're unpredictable, and you never know what they're liable to do."

She seemed unsure about saying it, but added, "Please forgive me, but your mother's passing removed another negative influence from our relationship. "At the moment, things seem to be going our way."

"They do."

Mai exited the Storrs fitness center in high spirits. She enjoyed her routine of working-out with weights followed by a run on the treadmill. That morning she had set a personal record of running for an hour. The release of endorphins left her with a feeling of euphoria. She wasn't going to Jake's. He and Bret were in the office. Her day was free. After lunch she might visit Frankie and swap gossip.

A car followed her into her driveway. Not wanting to go to the garage and be isolated from the few automobiles that traveled Lover's Lane, she stopped in the driveway and reached for her phone. The engine was running in case of the need for a fast getaway. Panic overcame her when she looked into the rearview mirror and saw two men leave their car and walk toward her.

"Oh, my God," she exclaimed as she recognized her uncles. They must know about her shameful relationship with Jake and were bent on restoring family honor. After signaling her to unlock the doors, one of her uncles sat in the front passenger seat and the other took a back seat. Mai tried to hide her nerves. She turned off the engine.

With a semblance of a smile, the uncle in the front seat said, "Good morning lovely niece. Happy to see you. It appears you have settled well in Windham." The one in back bowed toward her showing agreement with his brother.

Caught off guard and fearful of their intentions, Mai looked at each and said, "Glad to see you too, uncles. Please come in for tea."

"No time," said front seat uncle.

"Why have you come, then?" she asked him.

"Before she left for Macao, Jia asked us to visit you. To insure all is well."

Mai gathered her courage, and said, "You can see yourself that my husband and I live in this fine house. In my next letter to mother I will remind her."

"Please do," said front seat uncle. It was an order.

Back seat uncle said, "We have associates here in your village and have informed them about you."

Was it a threat? A warning of dire consequences if she was caught doing something wrong? "Why are you telling me this?"

"If you should require our help," back seat uncle continued, "you can contact them. They know how to get in touch with us."

"I won't need any…"

"Shhh," he interrupted. "We promised Jia, and it is our duty to protect you."

Mai knew not to argue.

He handed her a slip of paper, "Here is the number. Place it in your phone contacts under a fictitious name where it can be easily retrieved." When he saw Mai hesitate, he demanded, "Do it now, so I can destroy the paper."

"I will, uncle." Mai took out her cell and did as told.

The uncles said their goodbyes and left. Mai had to sit in her car until she stopped shaking and was able to drive to her garage.

No longer mourn for me when I am dead...

Windham, Connecticut: Spring brought astounding beauty to Windham Center. Warm weather melted the last dregs of soot covered snow enticing crocuses to poke their heads from winter hiding places. Forsythia followed, its yellow blaze scorching the earth. Grass, chameleon-like, went from dull brown to lush green, and trees began to don their summer coats.

New greenery decorated the pathway between the Manley and Grimaldi yards. Snow and ice had made winter use impossible. With the arrival of the new season, it became the main route of travel between the two houses. Frankie used the path to walk to the Manley back door on a Saturday morning in May.

Mai was sleeping, but Bret was awake and heard the rapping at the door. It had to be Frankie. On weekends she came to their house for morning coffee. Frankie's habit was to enter with the key Mai gave her and brew a pot of the special French roast that she ground at home and brought with her. The pungent aroma of coffee wafting throughout the house acted like giant elastic tentacles pulling the couple from their bed to the breakfast nook adjacent to the kitchen.

Bret put on his robe and went to the kitchen. Confirming it was Frankie, he opened the door. About to ask why she hadn't used the key, he realized she was distraught. Frankie was shifting from one foot to the other, unable to stand in one place on the porch, and tears welled in her eyes.

"Sorry to bother you," she said, "But I'm at my wits end." Her palm was cradling the left side of her cheek.

Bret approached, placed a supporting arm around her shoulder, and said in a reassuring voice, "Come in and have a seat. I'll take a look at you. The way you're holding your cheek, I'd say you've got an infected tooth."

Frankie's eyes were wide and sweat beaded her forehead, "I've had one heck of a toothache since last evening. And I woke up with this swollen face." She removed her palm from her cheek and turned the puffy area to Bret.

He used his hands to control her head as he did a visual examination. When finished, he said, "You should have called, or better, come over when it first started, no matter what time it was. The side of your face is all red and you're beginning to swell under your jaw." The latter was a serious problem. Bret wanted to examine her in detail. "Can I put pressure on the area that hurts?"

"Do whatever you have to do to get me out of pain."

He began to palpate Frankie's face and neck. At one point, she flinched from what she described as a feeling like a fiery jolt of electricity. When he finished his examination, Bret assured, "Don't worry, I can help you. You'll be fine soon."

"Oh, good. I can't begin to tell you how lucky I consider myself having an oral surgeon as a neighbor. Especially, one who's such a nice guy."

Although grateful, Bret let the compliment slide and continued his examination. "Just relax and let me take a look inside your mouth."

Using a small flashlight from what Mai called their junk drawer, he examined her mouth and confirmed what he suspected. "You have an infection caused by an impacted wisdom tooth. Have you ever had this problem before?"

"A few times, but not this bad. I always got better after rinsing with salt water. I'm sure you know my dentist, Dr. Belmont. He's been telling me for years to have my wisdom teeth out, but I've been too scared to do it."

"I'd like to take you to my office and get an x-ray. You're also going to need antibiotics."

Gesturing with her hands like a tap dancer during a

performance, Frankie said, "Whatever you say."

Bret woke Mai, and the three drove to his office where x-rays revealed an infected wisdom tooth in her left jaw. She had three other wisdom teeth that required extraction.

The sole negative finding in Frankie's medical questionnaire was a severe allergy to nuts. Bret couldn't resist saying, "It's such a common allergy we don't allow nuts in any form in the office." With a big smile, "That is, if you don't count the staff."

Mai and Frankie looked at each other and shrugged their shoulders. Realizing his attempt at humor was a flop, he cleared his throat and became serious. "How did you find out you were allergic to them?"

"By almost dying from an anaphylactic reaction. I'll never forget that day."

Mai let out a gasp. "Wow. How did it happen?"

"I was eating a peanut butter cookie at *Sally's* in downtown Willimantic when suddenly my entire body itched, and I began to have difficulty breathing. I guess I fell on the floor twitching all over, at least that's what they told me because I passed out." She shivered. "Even now, it scares me just talking about it"

Bret said, "You don't have to say any more, although I have to admit I'm curious about how you got adrenaline. It's the only thing that could have saved you."

Frankie answered, "I don't mind telling you. A man having lunch was allergic to bees and always carried an allergy kit. He used it on me. Saved my life. I found out later he was passing through the area on his way to Hartford. Lucky for me he happened to be there that day."

Mai exclaimed, "You certainly were lucky. Of course, you carry an allergy kit now?"

"I should, but I don't. I just try to stay away from nuts."

"I can prescribe an allergy kit if you want," Bret suggested.

"Don't bother, I'd just forget to carry it."

Bret said, "If you change your mind, let me know. In any event, I'll call in an antibiotic called Clindamycin. Should take care of the infection within a few days. You don't have a problem with it, do you?"

"Not that I know of."

With Frankie's immediate condition diagnosed and resolved, Bret recommended a permanent solution to her dental problem. "I'd like you to make an appointment to have your wisdom teeth out with an intravenous anesthesia. We can do it first thing Thursday morning. As you know, it's my day off, but I checked my schedule, and I'm completely booked every other day next week. Thursday would be perfect timing for the extractions, and I'd be happy to come in for you."

Frankie shook her head. Looking at Mai, she said, "I don't know. Never had anesthesia and nervous about having it. What do you think?"

"I think you should do what Bret says," Mai answered, "He'll take good care of you."

"You bet I will," Bret seconded, "Let me tell you all about it."

Frankie's "Okay," was reserved.

He went into the details of removing Frankie's wisdom teeth.

When Bret finished, Frankie looked at her two friends with trust in her eyes and said, "All right, it seems I have no other choice. You can schedule the surgery."

That afternoon Mai told Bret she was going to the East Brook Mall to replenish housekeeping supplies. She was in her car in a secluded part of the parking lot talking to Jake on her private pre-paid cell phone. A window was down to let in air.

"I could leave him and file for divorce," she said. "Connecticut is a no-fault State. You don't have to prove anything, but I can make up a good reason if I have to. It's not difficult."

An automobile drove into a nearby space. "Hold on a minute," she said, "Someone parked out in the boondocks with me. I'm guessing the driver wants to keep from getting dinged."

A woman with a child exited and walked hand in hand to the mall. Mai waited until they were out of range before continuing with her proposal.

"After the divorce and waiting a respectable amount of time, we could begin to see each other publicly."

Jake listened without interrupting.

"My parents back in Macao would never find out about us." Although Jake was sensitive about his mother's passing, she was obligated to say, "And there's nothing stopping us on your side of the family."

Mai took a breath before continuing. "When I devised our plan of using Bret as a sexual beard, it was to be until we found ourselves in a position like the one we're in. It's time to scrap it."

After a delay, Jake replied, "Believe me, I'd like nothing more than to do what you say, but don't forget your uncles. Without them in the picture, you could get a divorce, and we could start over someplace else. But doing that now, so soon after your parents left the country, would raise their suspicions. It would seem that you were waiting for the right time to dump Bret and hook up with me. They'd see through the scheme."

Mai sighed.

"It was you who said they would kill us if they found out we were going against your family's wishes. Sure, they may not be paying as close attention to us as when your parents were around, but we can't assume they'll ignore us altogether. It has to look as if you and Bret broke up because of what he did. Maybe cheated on you or caused some sort of a scandal."

Exasperated by their plight, Mai agreed, "I know, I know. I've been purposely ignoring them in my thinking. My uncles don't have grudges against Jewish people like my parents have and probably would tolerate our being together under the proper circumstances."

She gave another sigh, "You're right, though, if they suspected we were doing something underhanded, they'd find us no matter where we went. Once, they bragged about how their connections allowed them to track down some guy who double-crossed them and fled to Chicago. I can guess what they did to the man when they found him. And they have people here that might be watching me and reporting to them."

Speaking in a harsh manner, Jake said, "Look, you know how I hate the thought of Bret living with you, touching you," his anger was evident, "having sex with you. Truth is, I don't know how much longer I'll be able to bear it. But now isn't the time to do anything rash."

"So we do nothing?"

"Yes. For the time being, we do nothing. Don't give up hope. A solution is going to pop up. I can feel it."

Neither spoke.

After a while, Mai said, "Jake?"

"Yes?

"I've been struggling to keep some bad thoughts from my mind. No matter how hard I try, they keep coming back." She took deep breaths, "There may be something we can do, but we'd need more courage than we've ever needed before."

"What are you talking about?"

She explained, "Bret had to take Frankie Grimaldi to the office today."

"Why?"

"Frankie has bad wisdom teeth. On Thursday he's going to sedate her and take them out." She paused, "I can't help thinking that if something bad were to happen to Frankie during the procedure and it was Bret's fault, we would be rid of him. We could spread the word he didn't like her because she's a lesbian and thought she was interested in me. He would be blamed for what happened."

Jake was about to utter, "Not that lesbian thing again," when he had a eureka moment. "Hold on. I think I've got it."

"Got what?"

"I'll tell you when I've worked out the details." Aware Bret played tennis on Sunday mornings, he said, "Call me tomorrow when Bret's at the club." His voice couldn't conceal his excitement, "Just remember my words that we'll find a solution to our problems." He ended the call.

Jake recognized an exploitable opportunity. In an instant, he visualized a way for Mai and him to be together with society's and her uncles' approval. Murdering Frankie and framing Bret ... what Mai wanted ... was feasible. It required poisoning the anesthetic drugs Bret used and the help of Corrie Hunter. Corrie's help was critical.

Jake went to his office and reviewed Frankie's chart. He had been contemplating a specific solution to their problem, but the chart indicated a backup to his plan that would ensure the result he wanted.

From the office he went to the University of Connecticut campus. He had the key to the pharmacology laboratory, and it held the poison he needed. Grace Putnam gave him the key so he could visit her when she worked in the lab. Although they stopped seeing each other, she had neglected to ask for its return. It was on his key ring.

Potent drugs and poisons were kept in a metal cabinet that was supposed to be locked at all times. Although research students who used the cabinet were given keys, they tended to keep it unlocked for convenience of access. There was an excellent chance he would find the cabinet unlocked. If not, he would jimmy it open taking care not to damage it.

Pharmacology grad students had busy social schedules. Other than Grace, no one worked in the lab on a Saturday afternoon after two or three o'clock. She was the sole user at that time, because she wanted the privacy. Jake had spent several Saturday afternoons with her as she worked on a project before a date.

While getting coffee at a local Storrs bakery, he had run into her. She mentioned leaving for a semester of research at Roche Pharmaceuticals in Basel, Switzerland. With her out of town, the lab should be empty after three p.m.

A rectangular two-story building housed the pharmacology, chemistry, and physics laboratories. In addition, there were offices for professors and others in charge. Since research areas were available at all times, Jake could enter the building without anyone thinking it unusual.

The upper half of the door of the second floor laboratory was frosted except for a clear area with the name *Pharmacology*

Laboratory painted in black. The room was dark. Wearing rubber gloves, Jake unlocked the door and let himself in. Turning on lights might prove risky, so as a precaution, he brought a Mini Maglite for illumination. He found it wasn't necessary since the late afternoon light shining through the windows provided good visibility.

Jake went to the drug cabinet, and, as expected, found it unlocked. It contained labeled bottles and jars. He checked several until he found what he was looking for, a small jar containing a white powder labeled *Potassium Cyanide*. It was the potent and quick killer he wanted.

Taking care not to disturb the contents, Jake removed the rubber stopper. He wore a surgical face mask as breathing in a miniscule amount of the powder could be fatal. With a tiny spatula and a vial meant for drawing blood, he transferred a teaspoon of cyanide from the jar to the vial. When the transfer was complete, he closed both containers and rinsed the spatula and rubber gloves with hot water. Before returning the cyanide to the cabinet, he tapped the jar with the spatula handle to level the powder. He was confident a casual observer would not notice a change in the jar's contents. If it were discovered a portion of the cyanide was missing and unaccounted for in the log book, sloppy record keeping would be blamed. Graduate students were not known for meticulous records.

Keeping the gloves on, Jake placed the vial, spatula, and face mask in his pants pocket and walked to the entrance door. Opening it a few inches to ascertain the hallway was empty, he heard footsteps on the tile floor. Gripped by fear of being discovered, he closed the door and looked for a hiding place.

He made for a utility closet. It was tiny, and the stored mops, brooms, and buckets filled it with an odor of mildew. The door was thin and would allow him to hear what was happening in the room. It might be uncomfortable, but no matter the wait, he would remain in the closet until whoever was working in the lab left. His worry was the student might require something in the utility closet and find him hiding. If discovered, he'd be forced to take drastic action. A thick broom handle, the type that screws into a large push broom, was propped in a corner and could be employed if necessary. Jake took solace in the fact that such an encounter was unlikely.

The footsteps stopped at the entrance door. Trying to control his breathing, Jake was on the verge of hyperventilation and could feel the beating of his heart as if it rested on the outside of his chest. He considered praying, but the hypocrisy deterred him.

Opening the utility door a crack gave him a view of the main entrance. The handle of the lab door turned a few times before it squeaked open.

"Dumbasses. Always leaving the room unlocked," a deep male voice said.

It was the security guard doing his routine check of the offices and laboratories. Jake had met him a time or two. Friendly, but Jake wouldn't want to mess with him. He watched as the guard peeked into the room and saw no one. The noise of jingling keys signaled the man was locking the door before continuing his walkthrough of the building. With a sigh of relief, Jake left the closet and tiptoed to the entrance. He listened with his ear to the door. When confident the guard was gone and the hall was clear, Jake exited the laboratory taking care to lock the door. He took the stairs to the ground floor. Before leaving the building, he removed the rubber gloves, pocketed them, and went to his car parked in the adjacent lot. On the drive to his condo, he flung the laboratory key into a wooded area. The gloves and mask were destined for a MacDonald's trash bin.

That evening he met with Corrie Hunter. She was on the couch in his living room holding a glass of wine. Jake sat across from her. He could tell by her constricted pupils she had fortified herself before coming to his place. After evaluating her state of mind by engaging in small talk, he deemed her capable of understanding what he was about to ask.

"I need your help."

Corrie gulped a swallow of wine. "Me?" she said, bringing the glass to her lap. "What is it?"

Jake explained his scheme, her role, and the danger involved. There was the risk she would decline to help, or worse, threaten to expose him. He thought it minimal because of her dependence on him as a source of drugs.

When finished, he sat back in his chair, eyes fixed upon her. Corrie seemed unsure of what to make of the proposal until her eyes widened, and she said, "Wow. That takes real balls. You can count me in." She added, "There's a price for my help."

Jake expected a monetary demand and assumed a poker face. "How much?"

Corrie answered, "Fifty thousand."

"Fifty thousand dollars? How the hell did you come up with that?" Jake feigned shock.

Corrie shrugged, "Oh, I don't know. It just seems reasonable for what I have to do."

Jake pretended to be thinking. After what he deemed the proper amount of time, he shook his head as if what he was about to say was against his better judgment, "All right. I'll agree to it."

The risk Corrie had to take was tremendous and failure would be catastrophic for all. The money was worth the prize he and Mai sought and was less than he had been prepared to pay. If Corrie became a liability, he'd deal with her the same way he did with Larry Reid and planned to do with Frankie. Adding another murder to his count wouldn't make a difference. For him, murder had become a reliable method of solving problems.

Jake had anticipated the need for the help of his friend Carlton to pay Corrie. He called Carlton the following morning ... Sunday, but Carlton said to call anytime ... and when he answered, he was at the stables grooming his favorite horse for a day of polo.

Jake made his second request for money. "This time it's got to be a secret deal. It's important the money can't be traced. I'll need it in about six months." Being vague, "That's when I have to turn it over."

He had not told Corrie she'd wait six months before getting her money. If he had, she might not have agreed to help. Things had to cool before he gave her anything. Less chance of someone discovering the payoff and raising questions about why she received it.

"That's going to take time. I'll get back in a few days." Carlton ended the call.

When Mai phoned that morning, Jake said, "Come to my condo right away. We've got a few hours before Bret returns from tennis."

Jake outlined his plan as they sat at a small round table in the breakfast nook. Mai nodded several times.

When he finished, she asked, "Are you sure you want to do this?"

"Yes," he said, "It's what I think you want."

Mai lifted her head and fixed on Jake. She said nothing.

He continued, "The opportunity has fallen into our lap." Looking into her eyes, "It's a road we've taken before."

Mai gave another nod.

"I'm leaving it up to you," he said, "If you say it's a go, we do it. If you say no, we do nothing and wait for another opportunity."

The final responsibility for carrying out the plan rested on Mai's shoulders. She straightened in her chair and said, "You're right. We have an opportunity and should take it and do what you've outlined." Mai's expression hardened, "It's a go."

At the office the following morning before the first patients were scheduled, Corrie Hunter stood at the Formica counter in the hall outside the utility room. She was reviewing a printout of the weekly schedule. The other staff members were performing routine tasks in preparation for treating patients when the doctors arrived.

As Pearlie Perez passed, Corrie said for her to hear, "The nerve of that woman."

Pearlie stopped and turned to Corrie who was pleased her co-worker took the bait, "What are you talking about? What woman?"

Appearing bothered by an intrusion into her personal

thoughts, Corrie said in a snotty manner, "Well, if you must know, I'm referring to the fact that Frankie Grimaldi is scheduled to have her wisdom teeth removed by Dr. Manley this Thursday."

"Are you sure?" Pearlie asked. "Thursday is his day off. And what's your problem with Frankie Grimaldi?"

The conversation attracted the other staff members who sensed the possibility of a confrontation between Pearlie and Corrie. Everyone knew they disliked each other. Sandy, Sue, and Brittney joined them.

"What's going on?" Brittney said.

Corrie ignored the new arrivals and addressed Pearlie in the tone of one who's privy to insider information, "Yes, I'm certain of it. It says so right here." She pointed to the schedule. "Dr. Manley's going to come in especially for her."

Pearlie said, "So? It's his business if he wants to work on his day off. I'm asking again, what's wrong with Frankie Grimaldi?"

Corrie placed her face as close to Pearlie's as she dared without getting it slapped. "I guess you don't know Dr. Manley doesn't like the Grimaldi woman."

All eyes were on Corrie. "Mrs. Manley told me about it when we had dinner at Roscoe's." She paused for emphasis, "You know. The terrific bistro that opened a few months ago in downtown Willi?" Corrie enjoyed boasting to the others about her relationship with Mai Manley.

Pearlie rebutted, "That's a load of bull. Dr. Manley likes Frankie Grimaldi. He always says nice things about her, like she's a good neighbor and a friend of theirs."

"No, you're wrong," snapped Corrie whose facial expression was as condescending as she could make it. "He really doesn't like her. Hasn't for quite a while. Just tolerates her because she's a neighbor. That's what Mai, I mean, Mrs. Manley, told me."

"I don't believe it," Pearlie challenged as she rolled the pearl around her neck between her thumb and forefinger. Her equivalent of a security blanket was always within easy reach to calm her when she was nervous or angry. And she was angry.

Corrie had everyone's attention. "You see, the Grimaldi woman

... or should I say man, it fits her better ... made inappropriate advances toward Mrs. Manley."

The group uttered a collective "Oohhhh."

Having unleashed her shocking tidbit of gossip, it was time to press the attack in her effort to destroy Frankie's character and to sow the seeds of Bret's animosity toward Frankie. "Ms. Grimaldi is a lesbian, as you're all aware."

The listeners nodded in unison. The relationship between Frankie and Sara Cunningham was not a secret in Windham.

"According to what I've been told me, not long after they moved next door to her, Frankie began to make sexual overtures toward Mrs. Manley. Mrs. Manley quickly put a stop it, but when she told Dr. Manley what happened, he wanted to let Frankie know she wasn't welcome in their house any more. Mrs. Manley disagreed. Said they were neighbors, and it was important they keep up the appearance of friendship."

The jaws of each of the staff members dropped registering their disbelief.

"What happened then?" asked Brittney.

"Dr. Manley reluctantly agreed." Corrie had her audience hooked. "But he told his wife he would keep an eye on Frankie Grimaldi to make sure it didn't happen again."

"Then, you think Dr. Manley decided to treat her just to keep up the appearance of friendship?" asked Brittney.

Appearing to think about the question, Corrie said, "I'm not sure. Probably. I know Dr. Manley would never refuse to treat a patient who sought his help. No matter who they were." In a cynical manner she said, "You know oral surgeons. Principles, ethics, and patient care above everything else."

"You said it." It was Brittney, the unelected spokesperson for the listening group.

"One final thing," Corrie admonished, "Not a word of what I've told you to Dr. Manley. I'm sure he would be terribly embarrassed if he were aware of our discussion. Okay?"

The group nodded their agreement.

On Tuesday evening, Carlton called Jake. "Is the secure phone I overnighted you working okay?"

Jake said, "Yeah, fine. Got it this morning. I'll destroy it when we finish this call."

Carlton began, "I've arranged for a mid-level manager who works in our Hartford branch to utilize trusted intermediaries to open a Bahamian bank account in a fictitious name. I can rely on this manager. He owes me a big favor, something like the one I owed you."

Jake noted Carlton's use of the past tense.

Carlton explained, "When you give the go-ahead, the fifty thousand will be deposited in the account, and a debit card with a withdrawal limit of two thousand dollars per month will be issued. My man will make several withdrawals each month from ATM machines at various locations in Connecticut equaling the two thousand. The money limit is my decision. Safer that way. Won't attract anyone's attention like a large lump sum would."

"Right," Jake said. *Can't blame him, although it's another thing Corrie isn't going to like.*

"That's not all. Close to, but no later than, the last day of each month, the money will be left at a secure drop box we pulled strings to get. It's located in a private administrative office area of Union Station, the main Hartford train and bus station. The drop will always take place during a busy time in order to mask what's being done. Obviously, my manager knows something irregular is going on, but he's not the type to ask questions."

Carlton paused, "What do you think? Any comments so far?"

"None. It's clever, extremely clever."

Carlton continued, "Sometime during the first four days of the following month, the person getting the money must . . . emphasis on *must* . . . remove it from the lock box. That should also be done during a busy time at the station. Only the courier and recipient will have keys to the box."

Carlton's tone was serious, "This is important, Jake. Let the person getting the money know if my manager checks the box after the money was to be removed and finds it wasn't, no more will be left, and the entire arrangement will be cancelled. There are few extenuating circumstances that will make us resume the drops." Carlton chuckled, "Impress upon her . . . I assume it's a her . . . absolute secrecy is mandatory, and only she can be involved in the pick-up."

Jake knew Carlton was thinking he had gotten someone pregnant and didn't want Mai, his new love, to find out. He was paying for silence. His friend was aware of similar "female problems" in Jake's life. Carlton was wrong, but Jake didn't deny it. As close as they were, Carlton must never know the truth.

"When the time comes to make the bank deposit, we'll review everything again and you'll get the box key. As for repayment it can be done anytime. For security reasons you have to give it to me in person and in cash. Like your other loan, only principal is required." Carlton closed, "And Jake, this will square us."

Jake thought about the plan laid out to him. It was designed to keep Carlton's involvement hidden under layers of cloaking. It was the smart way to handle things. The weak links from Carlton's point of view would be the Hartford branch manager, Jake, and the person receiving the money. Carlton would have insured the manager couldn't implicate him in what was being done. Jake and the person receiving the money had no way of connecting Carlton to it. It was impossible to trace anything to him.

For Jake, Corrie was the problem. It would be difficult to convince her to accept the restrictions placed on receipt of the money. He'd deal with the issue when the time came. As for Carlton, he was certain the man would not grant him another favor. Carlton had done more than anyone should ask of a friend. Jake was grateful.

On Wednesday, Corrie approached Brittney at the scheduling desk.

"I'll be late tomorrow. Mrs. Manley is driving Frankie Grimaldi to the office and wants me to accompany them." She leaned and whispered, "I guess she feels a bit uncomfortable alone in a car with the woman."

Brittney raised her eyebrows, "Really? Does Dr. Warden know you'll be late?"

"Yes, he does. In fact it works out perfectly. He called me earlier and said he wasn't coming in tomorrow. Hasn't been feeling well lately and is going to take an extra day off. Said to tell you to cancel his Thursday patients."

That evening Corrie called Dr. Warden. Being cryptic, she said, "I cleaned the office like you asked."

"Thanks. Really appreciate what you've done."

Mai and Corrie drove into Frankie's driveway. As Frankie entered the car, Mai referred to Corrie who was sitting in the back seat, "I asked Corrie to come with us if it's okay with you. She has lots of experience with pre- and post-op patients. I feel better with her here."

Frankie looked at Corrie, smiled, and tried to hide her nerves by saying, "Sure. You know what they say, the more the merrier."

Corrie's smile was reptilian, as Mai shifted the lever into reverse.

Having spent the night tossing and turning, Mai drained several cups of coffee that morning. In spite of the caffeine jolt, she was worn and tired. Bouts of diarrhea added to her woes. Frankie's appearance impressed her. The normally unkempt hair was combed, and her face sported lipstick and make-up. In place of her trademark overalls were black designer jeans. On top she wore a lime-green, v-neck, lightweight sweater with a pale yellow blouse under it. Even her sandals were stylishly two-toned and worn without stockings.

Mai couldn't recall more than one or two times, like the past Thanksgiving, when she saw Frankie wearing anything other than paint stained overalls or grubby cut-off jeans. Frankie exuded electrifying sophistication and glamour, and Mai understood why Sara Cunningham was attracted to her.

Frankie's facial infection had responded to the antibiotics, and the associated swelling and pain were gone. As she sat in the front passenger seat of the Camry, Frankie turned to Mai and said, "I can't wait to get this thing over with and put my tooth problems behind me."

Chuckling, Corrie chimed, "Well, I'm sure it won't be long before you'll have nothing to worry about."

Mai was angered by the double entendre and could feel the reddening of her face. *Just what we need, a wing-nut like Corrie trying to be clever. It's bad enough I can't look at Frankie without conjuring up ghastly images. Corrie better keep her mouth shut, or I'll shut it for her. God, I hope I don't have to stop to go to the bathroom.*

They pulled into the office parking lot five minutes before the nine a.m. appointment. Mai remained in the reception room on the pretense of waiting to take Frankie home after the surgery. She paced.

No other patients were scheduled, and preparations for Frankie's surgery had been completed prior to her arrival. She was taken to the operating suite. A covered tray of sterile instruments rested on a stainless steel stand next to the dental chair, and on one of the walls a six-inch wide shelf held vials of anesthetic medicines and syringes. Midazolam, a tranquillizer, fentanyl, a narcotic, and propofol, a general anesthetic, were the drugs used in various ratios to obtain the degree of sedation required for surgery.

Frankie's vital signs were taken and recorded. After reviewing them, Bret remarked, "In spite of your smoking, your lungs are fine, and you're in excellent shape. This should be a piece of cake."

"I hope so," was the anxious reply.

To keep Frankie occupied, Bret said, "One of these days, I'm going to get you to stop smoking."

"Good luck with that," was accompanied by a soft chuckle.

Oxygen was administered via a nasal cannula, and Bret started an intravenous line in Frankie's left arm.

"The first medicine I'm going to give you will dry your mouth so don't be nervous if you notice it." As Frankie watched, he injected the drug into the intravenous line and followed with two milligrams of midazolam saying. "This second one will take the edge off your nerves."

From a third syringe he administered fifty micrograms of fentanyl to diminish pain. Frankie yawned. She was in a light sedative state. Although Bret knew Frankie was unable to respond in a coherent way, he said, "Pretty soon you'll be in la-la land."

Bret checked his patient's vital signs to confirm no untoward reaction to the initial medications before administering a dose of thirty milligrams of propofol to deepen her sedation.

In spite of their awesome power, the anesthetics were innocuous looking liquids. The syringes of midazolam and fentanyl appeared to be filled with water, and the propofol looked like the cream you put into coffee.

"She's doing great," Bret said to Pearlie and Corrie who were in the surgical room with him.

Pearlie was assisting with the extractions and Corrie was keeping the anesthetic record and monitoring Frankie's vital signs. Corrie was doing Sandy's job, but Bret decided to use her since she was the most experienced of the staff. Jake's absence from the office made her available.

Less than two minutes after the procedure began, Frankie had a mild convulsion that ceased after a few seconds. At the same time her face took on a grayish pallor. A small amount of frothy saliva dripped from one side of her mouth. Bret, on the alert for potential problems, checked Frankie and the monitors to see if anything abnormal was developing. There was a slight duskiness to her skin, but all readings and recordings were within normal ranges.

He let out a breath to relax himself and, as was his habit, checked his impressions with his assistants. "Do either of you see anything wrong?"

"Everything seems fine to me," said Corrie.

"Same here," said Pearlie as she suctioned the froth from

Frankie's mouth, "Except I smell something like the hand cream my mother used to use."

Bret sniffed the air, "So do I. Most likely its Frankie. Probably put it on before she came."

Corrie was monitoring breath sounds with a stethoscope taped to Frankie's chest. She alerted Bret, "Her breathing has diminished. And take a look at the oximeter"

Bret glanced at the Pulse Oximeter which measured oxygen in the blood. The reading had dropped from one hundred percent to ninety two percent. *What the hell's going on?* "Keep an eye on it, Corrie, and let me know if it falls below ninety." He put the instruments he was using on the tray. "I'll check her airway."

To ensure Frankie's breathing passages weren't blocked, he repositioned her head and inserted a plastic device into her mouth to keep her respiratory tract open. Frankie didn't respond to the placement of the device indicating she was in a deeper level of anesthesia than he intended at that stage of the procedure. Realizing something untoward might be happening, he instructed Corrie, "Connect the oxygen to the Ambu bag and assist her breathing. Run the oxygen at six liters."

Corrie grabbed the Ambu Bag, connected it to the one hundred percent oxygen line, and augmented Frankie's shallow breaths. "The oximeter's down to eighty-eight and falling," she said.

As trained to do in emergency situations, Pearlie pressed the intercom button and called for assistance. "We need help in Surgery One."

Sandy was working in the sterilization room and heard the ruckus in the operatory. Realizing there was a problem, she hand-signaled Sue and both were on their way to the operatory when Pearlie summoned. The staff was trained in handling emergencies. Each had a specific role in the management of problems like the one they were facing.

"I can take over breathing for her," Sandy said as she relieved Corrie of that duty. It freed Corrie to concentrate on monitoring Frankie's vital signs and to record medications administered to correct the problem they were facing.

Remaining on standby and prepared to be of assistance, Sue said, "I'm ready to help, Dr. Manley."

"Thanks Sue," he said without looking at her. Perspiration dripped from his face and sweat stains darkened the brim his surgical cap and the underarms of his surgical shirt.

The most common cause of what was happening to Frankie was improper head position resulting in diminished oxygen flow to the lungs. Bret knew if that were the case, the placement of the airway device and the use of the Ambu bag with one hundred percent oxygen would have corrected the problem. Those steps hadn't resulted in improving Frankie's condition. He feared he was overlooking something, something obvious he should recognize and correct.

The frothy saliva Pearlie continued to suction from Frankie's mouth remained unexplained, and Bret turned his attention to it. He ordered, "Sandy, turn the oxygen all the way up." Sandy twisted the knob on the oxygen valve to its highest setting. Ten liters per minute of one-hundred-percent oxygen flowed through the Ambu Bag. It hissed as it surged into the unconscious woman's lungs.

Frankie's color darkened to a bluish-black indicating a serious lack of oxygen in her body.

"If I don't assist her breathing, her breath sounds are almost nonexistent," Sandy reported.

"Her blood pressure is dropping rapidly, sixty over forty, and her pulse is forty-eight with occasional extra beats." Corrie said.

Bret's mind and heart were racing. Frankie's condition was inexplicable. She was healthy and had been given minimal drugs. There were possible esoteric causes for what was happening, but they were unlikely. Established procedure demanded he look for the most probable ones. His patient seemed about to go into cardiac arrest for no reason he could discern.

"Sue, get the Automatic External Defibrillator and make it ready for use."

Without answering, Sue hurried from the room to fetch the device.

Frankie began to develop bright red swellings over the exposed parts of her body.

"Now, I'm hearing wheezing and I can feel resistance when I bag her." said Sandy.

Frankie began another short period of convulsing.

Bret pushed on Frankie's shoulder saying, "Can you hear me?" She remained unresponsive. The stench of feces began to waft about the operatory. A urine stain appeared on Frankie's jeans. She had lost control of bowels and bladder.

Bret administered another two milligrams of midazolam to quell the seizures.

"I can't get a blood pressure or pulse," Corrie said.

Sandy followed, "She's not breathing on her own."

"This can't be happening," Bret said. He looked to his helpers as if unsure of what to do and wanted advice. He turned to Pearlie, "Bring the chair all the way back," The dental chair was flattened to stabilize Frankie.

"We need to start CPR," he said, as he began to compress Frankie's chest at the rate of one hundred compressions per minute. Pearlie positioned herself across from him, prepared to relieve him when he tired. Meanwhile, she continued to suction the froth that dripped from Frankie's mouth. Every six to eight seconds, Sandy was giving a breath with the Ambu bag.

The defibrillator arrived.

Bret said to Sue, "The electrode pads have to contact skin. Cut her clothes out of the way."

Sue grabbed a blunt-nosed bandage scissors taped to the side of a cabinet and made a vertical cut through Frankie's sweater, blouse, and bra. When the task was completed, the clothing was pushed aside. Frankie's torso was exposed allowing the two defibrillator leads to be attached. Chest compressions were discontinued to enable the defibrillator to analyze her heart rhythm.

"Shock Advised," a mechanical voice announced.

"Everyone stand back." Bret had to insure no one other than Frankie would be shocked. After confirming all staff members were out of danger, "Now, Sue."

Sue pressed a button and a shock was delivered. The electrical charge shot across her chest. Frankie's body, as if a rag doll, went into a violent spasm. CPR was reinstated until time for the defibrillator to analyze the cardiac rhythm to determine if the shock had returned Frankie's heart beat to normal.

Although terrified, Bret forced himself to control his emotions to keep his assistants from panicking. After a cycle of cardiac compressions, the defibrillator was allowed to reanalyze Frankie's cardiac rhythm. Sandy maintained a proper breathing rate with the Ambu bag.

Bret considered alternative causes of the current dilemma. The red blotches on Frankie's body and subsequent high-pitched breath sounds indicated she had suffered an allergic reaction. Adrenaline was the treatment of choice.

"Sue, get me an adrenaline syringe for the I.V. line . . . one to ten thousand concentration."

"On it," she said and rushed to the emergency drug cart. For easy access syringes of adrenaline were kept in the top drawer. Sue searched the cart. With disbelief in her voice, she said, "Doctor Manley, they're not here. I can't find them."

"What!" Bret said. "Pearlie, help her."

"I'll help too," said Corrie.

"No. Take over for Pearlie and suction Frankie's mouth," Bret ordered.

As Pearlie and Sue looked for the adrenaline syringes, Pearlie shouted, "Corrie, it's your job to see that they were in the top drawer. What happened?"

Corrie was defensive and hesitated. "I . . . I don't know. They were there the last time I looked. Someone must have moved them."

"Shock Advised," the defibrillator interrupted. A second shock was delivered.

Although tiring from the exertion of the chest compressions, Bret continued CPR. Pearlie and Sue were looking for the adrenaline, Sandy was providing breaths for Frankie, and Corrie was busy suctioning her mouth. No one was free to relieve him.

Another defibrillator evaluation revealed Frankie remained in cardiac arrest.

A siren was heard. Brittney had summoned the Windham Hospital paramedics as soon as Pearlie called for help. Bret glanced at Corrie's record of events. Although it seemed longer, the record showed seven minutes had passed since Frankie had convulsed and froth issued from her mouth. More important, she had been unresponsive and without recordable vital signs for more than four minutes, the time within which a person in cardiac arrest must be resuscitated to prevent brain death.

"I've found the adrenaline," Sue shouted. "They were mixed in with the steroids. The syringes all look alike." She handed a syringe to Bret who injected the contents into the I.V. line. The potential lifesaving liquid poured into Frankie without effect.

The paramedics arrived and accessed the situation. To Bret's relief, they took over the care of his patient. The paramedics continued CPR, defibrillated, and medicated Frankie without success. Continuing their resuscitation efforts, they placed Frankie on a stretcher, wheeled her to their ambulance, and transported her to Windham Hospital. Covered in sweat and tears, Bret accompanied them.

Despite his emotional state, he was impressed by the abilities and professionalism of the Windham Hospital paramedics. On the way to the hospital, with a breathing tube in her throat, an intravenous infusion in her lower leg bone, and several monitoring devices attached to her, the consensus of those involved in Frankie's care was she was beyond saving.

After several minutes of resuscitation in the emergency department, the physician in charge said, "Stop everything. She's gone."

I'm responsible for the death of my friend. The thought flooded Mai's mind as she paced the reception room. She dreaded taking Frankie to the office that morning. Vital Frankie had no inkling her life would end that day. Every time Mai had looked at her, she visualized Frankie dead and lying in a coffin. To get rid of the morbid visions, she forced herself to concentrate on driving, the road, and her future with Jake.

I don't care if I'm a monster. It had to be done. There was no other choice. Her hope of being with Jake had been theoretical, a future event. Today, their dream was to become reality.

Frankie and Bret must pay the tab for their happiness. Frankie's part of the bill had come due. It saddened her to think Frankie would not see another sunrise. Never see the flowers in her garden. Never paint on a canvas.

Her life is being taken because of a decision I made. She agreed with Jake when he told her what he proposed to do. She had planted the seed of Frankie's destruction and knew Jake would follow it to its logical conclusion. Logic and her heart said Frankie must die, if she and Jake were to be free. Freedom's price was premeditated murder and placing the blame on an innocent person.

Mai stopped pacing and looked through the receptionist's window. She saw people scurrying about. *It's happening. I can tell by their actions and the fear on their faces. Our plan is being executed.*

She was startled by the opening of the reception room door. Corrie entered to tell her of the tragedy. Mai sensed a smile under Corrie's phony sadness. *Did she wink before beginning to explain what she knew? Did Corrie think she was more than someone to be used by Jake and her?*

"Something terrible has happened," Corrie said. She regurgitated her practiced rendition of the tragedy for anyone within earshot to hear. Mai wanted to leap and scratch her impertinent eyes out. Corrie would never give another sly wink.

She didn't hear a word. It didn't matter. It was to deceive the staff and make them think Mai was without guilt. In the coming investigation, it would be important they feel she had no knowledge of her husband's plans. She was under the impression Frankie and Bret had resolved their differences.

Desperate people make desperate decisions and do desperate

things. Corrie personified her desperation. Although critical to their success, Mai hated her. After the present affair was over, Corrie would be barred from their lives. She'd put the presumptuous bitch in her place.

When finished with what she had to say, Corrie placed a consoling arm around Mai.

"Get away from me," Mai screamed and pushed her with both arms. An observer would believe the reaction was consistent with someone in shock.

Pearlie was in the doorway leaning into the waiting room. Having witnessed Mai's outburst, she offered, "Can I help? What can I do? Do you need a ride home?"

Mai looked at Pearlie, turned, and ran from the office.

Pearlie began to follow. With a hand signal Corrie stopped her saying, "Don't worry. I'll handle it and take her home. Frankie was her friend, and she needs to grieve."

Mai went to her car and sat. She thought about the legal barrage that was going to fall upon them. She must be strong. They couldn't undo what had been done.

Bret, distraught beyond description, was assisted by an emergency department nurse to one of the private rooms reserved for people who received tragic news. The room was small, and a family grieving the loss of a loved one might feel cramped.

A counter held informational pamphlets on religious organizations, hospice care, and funeral services. Above the counter were two large windows that provided a claustrophobic view of an adjacent wing of the hospital. He had closed the blinds.

The nurse poured him a cup of black coffee from an urn also on the counter and put it on a wooden coffee table. Bret sat in one of the leather chairs arranged around the table. Wretched thoughts invaded his mind. He put his hands to his face and sobbed.

Jake burst into the room and rushed to him. On a knee at Bret's side and with an arm over the weeping man's shoulder, he said in a soft voice, "How are you doing, buddy?" He oozed deep sympathy.

Bret made no attempt to respond.

"I'm here with you. Behind you all the way." After patting Bret on the back, Jake stood, went to an empty chair, and slid it in front of Bret before sitting. He watched his friend in silence.

Minutes passed before Bret lifted his head. His eyes were red and watery and his voice cracked, "Frankie's gone. I've been thinking and thinking and still can't figure out why or how she died." Taking a tissue from the container on the table, he wiped his tears and blew his nose.

"We'll get an answer," Jake encouraged. "They'll examine her." He knew Bret was aware of the required procedures for handling an unexplained death. He avoided the unpleasant word, autopsy. If the cyanide and peanut oil were going to be discovered as he planned, Frankie Grimaldi's body had to be examined and her blood and body fluids tested.

It wasn't easy for Jake. A sweet and kind young woman was dead, and a good man was going to suffer because of what he did. It was impossible not to feel guilt, but the remorse in his heart didn't matter. Like Mai, he had made a desperate decision to live by the Machiavellian principle of the end justifies the means.

"Come on, let's get out of here. I'm going to take you home." He helped Bret stand and assisted his distressed partner from the room.

In the month since Frankie's passing, Bret remained in a self-imposed house arrest. The one time he ventured from home turned disastrous. It was when he observed Frankie's funeral from a distance. The burial was held at the cemetery on Catholic Cemetery Road across from a golf course. It was a strange juxtaposition of happy golfers on one side of the street and unhappy mourners on the other.

As he watched the proceedings, a large and burly member

of Frankie's family recognized him and shouted, "What are you doing? Get the hell out of here. We don't want you near this place." Those on both sides of the street heard.

Recognition led to a maelstrom of verbal abuse from Frankie's relatives. Several began to approach while hurling curses and insults. Bret feared for his life, and fled what threatened to turn into an uncontrollable mob. If a pile of rocks had been available, the family would have tossed them in place of the vile invectives. It hurt him that Frankie's family didn't realize he was as devastated as they. Since the incident, he hadn't left his house.

The situation at home was bad. Mai offered no pity for his plight. Speaking was kept to a minimum. The couple avoided each other by cooking and eating separate meals and sleeping in separate bedrooms. With the exception of a few trips to a local convenience store to purchase groceries, Mai was as housebound as he. Bret was chafed by Mai's aloofness and her failure to try to soothe the pain he felt over Frankie's death.

His family visited him, although when they called, Mai avoided them by remaining in her bedroom and not emerging until they had gone. Time spent with his family was short, but Bret gained strength from their presence. His uncle Hubie, who acted as a bulwark against what Bret perceived as a cruel world, was his most welcome visitor.

During the period of isolation, Jake called and visited under the pretense of attempting to convince Bret to return to work. On one visit he said, "After all, in the United States there are a number of anesthetic deaths every year. It can happen to any of us. It's a risk we all take."

Bret replied, "I can't face patients, Jake. I'm done with oral surgery."

Jake responded, "Look, other doctors have gone through what you have and survived the ordeal. They've returned to work. Besides, I'm sure you're going to be exonerated of any wrongdoing. Most likely, they'll find Frankie's death was the result of some medical condition she had and didn't know about. Your anesthesia just uncovered it. She smoked and, most likely, used drugs. My guess is she was a time bomb waiting to explode."

Angry at the allegation, Bret said, "Frankie didn't do drugs, and I don't want to hear that again."

Jake backed-off, "No offense."

Bret calmed a bit and said, "Look, I know you're trying to make me feel better, but it's not working." Displaying frustration by hand gestures, "No matter what you or my family says, I'm not going back. The only thing concerning me now is what's going to become of Mai and me. Our relationship is in jeopardy."

Jake' final words were, "Well, I'll be back. Maybe the next time you'll change your mind." He left, and Bret didn't see the grin on his face as he walked out the door.

A little before ten a.m. on the Monday of his fifth week at home, the noise of multiple automobiles speeding into the driveway was heard. Mai and Bret rushed to the picture window. There was a screeching of brakes as a Willimantic police cruiser with lights flashing and an unmarked gray Ford sedan stopped in their driveway. The cruiser held two uniformed officers, and the sedan contained two men dressed in conservative suits. The four exited and walked to the front door. Their slow approach contrasted with their dramatic entrance into the driveway.

Mai turned and leaned her back on the window. With her hands over her face she sank to the floor muttering, "It's happening."

Bret wondered what she was saying. He felt Mai was on the verge of mental collapse and was talking nonsense. Ignoring her, he watched the approaching men whose countenances and bearing communicated they were not bringing glad tidings. On the first knock, he opened the door and was in the process of asking why they had come to his house, when the shorter of the two suits asked in a severe manner, "Dr Manley?"

With shaking knees and in his most placating but trembling voice he replied, "Yes, that's me. How can I help you?"

The man spoke as the others paid close attention. "My name is Detective Powell. We're from the Willimantic Police Department. We're here to arrest you for the murder of Ms. Frankie Grimaldi. You have the right . . ."

In total shock and disbelief over what was happening, Bret didn't understand why four men were leading him from his house in handcuffs.

'Tis better to be vile than vile esteem'd,
When not to be receives reproach
of being ...

———

Brooklyn, Connecticut: Bret was booked and processed in the Police Department in downtown Willimantic. The building's modern design and brick construction clashed with its older neighborhood. In the months Bret had been a resident of the town, he never gave it more than a cursory look. He considered himself a model citizen and never envisioned being forced to inhabit it.

The men in suits who arrested him were in charge of his interrogation. Booking included another reading of his rights, fingerprinting, and photos. When these preliminaries were completed, he was taken to a large rectangular room with a black vinyl floor. What he assumed was a two-way mirror covered a large part of one wall. Furniture consisted of a rectangular wooden table in the center and several chairs strewn about. Bret noted the legs of the table were screwed into the floor. Although there were flush mounted lights in the ceiling, the light being used was a single, green metal shaded lamp about three feet above the table. The smell of cigarettes and stale tobacco emanated from ashtrays full of debris.

Pointing a finger at a chair, Detective Jablonski, the taller and friendlier of the detectives, said, "Sit, please." Jablonski's superior, Detective Powell had accompanied them. The latter exhibited a military bearing and, although of less than average height, he was a powerfully built Black man.

As told, Bret sat in the assigned chair. He thought it had to be the perp's side of the table as someone on the other side of the two-way mirror would have a clear view of him. The light from the hanging lamp shined in his eyes. No attempt was made to adjust it. He thought of repositioning the lamp but decided not to.

Attached on the upper part of each corner of the room were cameras on rotating arms. They appeared able to provide front, side, and back views of everyone. There were three circular grates in the ceiling that Bret would not have been surprised to learn concealed microphones and additional video recording devices.

Detective Powell placed an audio recorder on the table, pointed to a corner camera, and said, "Dr. Manley, for your information, we'll be recording this interview. I'm going to remind you that your rights have been read to you. Can we agree there's no question about your having gotten them?"

Bret nodded.

"Speak up, please." The detective said in a louder voice, "Have you been read your rights and do you understand them?"

"Yes, I have," was the meek reply.

Detective Powell continued, "As you've been advised, if you want an attorney present, you can call one. If you don't have an attorney, we can and will provide one."

Bret pleaded, "I told you several times, now, you've made a big mistake." He repeated, "A big mistake."

"Nevertheless," Detective Powell persisted, "I'm obligated to tell you it may be in your best interest to call a lawyer."

After taking a moment to think about what Detective Powell advised, Bret said, "I could call my uncle. He's an attorney but lives out of town. I don't want to bother him if someone local is available to help. Maybe I can call Harvey Baronet. He was a patient of mine, and I've heard good things about him. He should be able to straighten out this mess."

The interrogation was deferred, and Bret was allowed to summon Attorney Baronet who arrived in forty-five-minutes. Before the official questioning began, Bret and his attorney had a private consultation in a room with a guard at the door.

When he called the attorney, Bret said his arrest was a gigantic misunderstanding and general screw-up, and he required an attorney to help untangle the mess so he could be released as soon as possible. Upon hearing Bret was being charged with the first degree murder of Frankie Grimaldi, Attorney Baronet made it clear he would represent Bret until he found an experienced criminal lawyer. The attorney added, "And I mean with plenty of experience."

For an hour he and Bret reviewed questions likely to be asked and how they should be answered. When finished, they were led back to the interrogation room and Detective Powell, the primary interrogator. After laying the groundwork for what was to come, the detective went to the heart of the matter, "Why did you murder Ms. Grimaldi?"

Bret looked at his attorney. With a nod, Attorney Baronet let him know he should answer the question as they had prepared. "I didn't murder Frankie Grimaldi. If she was murdered, someone else did it and is trying to place the blame on me."

"Who'd want to pin the murder of Ms. Grimaldi on you, and why?"

"I have no idea. It's unthinkable anyone would want to do such a thing to either one of us."

Detective Powell asked these and other questions in many ways and forms. Bret supplied the same answers. The interrogation lasted until late afternoon, when Bret, accompanied by his legal representative, was brought before a judge who ruled he be held without bail in the State Jail in Brooklyn.

Not until he was being transported in a van to the jail did the horrible reality of his situation hit him. The authorities were accusing him of premeditated murder. It was a crime in which life without parole could be imposed. The possibility of being incarcerated for the rest of his life for something he didn't commit petrified him. Attorney Baronet was correct when he said a good criminal lawyer was needed. The one silver lining in the horrible black cloud hanging over him was he knew the man, who many believed was the best criminal attorney around, his uncle, Hubie Santos. Bret was in dire need of his services.

That evening, he and his cellmate, Roman Hernandez, a scary looking dude about twenty-five years old who arrived at the jail that day, watched the news of his arrest on TV. The known details of the heinous crime for which he was accused were released to the people of Connecticut by talking heads whose solemnity and sincerity he doubted. Film of him in handcuffs being escorted to the jail van was difficult to watch.

Roman turned to him, raised his hand, and said, "Gimme a high-five, bro. You're famous."

Bret returned the gesture out of fear of what might happen if he didn't. One look at Roman told you he wasn't to be trifled with. Roman was hard and tough looking. An assortment of facial scars reinforced the impression that he was acquainted with the area's mean streets.

"What are you in for," Bret said in an effort to establish a rapport with the man he was sharing a cell with.

"I almost cut the cojones off the maricon who lives next door to me. He made kissing noises at my bitch." Roman smacked his lips mimicking the kissing noises. "Like he wanted to kiss her *you know what*. Too bad I didn't cut them all the way off. I shoulda cut his tongue out at the same time."

Over the years Bret had acquired a working knowledge of Spanish, including street slang, and understood Roman had attempted to cut off the testicles of a fellow he referred to as gay but wanted to have oral sex with his girlfriend. It didn't make sense, but what counted was it made sense to Roman. "Will they give you a long sentence?" Bret asked, curious what the sentence was for that type of crime.

"Nah, bro, I didn't do that much damage. I heard they stitched him up in the emergency room and let him go. Scared the shit out of him though. With prison crowding as it is, they shouldn't give me more than six months. I can do that standing on my head."

Aware prisons were full of men like Roman, Bret desperately wanted to avoid being placed in one. A great concern was Mai made no attempt to visit him at the police station or the jail. They had taken his cell phone, so he couldn't contact her. Given his plight, he couldn't dwell on what was going on in her head. Recent events had made her a psychological wreck. *Well, she'll have to put on her big girl panties and get over her doldrums. I'm dealing with more pressing problems.*

It was his mother, Rose, who came to the rescue. Her friends had seen television news of Bret's arrest and alerted Rose to his plight. Because of side effects of medicines she was taking, driving long distances alone was difficult. A neighbor drove her to the jail. Although she arrived after visiting hours, Bret's mother demanded, and was granted, a short visit. They met in the room reserved for inmates meeting with their lawyers. A corrections officer monitored them.

"Calm down, Mom," Bret said when he saw her. His mom was close to being overcome with worry, and he was concerned the strain might be too much.

"Don't be bothered about me," she assured him. "I'm strong and not about to complicate things with a medical problem." After making herself comfortable in a chair, she said, "I want to help. What can I do?"

"Just contact Uncle Hubie and tell him I need him. He might not know what's happened."

"Of course. He's away, but when he gets back, he'll help you get out of this mess."

Bret's first night at the jail was difficult. He was wrestling with concerns about who killed Frankie and about Mai's behavior. Although she had been cold at home, he felt that because he was in jail, she should have attempted to contact or see him. He was annoyed that she hadn't done either.

Another worry was what Roman might be thinking. He had been friendly. Too friendly. Was he trying to get Bret to lower his guard? When least expected, he might pounce on his defenseless cellmate. Street smart and street hardened, Roman Hernandez would have no trouble overpowering him.

It wasn't a sexual assault he feared. After all, the man had a girlfriend and had been in jail a day. What scared him was the possibility of a jailhouse code of ethics of which he wasn't aware. Such a code might demand Roman prove he was the alpha male in the cell.

Adding to Bret's woe was the temperature in the facility. Although it was the latter part of June, the heating system was working, and it felt ten degrees above what would be considered comfortable.

The result was a sweaty, restless night filled with thoughts of Frankie and Mai and concerns about what Roman was contemplating. It was dawn when he fell asleep.

A crazy series of nightmares was terminated by Roman pushing on his shoulder. "Wake up, wake up, you need to wake up," Roman urged.

Thinking he was being attacked, Bret sprang to a defensive sitting position and covered his face with his arms. His heart was beating a tachycardiac tune.

Smiling, Roman said, "Take it easy, bro, we've got to get ready for breakfast. You don't want to miss breakfast here. It's the best of any jail around."

Thankful he was wrong in his judgment of Roman, Bret got out of bed. *So much for the alpha male thing.*

That morning a corrections officer rapped on Bret's cell door with his baton. "Manley, come with me."

"Why," he asked.

"We're going to the visitor's reception room There's someone who wants to see you."

"Is it my wife?"

"Can't say. All's they told me was to take you there."

The officer walked a half-step behind Bret keeping his baton at the ready and giving an occasional shove with it. Bret retaliated with nasty stares. He wanted it to be Mai waiting for him. A voice in his head told him it wouldn't be.

When they reached the room, Bret's escort opened the door and said, "You can go in. I'll wait here. The officer inside will give you about a half-hour, no more."

The Visitor's Reception Room appeared to have been copied from the set of a 1950's prison flick. A wall with thick glass partitions divided the room. On both sides of the glass were cubicles that faced each other. Each cubicle contained a counter and a chair. Side walls provided a modicum of privacy. Circular metal grates in the glass partitions allowed visitors to speak to each other.

It wasn't Mai but a white-haired older man sitting in one of the cubicles on the other side. He wore a blue pin-striped suit with a power-red tie. While disappointed it wasn't his wife, Bret figured the fellow was from his uncle's office. The officer stationed in the room led him to the chair across from the visitor. Bret greeted him with a friendly, "Hi."

Without a word of acknowledgement, the stranger nodded to the corrections officer who had remained standing at Bret's side. The officer walked to his duty station desk, picked up a large thick envelope, and brought it to Bret. Confused, Bret took it as the stranger spoke, "This service has been recorded in the jail logbook." The man rose from his chair and left without another word.

Bret opened the envelope and reviewed its contents. The papers fell from his hands, and his vision blurred. He was surprised. Or was he? Mai had been acting strange since before Frankie's death. It was official, she was filing for divorce.

As he sulked in his cell, ignoring Roman's attempts to raise his spirits, Bret was notified of a telephone call, and was taken to the room he and his mother had used. It contained a landline. He picked up the phone and recognized the cheerful voice.

"Bret, its Uncle Hubie. Hang in there, son, I'm going to help you." Hubie Santos paused a moment. People in Bret's emotional state required information to be provided in small bites. "I'll be in personal touch after I research the charges against you and think about our defense. It may take a day."

Bret's emotions threatened to overwhelm him.

Hubie continued, "In the meantime, one of my staff will meet with you today. If you want to talk to me, call anytime. I've arranged for you to have twenty-four hour use of the jail's landline. If I can't answer my cell because I'm in court or something, I'll get back as soon as possible."

As he held the phone to his ear, Bret began to sob. "Sorry for crying, but, until now, I had no hope of surviving this ordeal."

Hubert Santos, everyone called him Hubie, was a well-known criminal defense attorney who had defended numerous high profile clients. He argued cases in state and federal courts. It was not unusual to read a newspaper or watch a television news program with mention of him and his firm in their current legal battle. Those who had to have the best hired Hubie.

Because of age differences and divergent and busy career paths, Bret saw his uncle on rare occasions. Hubie would visit him whenever he was trying a case in New York, but for the most part, they met at events that bring together far-flung families and distant relatives. Christmas, weddings, and funerals led the list, but no matter the occasion, Bret welcomed the opportunity to visit with his uncle.

Hubie Santos was a raconteur extraordinaire who had the ability to tell a story and hold an audience as no other. When he entered a room, people flocked to him hoping to become privy to the latest "Hubie tale." As a listener, you expected to be belly laughing one moment and shocked into stunned silence the next. Hubie laughed with you, patted you on the back, or put an arm about your shoulder as emphasis to his narrative. Although Bret had never observed his uncle in a courtroom, he felt these stories gave him insight into Hubie's power to mesmerize a jury.

On Friday afternoon, Bret and his uncle were sitting at the table in the consultation room. Bret shaved, combed his hair, and wore the clean uniform that was issued for the meeting.

As he was setting up a recorder and booting his laptop to

connect to the wired internet service provided, Hubie asked, "How're you getting along with your cellmate? Hernandez is his name, right?"

"Yes, that's it. He's a pretty good guy, actually. He says his lawyer got the prosecutor to agree to a reduced plea, and they're going to give him the six months he was hoping for. They're also going to let him serve his time here, and he's ecstatic about that. When the sentence is official, they'll move him out of our cell to one of the dormitories. I'll be sorry to see him go. Believe it or not, in the short time we've bunked together, we've become friends. He even told me to look him up when I get out of this mess."

Hubie kept his gaze on Bret. "I'm going to do everything in my power to see that you keep that date.

When his equipment was in order, Hubie began the session. "Because of the gravity of your charges, I'll request the administration not to assign anyone to your cell. That will give you more time to concentrate on helping with the upcoming trial. I'm pretty sure they'll agree. They don't want to give me any reason to say your defense was unfairly hindered and to ask for a mistrial should we need one."

Hubie was tall and broad with close cropped salt and pepper hair and compassion in his eyes. He gave the impression of a man who could be trusted to defend your life.

"Tell me everything that happened the day Ms. Grimaldi died. Don't leave out any detail no matter how unimportant you might think it is. What seems unimportant now may turn out to be critical to our case."

Bret related the circumstances of Frankie's death, giving as much detail as memory allowed. Hubie asked for clarification when appropriate.

When the recitation was finished, the attorney said "That was good, Bret. You've told me what you believe is the truth." He stood and went to his nephew who remained seated. Placing both hands on Bret's shoulders, he began in a gentle manner, "I've never known you to lie. Even when being honest resulted in punishment. I'm thinking of the time you were a kid and threw a rock that broke a window in the new house being built next to yours. If you had denied doing it, you wouldn't have been caught. Instead, you admitted breaking the window and took your lumps. I've always admired you for that." He removed his hands from Bret's shoulders.

Hubie finished rough and to the point. "But, I have to tell you some person or persons went to great lengths to make you look guilty. And, they've done a good job."

He returned to his chair and cradled his chin with his hand. "Yes," he said, "a really good job."

Turning to Bret, he posited, "Let's see if I have it. It's complicated, but hear me out. The prosecution says Frankie Grimaldi died from a combination of peanut oil and cyanide you added to the medicines typically used by an oral surgeon when giving intravenous anesthesia. They speculate the cyanide was meant to poison her and the peanut oil was used to insure death by causing an anaphylactic reaction. Of course, the cyanide alone should have been enough."

"No, no, no. That's a lie," Bret insisted, shaking his head.

Hubie's voice was firm, "Hold on. I said to hear me out."

Bret fixed upon his uncle.

"You have to know everything if you're going to assist with our defense. I understand it's difficult to hear. Be tough."

Bret shook his head, "This whole thing is unbelievable."

Hubie continued, "They say you took the further precaution of putting the adrenalin syringes, crucial to treating cardiac arrest and stopping allergic reactions, in a different place from where they should have been in your emergency kit. That made them hard to find. Delaying treatment and increasing the chance of death."

Bret listened without comment to his uncle's words.

Hubie stood and paced the room, his eyes never leaving his young client. Pointing a finger in the air, he continued with the prosecution's theory, "You would have gotten away with the murder had not Corrie Hunter, the office manager, accidentally walked in on your alleged drug switch in the room where such medicines are kept. She claims you were acting suspicious."

Hubie stopped pacing and paused as if thinking, "Ordinarily, there would have been no drug testing other than for the standard anesthetics used. The blue color of Frankie's blood caused by the cyanide would be chalked up to lack of oxygen from what happened. Even the almond odor of the cyanide you and the assistants smelled was assumed to be from a cream or lotion Frankie used."

Shaking his head in disbelief, Bret couldn't fathom why anyone wanted to do what had been done to Frankie and him.

As if reading his mind, his uncle said, "Whoever did this terrible thing wanted to kill Frankie Grimaldi and get away with murder by implicating you." As if he had an inspiration, "Or, maybe they wanted to get rid of you and used Ms. Grimaldi to do it. Who knows, perhaps, it was both. Can you think of anyone who would harm either of you?" He returned to his chair.

"Only Corrie Hunter. That's because I know she's lying when she says she saw me switching the intravenous drugs. I don't know why she would do such a thing. I thought we had a good working relationship." He gathered his thoughts, "If she was acquainted with Frankie, it wasn't very well. She never mentioned anything about her. Maybe something happened long ago, and she's been carrying a grudge."

"Perhaps," was Hubie's noncommittal response. He leaned forward, and with a grave expression on his face said, "Remember what I said earlier about being tough."

Bret responded with a firm, "Yes, and I'm trying to be."

"What I'm about to tell you will hurt, but I believe it to be fact."

Shivers rattled Bret's spine.

"We have to go where the evidence leads. In my mind there's no doubt your wife had a role in setting you up for a murder rap."

Feeling as if he had been hit with a sucker-punch and had the wind knocked from him, Bret banged his fist on the table and shouted, "How can you say it?" He was seething and didn't want to admit his uncle might be correct. After a while, he calmed and said, "You don't know her. She could never do this. Even though she's filed for divorce, I know down deep she still loves me."

The angry outburst caused the guard at the door to look into the room to see what the noise was. As nothing untoward was happening, he returned to his chair and girlie magazine.

With a quick movement, Hubie reached across the table and grabbed his nephew's wrist. His grip was a vice. "You've got to believe it," he said in a normal tone that belied the strength in his hand, "The evidence irrefutably points to it. I'll explain."

He released his hold, and Bret rubbed his wrist. "Think you're ready to hear what I have to say?"

"Yeah." Bret squirmed in his chair as Hubie Santos, prominent criminal attorney, his uncle, and a man who Bret admired and loved, spent the next several minutes destroying the life he had come to know.

"Corrie Hunter was certainly part of the scheme, but was, most plausibly, being used by the originator of the plan to kill Frankie and place the blame on you. My private investigator is working day and night on the case. To date, his findings are preliminary, but it seems, as you suspected, Corrie Hunter and Frankie Grimaldi had no prior interaction other than to be aware each existed. It's unlikely Corrie initiated the plot to murder her . . . I doubt she's smart enough . . . but was somehow enticed into being a part of it. Maybe paid, maybe blackmailed, maybe both."

Hubie posed the hypothetical question, "Who benefited from Frankie Grimaldi's death? Our initial investigative results indicate Frankie was well-regarded in both the gay and straight communities. Nobody has a bad word to say about her. She owed money to no one, had a small life insurance policy with her parents as beneficiaries, and by all accounts lived a private and laudatory life. No one, it seems, would want to murder her."

Hubie changed tacks. "Let's consider this," he stared at the ceiling and appeared to be thinking as he spoke. "Say, for instance, you were the intended victim of the crime, and Frankie was a poor unfortunate lamb who had to be sacrificed to get at you. Puts a new perspective on what happened, doesn't it?"

Bret, accepting Hubie's reasoning, interrupted, "It's horrible to think an innocent person was murdered because someone has a grudge against me."

"It certainly is. Just remember, what I'm telling you is a work in progress. Nothing's proven."

Hubie lowered his head and said, "How about Mai? Lets parse her. Don't you think she was a little too quick on the trigger in filing for divorce? If you make the assumption she thought about divorcing you prior to and not because of the present mess, your going to prison for a long time would fit perfectly with what she was seeking."

Bret didn't want to believe Hubie. How could he have been so deceived, so wrong in his judgment of her? He was a mountain climber who made an arduous and dangerous climb to a summit and found he climbed the wrong mountain. Bret would rather have been hit by bricks falling from a building than believe what his uncle was suggesting.

Hubie wasn't done stripping him of everything that mattered. "Mai doesn't have the type of background necessary to commit a murder such as the one we're dealing with. She would need the help of someone, say, for instance, Jake Warden, a man we know to be expert in intravenous anesthesia and knowledgeable about the drugs that killed Frankie. If you look at the facts objectively and follow where they lead, it isn't difficult to come to the conclusion your wife and your partner must have acted in concert to pull off the murder.

Hubie left his chair and began another pace of the room. "Sorry, but those are the facts as I see them." He stopped moving and with arms folded faced Bret. "I know you're upset. You wouldn't be normal if you weren't. It's okay to vent your anger. You'll feel better if you get it out."

Bret was unable to vent. He remained immobile, akin to the day Frankie died when he was sitting in the room at Windham Hospital. All the strength in his body evaporated into an unseen ether. He couldn't raise his hands from where they were glued to his lap, and it felt as if he was going to fall from his chair. Instead of the outburst Hubie advised, Bret stared at the floor.

Hubie went to his nephew and patted him on the back. There were things to say, but the time for talking had ended.

While Bret was in the throes of depression that Friday afternoon, Jake Warden and Mai Manley were in Jake's Storrs condominium. He was sitting in one of his stuffed leather chairs, and Mai was in his lap. Waterford crystal glasses on the table next to the chair held red wine for him and white for her. In the background, a Mozart sonata played.

Jake picked up his glass and lifted it in a toast. Mai did the same, and the clink of the colliding crystal created the pleasing high-pitched sound of a wedding bell. "To the ex-Mai Manley. Soon to become Mai Faca again, and as soon as socially appropriate, Mai Faca Warden."

Mai turned in his lap to face him. With a puzzled look, she said, "I'm not sure it was a good idea to serve Bret with divorce papers so quickly after his arrest? Shouldn't we have waited?"

Jake replied, "It's somewhat of a gray area. I thought he should be served because according to the chief prosecutor, if you were planning a divorce prior to the commission of the crime, it's possible you'll be permitted to testify against him in a case like this. I'm pretty sure the prosecutors are going to request the judge let you."

Mai became agitated. "No. Don't make them force me to testify," she pleaded as she straightened herself, although remaining on her lover's lap. "I don't think I can do it. I don't want to testify against Bret."

"You must, if they want you to," he insisted. "Your testimony will cement the case against him. All you have to do is say yes when the prosecutor asks if Bret hated Frankie for making lesbian overtures toward you." Jake thought the lesbian thing was a nice touch. It added hate crime aspects to what was a bizarre crime. Another obstacle for Bret to overcome.

Mai got off Jake's lap and stood, bending so her face was a few inches from his. "How will I be able to look at him? I couldn't do that and lie. Everyone in the courtroom would see I was lying."

Like a child anxious to share a secret he'd promised not to reveal, Jake answered, "No they won't. You won't have to look at him. You're going to appear so distraught, you'll spend most of your time in the witness chair crying into a handkerchief. You'll have one in your hand at all times." He added, "Very feminine. Should make the male jurors and the motherly female ones want to leave their box and come and wipe away your tears." He concluded, "Don't worry, with your face in your hanky, you won't have to look at the jurors, Bret, or his damn lawyer."

Jake knew she was scared. He'd help her. "I can see the goal line," he said and kissed her on the cheek. "Admit it. So can you."

Mai gave a reluctant nod.

Jake said, "Once we get past the trial and Bret is out of the way, we'll have the rest of our lives to enjoy together. Think of that when you get nervous about what you have to do. We've already been through the hardest part of our ordeal."

Unsaid was that they were in great danger. If their scheme was uncovered, it would be they, and not Bret, on trial. They'd lose each other forever. Whether Jake got life without parole or a lesser sentence, being without Mai would be unbearable. He couldn't exist without her.

Bret had composed himself, and Hubie completed what he was obligated to say. The sad young man who had been misused by those he trusted had to be informed of the legal severity of his circumstances. "Although we know you are innocent and who most likely committed the crime you've been charged with, the case against you is extremely strong. The prosecution will ask for the maximum of life without parole. They're not willing to settle for a plea deal and a lesser sentence. The only good news is it's not death."

"I don't care. Nothing matters now." Bret was dejected.

Hubie ignored him and held to the subject, "Anyway, Corrie Hunter is a credible witness. So far, she's sticking to her story. We'll depose her and see if we can break it down, find inconsistencies, but my gut feeling is we won't succeed. If so, she probably won't crack under cross examination during the trial. Her testimony might be enough to convict you." As an afterthought, "I bet she was paid well."

Bret interrupted, "I still can't believe she would say those things against me."

The attorney said, "Who knows why people do what they do." He scratched his head, "The two great unknowns are Mai and Jake. Given that Mai is already suing for divorce, I can only surmise they are going to come at you with guns blazing."

Bret asked, "Can she testify against me? We were married when Frankie . . . " he had difficulty saying the words . . . "passed away."

"I fear the prosecuting team thinks so. They're pushing for a quick divorce. I can delay it, but it's inevitable. And the prosecution can easily delay the trial until the divorce is final. Meanwhile, you're in here counting the minutes, hours, and days, right?"

With a nod Bret indicated his agreement.

"I say we let them have the divorce. She'll get everything, of course, but that doesn't matter. We have more important issues to worry about. After the dissolution is final, we should be able to see what they're up to. Once I know their game plan, I can develop countermeasures."

Hubie summed with, "Let's focus on where we should have the trial. You never know how a judge or jury will react in a hometown case such as this. Though Windham is small compared to Hartford or Manchester, I've argued enough cases here to believe we can get an impartial jury and a fair trial. I don't think we should ask for a change of venue. Do you?"

Bret's answer lacked enthusiasm, "Whatever you feel is best."

"I'll take that as a yes."

The meeting was over and Hubie began to pack his briefcase with the legal papers that had cluttered the table. He saw the hopelessness on Bret's face. He went to the door as if intending to signal the guard to unlock it, but before doing so he turned to Bret. "One of these days you'll meet my private investigator. You know, what they call a private dick." Chuckle, chuckle. "He'll remind you of Columbo. I make him wear a well-used trench coat with the collar up. And when he's interviewing someone, I insist he walks away and then turns back and says, 'Oh ... just one thing bothers me ...'" The latter was spoken in Columbo-ese. Bret smiled. "Only kidding, of course. He isn't like Columbo at all. His trench coat is much newer." Another chuckle.

Hubie summoned the guard who opened the door. His parting words were serious, "His name is Bob Dillon. He's a good man and has been instrumental in getting the verdict I wanted in many cases. You can be assured he's working hard on your case. He gave a wave of his hand and left the room.

That's Hubie for you, Bret mused. He was never one to waste an opportunity to create a bit of humor. If he were about to be hanged, no doubt he'd quip that he hoped the hangman passed the knot tying test when he was a Boy Scout.

Bret spent six months in the Brooklyn jail as the prosecution and defense worked their cases. He accepted and acclimated to his environment. A big challenge was getting used to his mattress, clearly not a Sleep Number bed. Guards weren't abusive, and because of his celebrity, he received a higher level of care, attention, and perks than the average car thief or mugger. When Roman was transferred to the dormitory, Bret missed the happy-go-lucky fellow who had the knack of cheering him. It wasn't long before he came to appreciate the extra living space, not to mention the silence and thinking time that resulted from being alone.

With the continuing news coverage of Frankie's bizarre death, his arrest, and the upcoming trial, Bret's notoriety had become national. He was mentioned on the well-known "Fair and Balanced" channel as well as a plethora of other news organizations.

When not working on his case, Bret read, played solitaire, and began to study chess. Hubie brought him a board and pieces as well as books on the subject. Learning the technical and historic aspects of the game and playing both sides of the board brought short periods of peace to Bret's troubled mind.

Whenever Hubie's group or the prosecuting team made a move in what could be considered their legal game of chess, headlines resulted. The maneuvers had to do with allowing or disallowing a witness or piece of evidence. They were thoughtful and made with consideration of what the opposition might do in response. The defense would outfox the prosecution on one issue and be bested by them on another. The goal of both was to sway a jury into believing their argument was valid. It was the jury that was going to render the final *Check* and *Mate*.

During this period Bret became single. It resulted in a week of greater than usual depression. Neither Jake nor Mai had visited him, and after the divorce, it was confirmed they were going to testify for the prosecution. It was validation that they had masterminded Frankie's murder. Bret might have been able to accept what they did to him. It was an affair of the heart and such things happened in the name of love. What they did to Frankie could never be understood, accepted, nor forgiven.

Bret received information concerning events in his former world from Hubie's private detective. In the detective's words he was hard at work trying "to expose snakes hiding under rocks."

When Bob Dillon, the P.I., introduced himself, he noted the spelling was D-I-L-L-O-N, not D-Y-L-A-N like the singer. Bret couldn't resist saying the singer, Dylan, was not born Dylan, but Zimmerman.

He didn't look like Columbo, as his uncle had joked, but was perfect for his job. He was middle-aged, average in looks, build, and height and wore clothes of last year's style. The P.I. was so common in appearance he would be unnoticed in a crowd of two people. In addition, he was friendly, intelligent, and, like Hubie, quick with the quips. To Bret, his uncle and the investigator were kindred spirits.

Bob was talkative and in short order, Bret learned a great deal about the man. At one time he had been part of a P.I. group, but the relationship didn't last. None of his partners shared his intense work ethic. The situation led to arguments and the dissolution of the firm. He worked alone and provided his services to attorneys, not the general public. Working with Hubie's group was what he most enjoyed. "The firm has interesting cases and the folks are easy to deal with. Unfortunately, your case is an interesting one, but don't worry, I'm on your side. How could we lose?" he boasted. Bret liked the attitude.

Members of his family visited when able. Age and distance made the visits infrequent, but he spoke to his mother by phone several times a week. The most regular visitor and one of his few remaining Windham friends was Pearlie Perez. Her belief in his innocence was unwavering, and she helped the defense team in every way she could. She was his main source of local news. Although no longer employed by Jake, she was kept apprised by Sandy of what was happening in Jake's life. Pearlie reported on the exploits of his ex-wife and former business partner. The reports were important to Bret. Although he had come to loathe the pair, he developed a perverse interest in the updates.

As he lay in his bunk, Bret conjured abhorrent images of Mai and her lover. Violence repulsed him, and he became sick to the point of vomiting when thinking of Frankie's death. Yet, he fantasized taking the lives of Jake and Mai by pouring gasoline on them and lighting it, whacking them Mafia style with bullets fired into each of their brains, or suffocating them by tying thick plastic bags about their heads. He never considered poisoning or causing anaphylactic allergic reactions. His psyche wouldn't allow it.

In early winter jury selection began. Both the selection and the trial were scheduled to be held in the brick and glass Superior Court building in Danielson.

"Picking the proper jury is considered by many to be the most crucial step in the successful defense of a client," Hubie told his nephew. "Some lawyers specialize in the process and are hired only to help pick the jury."

"Are we going to hire one?"

"No, I have people in my group who are experts. They'll give us the advice we need."

"Good, I'd rather work with your people."

"I appreciate your confidence, but if I thought we needed a specialist, we'd get one. With a sympathetic jury, no matter how damaging the evidence, there's always a chance of acquittal. Everyone has heard about famous cases where the evidence against the defendant seemed overwhelming, yet the verdict ended up being not guilty."

"Yeah, you mean like the O.J. and Casey Anthony verdicts. A lot of people thought they were guilty.

"True, those are two of the most memorable. The juries in both cases were able to be convinced of reasonable doubt. But never forget, it was defense attorneys that led them to the reasonable doubt. So after we get the jury we want, we can't assume our job is done. We'll still have to work hard."

Hubie went on, "The prosecutors are aware of the importance of jury selection. The battle over our jury is going to be down and dirty, but I'm ready to engage in hand-to-hand combat with them." He grinned as he said, "Figuratively speaking, of course."

They were in the attorney-client room. The guard on the other side of the door was familiar with the many rendezvous between Bret and one of his attorneys or Bob Dillon and ignored them. Hubie had arrived in a blue pin-striped suit with a light gray shirt and conservative tie. Within a short time the suit jacket was rumpled and hanging on the chair, the tie was loose, and upper buttons of his shirt were undone.

The process of jury selection, including the ability to reject some potential jurors without explanation, had been reviewed. "I want you present when the jury is selected." It was not a request.

"Why? I thought I didn't have to be there for the selection," Bret challenged.

"You're right. We can keep you out of the process, but there are good reasons for you to be there. Potential jurors will get to see you before the trial. Maybe one will bond with you. Another reason is you resided in this area. You may be aware of an important fact about a candidate I'm not familiar with or may notice something I've overlooked. As I said, winning or losing is often a function of proper jury selection." With a sympathetic expression, he added, "We're talking life without parole."

Although his hands and feet would be, as Hubie put it, "tastefully cuffed," he said Bret would be allowed to wear civilian clothes, not the orange jump suit he had been wearing in the courtroom.

"There will be the normal contingent of security officers near the exits. If you don't give them any trouble, they'll let you be."

Hubie continued, "You'll be sitting in the back of the selection room off to one side where I have a clear view of you. If for any reason you're adamant someone should not be on the jury, casually rest your hands on your left knee. I'll arrange for that person to be disqualified. Remember, it's the only time you should place your hands on the left knee." With a chuckle, he said, "Otherwise, you might have me disqualifying the entire pool. Good jurors, by that I mean those who will vote not guilty, are hard to come by."

He became serious, "Lots of people try to get out of jury duty. On the other hand, there are those who want to become part of the jury in a well-publicized case like ours. They plan to get rich writing a book. We try to avoid people like that if we can. A guilty verdict sells more books than an innocent one."

Bret snickered.

"I should mention another thing. Some candidates will say what they think you want to hear in order to get picked. Often, they're lying because they have an agenda. We'll avoid them, too, if they can be identified."

Shaking his head, Bret said, "I never realized picking a jury was so complicated."

Hubie said, "I guess all we can hope for is to find people willing to keep an open mind about our side of the argument. In any event, I'll periodically confer with you to ensure we're on the same page."

"Why will I be so far away from you? Why the secrecy?"

"Because if someone we object to gets picked anyway, I don't want him or her to know it was you who objected. I'd rather have them think it was me. I'm a lawyer and used to being disliked. Jurors are human, and the one you wanted off the jury might get even by finding you guilty."

Bret accepted the wisdom of his uncle's words and said, "I'll help. It will be sort of like a catcher giving signals to a pitcher."

Hubie's wry answer was, "Sure, just like that."

The day's work had ended. Hubie retrieved his jacket, buttoned his shirt and tightened his tie before going to the door and signaling the corrections officer to open it. He turned to Bret, "Of course, if you have something better to do, I would understand."

As his uncle exited the room, Bret quipped, "Ha, ha, you're so funny." It was another proof his uncle was a graduate of the *Leave Them Laughing School for Lawyers* who thought they were stand-up comedians as well as officers of the court. He knew the reason for Hubie's humorous asides. They were part of his uncle's many techniques, which included the chess set and bringing the occasional pizza to their meetings, to keep his spirits up. It was critical that he be able to withstand the coming ordeal.

Selecting a jury took eight business days. There were moments when Bret thought the prosecutors and Hubie's people were going to come to blows. It never happened. Each side knew when to back off. Bret looked upon it as the legal equivalent of a game of chicken. The last juror was selected on Wednesday and the trial was scheduled to begin the following Monday. The panel consisted of seven women and five men.

Hubie was pleased more women than men had been picked. "It's a generalization, but jury research indicates women are more likely to wait until all the evidence is in before making a decision. That means I have the whole trial to plant seeds of doubt."

The jurors were admonished to avoid anything pertaining to the case until reporting to the judicial building. They were to be prepared for sequestering for what promised to be a long trial. As for Bret, his stomach was churning acid in increasing amounts as the day of the trial approached.

The trial was destined to be four and a half weeks of pure agony for Bret. Before it began, prosecutors appeared on most of the news shows hawking their air-tight case. He was certain it was part of a strategy to push his buttons and bring havoc to his sleep patterns

He was to wear his most conservative suits and was given the herculean task of appearing attentive, relaxed, friendly, and nonaggressive. Angry outbursts were forbidden as was whispering in the ear of any of his defense team.

The first morning, a small but vocal lesbian group marched in a circle in front of the Superior Court building. Their placards proclaimed Bret was a homophobe and deserved the nastiest of punishments. For them, burning at the stake would have been inadequate retribution. Authorities disbanded the lesbians when it was discovered they didn't have a permit to protest, but not before they were interviewed by what seemed every media outlet in the world.

Most of the faces in the courtroom were unfriendly. The pleasant ones consisted of his family and the few true Windham friends who believed in him. Bob Dillon attended a portion of most morning sessions. He sat in an obscure area of the courtroom and monitored the proceedings. The purpose was to refine areas of his ongoing investigation. True to his profession, he took pains to appear he was one of the interested public allowed to observe the trial. Many of Frankie's relatives were in attendance and their unhidden anger caused a negative atmosphere to permeate the room.

The morning of the second day, he and Hubie were sitting at their table reviewing strategy. The judge hadn't arrived and the courtroom was empty except for security personnel. Hubie turned to Bret and said, "You did a good job yesterday by keeping your cool and basically looking innocent."

Shaking his head, Bret said, "It isn't easy when you are constantly being referred to as the most dastardly human being since Jack the Ripper. A few times it took all my effort not to jump out of my chair and shout that the witness was lying." Bret was agitated, "Especially when they brought up how I supposedly got the cyanide. Their drug enforcement agents testified I could have purchased cyanide when I was in Las Vegas and sneaked it on the plane. As long as I had the money, they said, I could have bought just about anything there, including cyanide. They had the record of my ATM withdrawal, and no one, including the investigators you have on the case, was able to find the call girl I paid with the money, or Sal the Bellman. He no longer works there and left for parts unknown. God, that didn't endear me to the jury. What must they think of me?"

Bret shook his head several times, "They don't know me. I'm a decent man," he slapped his hand on the table, "As for the cyanide, I'd be afraid to handle it or even be near it. A whiff could kill you."

Bret stopped talking, and Hubie gave him a light pat on the back. "Be strong and continue doing what you're doing. It's part of their plan. If they break you, they win."

Bret continued, "It seems they want the jury to have the impression I've been a bad seed since birth, a regular *Baby Scarface* born with a cigar in my mouth. And what happened to Frankie was the inevitable result of a process begun long ago." He took a sighing breath, "I'm just hoping you can undo the damage they've done." He placed his hands on the table and rested his head in them.

The prosecution had presented a flawless case against the young doctor. Their schedule called for more of the expected background witnesses followed by Dr. Moses Grant, the State Medical Examiner. Dr. Grant was known throughout the country for his excellent work in forensics. When a gruesome murder had been committed, he was sought as a talking head on all the major news programs. He never refused an opportunity to give a public rendering of his opinions. Books written by him that dealt with slayings of or by the rich and famous added to his reputation.

During a recess prior to Dr. Grant's testimony, Bret and Hubie were in a small conference room reviewing upcoming witnesses. Hubie said, "They're putting Grant on the stand just to cover their bases." Rummaging in his witness folder, "He's not going to add anything to their case. With the well-documented coverage of what happened, everyone on the jury knows Frankie died from a form of cyanide poisoning and an allergic reaction to peanut oil and how they were administered. Only a monk living in a cave wouldn't know it. But he's a grandstander, and will put on a good show for them."

Bret shifted in his chair at the mention of Frankie. "I dealt with Dr. Grant once," he informed his uncle.

Hubie appeared interested, "How so? Maybe you know something that'll help us?"

"I identified a burn victim from dental records. A Windham man was in an auto accident in Massachusetts and burned beyond recognition. From the car's registration they knew who he was, but not officially. Dr. Grant personally contacted me and pretty much begged me to do it. Said he couldn't get anyone else to go. So I picked up the x-rays from the victim's dentist and drove two hours to a hospital where I made the I.D. The kicker is he promised to reimburse me for doing the job, but never did. I hadn't intended to ask for money, but was pissed he didn't pay after he offered."

"Interesting story. Unfortunately, there's nothing we can use."

"I just thought it would give you some insight into the man when you cross examine him." After a moment, Bret said, "You know what my most lasting memory of the incident was?"

"What?"

"When I walked out of the hospital, I took in a deep breath of the clean autumn air and was glad to be alive."

As predicted, the medical examiner's testimony added nothing to the prosecution's case although the witness' flamboyant style provided good theatre and sold books.

Corrie Hunter was the prosecution's first damaging witness. Sitting in the witness chair, she was calm and deliberate. A dark conservative suit gave her the demeanor of a modern business woman, and hair held in place with an attractive hairclip exposed her full face. The overall impression was of consummate professionalism.

When questioned, Corrie claimed on the day Frankie Grimaldi was scheduled for wisdom teeth extractions, she went to retrieve the anesthesia drug vials from the drug room as was her custom. She encountered the accused with the vials and syringes filled with what appeared to be anesthetic solutions.

"What are you doing?" she queried. "The drugs are supposed to be drawn in the operatory."

"An inventory," she claimed Bret replied. "I want to be sure there'll be enough if the surgery lasts longer than anticipated."

At the time, she accepted the explanation without question. "It wasn't until Ms. Grimaldi reacted so badly to the anesthesia that I became suspicious about what Dr. Manley was doing in the drug room. That's why the next day I went to the police and reported what had happened."

As to what she knew of Bret's relationship with Frankie, she said, "He disapproved of Frankie Grimaldi's lesbian lifestyle and wanted his wife to stop having anything to do with her."

Hubie's objection was sustained, but once out, Corrie's words couldn't be unheard.

Upon further questioning, she boasted, "Mrs. Manley and I frequently go to restaurants together. She confided to me that the doctor had a great dislike for Frankie Grimaldi. He suspected Ms. Grimaldi was making lesbian overtures toward his wife." She looked at the jurors and explained, "Mrs. Manley being so pretty and all." Corrie took a sip from a glass of water before adding. "Mrs. Manley also said when she told the doctor they were simply good friends and Frankie had never approached her in a sexual way, he wouldn't believe it."

These last bits of information caused a loud drone from the pro-Frankie Grimaldi audience, and the judge asked the bailiff to restore order. The defense's objection was lost in the noise.

At one point in her testimony, Bret broke the rule and whispered to his uncle, "I can't believe the load of shit she's slinging."

Betraying no emotion, Hubie turned, looked at him, and gave a soft, "Shhh," with unmoving lips.

When cross-examined, Corrie didn't budge. As Detective Powell had done during Bret's interrogation, Hubie pursued a series of questions and repeated them in a different format. Corrie never contradicted herself, insisting she was reporting what she saw and heard. There was no confusion in her mind regarding what had happened on the day of Frankie's death. When she entered the drug room, she caught Bret placing cyanide and peanut oil in the vials of anesthetic drugs in order to put those tainted fluids into the syringes that would be used on Frankie.

At the conclusion of her testimony, she walked from the courtroom giving the impression of having accomplished an important mission. Bret feared the poisonous lies that spewed from her mouth would be as deadly to him as the cyanide and peanut oil had been to Frankie.

In contrast to Corrie's look them in the eye style of testimony, Mai spent her time in the witness chair sniffling into a white handkerchief. Attired in a simple and tasteful black dress, she radiated an aura of absolute beauty wrapped in a cloak of sweetness and demure bearing.

Prior to the beginning of the prosecution's questioning, Hubie said to Bret, "Any last minute advice you might want to share about her."

Bret replied as if resigned to the inevitable, "She's going to fool all the men of the jury, and they're going to fall in love with her like I did. Our only hope is at least one of the female jurors will want to strangle her in a jealous rage over the power she wields over men."

If academy awards were given for Best Actress While Performing On A Witness Stand, Mai would have gotten one.

Her emotional distress was enough to engender pity in the hardest heart. Mai's infrequent looks toward the jury box were tearful. In spite of her suffering, when confronted with the tough questions of the prosecution, she was able to muster courage and provide information that corroborated with Corrie's. As she gave answers incriminating Bret in Frankie's murder, there was absolute silence in the courtroom. An occasional cough from a spectator was all that broke the stillness. She never looked in Bret's direction.

At the conclusion of the prosecution's questioning of Mai, Hubie decided to defer his cross. She had won the affection of the jury and the courtroom audience. Cross-examining her would make him a bully picking on a defenseless woman.

When dismissed from the witness chair, Hubie and Bret half-expected a standing ovation for her performance. As she passed the defendant's table, Mai flashed Bret a glance lasting no more than a nanosecond. In that instant of time, he saw in her eyes the lowest depths of the *Inferno*, and the blood around his heart froze.

Jake was the final member of the conspirators summoned to the chair. He was neither as unwavering as Corrie nor as dramatic as Mai. He completed the final act of their rehearsed three-act play by tossing the jury his version of the pack of lies they were disseminating.

"What did the defendant tell you about the relationship between Mai Manley and Frankie Grimaldi?" the prosecutor asked.

"On several occasions he said he wanted his wife to have nothing to do with Frankie ... or the half-man, half-woman as he often referred to her." Gasps were heard in the audience and a juror shook her head at the slur. "He was obsessed with keeping Frankie Grimaldi out of his wife's life."

Hubie objected, and parts of the answer were stricken.

"Did you ever hear the defendant say he wished Ms. Grimaldi was dead?" The prosecutor paused for dramatic effect. "Or that he wanted to kill her?"

Another objection was sustained requiring the question to be asked in a different way.

It didn't matter. Jake had a prepared answer. "As I recall, I don't think I heard him say he wanted to kill her, but, I remember him once mentioning he and his wife would be a lot better off if she was dead."

Although Hubie's cross examination of Jake was brilliant, Jake gave no ground to the attacking defense. Hubie let two days pass before he recalled Mai to the witness chair. In contrast to her previous appearance, she was in control of her emotions. When she turned to the jury, she appeared to talk to each individual and made eye contact as she spoke.

A time or two, everyone in the courtroom was on the edge of their seats thinking Hubie had her on the ropes and was bearing in for a knockout blow. Audible sighs of relief could be heard when, as any champion boxer, she came off the ropes swinging. It was an encore performance as effective as the first.

Of all the witnesses, Mai was the most difficult. When Hubie was finished, he returned to his seat at the defense table. His hand covering the corner of his mouth, he said to Bret, "Cross-examining her is like trying to catch a soap bubble. It requires extremely gentle handling."

"I want you to consider the possibility of your testifying," Hubie said to his nephew. The trial had recessed for the evening and lawyer and client were in the Superior Court Building's consultation room. They were drinking diet sodas and munching on potato chips.

"I thought you didn't want me to testify, so the prosecution won't be able to grill me."

"I didn't and still don't. But we kept the option open, remember, and now that we're coming to the end of the trial, I believe it would be helpful if you testify."

Sitting in his chair, Bret looked at the floor and began to shake his head. "Most of our witnesses were as good as theirs. My former office staff, especially Pearlie Perez, seemed a distinct positive for our cause. None of them ever heard me say a negative word about Frankie. None of them believed I could have killed her."

With his usual rolled-up sleeves and tie undone, Hubie paced as he spoke. "You're correct. We've attempted to convince the jury that some person or persons other than you committed the crime. We've implied, but not proved, that the main witnesses against you could very well have been involved in Frankie's murder."

He stopped pacing, "And as you say, it's true, the testimony of our witnesses was a plus for our side. We countered or negated much of what was presented against you. We did all that, and well."

In a voice that conveyed the gravity of their situation, "Under most conditions I would feel we have an excellent chance of an acquittal. That is, if it wasn't for the unholy triumvirate of Corrie, Mai, and Jake. In my opinion, their testimony has been extremely damaging. They've painted a credible picture of your intense hatred toward Frankie Grimaldi. Of your insane jealousy over a lesbian relationship you thought she was trying to form with your wife. It leads to the logical conclusion you wanted her dead and planned and carried out her murder.

In addition, they've covered their tracks well. Dillon hasn't been able to find a shred of provable evidence of their complicity in the murder or scandal in their relationship."

He gave Bret a concerned look, "There's no other way for me to put it. The fabricated tale they've told is going to make it difficult for a jury to find you innocent. Having you testify may be our only chance."

Bret pleaded, "Now that I've seen what cross-examinations are like, I know I'm not tough enough to withstand one."

Hubie said, "Look, we can prepare you. Yes, their cross will be rough, but your testimony may uncover a weakness in one of their accounts. Their stories are so intricately interwoven, a flaw in one would point to flaws in the others. It could be enough for a not guilty verdict."

"Can I think about it?" Bret asked.

"Of course. Sleep on it. We'll talk again in the morning. If you agree to testify, I'll delay things until we can whip you into shape.

Once you're ready, I'll put you on the stand."

Bret had another of his many sleepless nights since he had become a guest of the Brooklyn State Jail. It wasn't that he didn't want to tell his story and let the truth be known. It was that he felt he would crumble under cross-examination by one of the prosecution's many cagey attorneys. He had seen witnesses break during questioning, and each time he was certain he would have done the same. If he broke, his entire testimony would become suspect. He and his legal team were walking on a high wire, and there was no safety net.

The following morning before the trial began, Hubie and Bret were sitting at their courtroom table. He didn't want to broach the subject of the previous afternoon's discussion and pretended to be preoccupied. He waited for his uncle to take the initiative.

After a time, Hubie said, "Did you think about what we talked about yesterday? About testifying?"

Meeting Hubie's gaze, Bret said, "Yes . . . and no. I can't do it."

Sensing his uncle's disappointment with the decision not to testify, he explained no matter how prepared, he would not be able to handle the attack that would come from the other side. He ended with, "I don't want to be responsible for losing the case."

"I can work with it, Bret," Hubie said as he put an arm around Bret's shoulder. "I'm your attorney, but I'm also your uncle, and there are times when you need me to be an uncle. This is one of those times. I understand how you feel and support your decision. And I'm really proud of the way you've held up during this wretched affair." Moisture in his eyes, Hubie returned to his legal papers.

Bret was aware his refusal to take the stand might result in his conviction, but there was no doubt in his mind he would be unable to bear the weight of the cross.

The lawyers presented their closing arguments. The defense was first, and Hubie's partner gave an eloquent attestation of Bret's innocence. She was followed by the prosecution lawyer who handled most of their case. He did a credible job of attempting to convince the jury there was no doubt of premeditated murder. It was the jury's job to decide which was the correct version of the cause of Frankie's death.

After four days of deliberation, the jury informed the court it had reached a verdict. Neither the defense nor prosecution could glean anything from the time it took for a decision. To Bret, they were the worst days of his life. Time passes slow when you are hoping every minute that goes by without a verdict means you are more likely to be found innocent. Bret's existence consisted of pacing his cell, learning to smoke cigarettes, and living with a constant pain in his stomach. Sleep was filled with nightmares.

If found not guilty, Bret would leave the Superior Court Building a free man. If convicted, he'd remain in the Brooklyn jail until he was sentenced and sent to the MacDougall-Walker Correctional Institute in Suffield.

Hubie was standing with him as the jury announced its verdict. The next thing he remembered was leaving in the barred van that brought him. The jury found him guilty and recommended life without parole. When the verdict was delivered, Bret heard screaming and moaning before he passed out.

How like a winter hath my absence been
From thee, the pleasure of the fleeting year...

———

Suffield, Connecticut: It didn't matter that the sentencing hearing was to be held in two months. Life without parole was a *fait accompli,* and the hearing wouldn't change Bret's fate. Hubie began the appeals process, but Bret knew to any sane person he seemed guilty as hell.

Until the official sentencing, he was to remain in the solitary confinement ward of the Brooklyn Jail. His cell was one of three in the solitary ward. It was in better condition than his previous one because its sole uses were for those in Bret's situation or when the jail was overcrowded.

A suicide watch was instituted. Humorous because he hadn't thought of suicide until they brought it up. He was denied shoestrings and a belt, ate on paper plates with pressed paper spoons, and wore a breathing monitor. The most odious of the precautions was a corrections officer stationed by his cell at all times. He had no privacy. One hour of solitary recreation in the yard was allowed each afternoon. The officer at his cell accompanied and remained with him during that time. As he exercised, his cell was searched for dangerous items.

Special attention was paid during meals. Were they worried he might jam the paper spoon into his heart? The precautions would not prevent him from killing himself if he wanted to. He'd find a way. But Bret was not in the mood to leave this world. There was hope his defense team would uncover new evidence to prove his innocence and the guilt of those he was convinced committed the crime.

March was behaving like a lion when his penalty was made official. As the verdict was a foregone conclusion, there was little media interest. Reporters who attended the proceedings seemed anxious to jump into their next assignments. Bret had become old news.

No matter how many movies you've seen, you can't appreciate what a scary place prison is for someone like Bret who had lived a sheltered life. MacDougall-Walker's size was overwhelming. As he was escorted from building to building via the open central area, he had to strain to see the fortified stone walls that formed the rectangular footprint of the facility. A huge open area contained basketball courts, bodybuilding spaces, and two large multi-use fields. Chalked lines on the latter indicated they were used for baseball and soccer. It was chilly, and most of the inmates he saw were in groups or in sheltered areas trying to keep warm.

Processing took hours. Most humiliating was the full body search for contraband. No orifice went unchecked. After processing, two corrections officers, a female at his side and a male following, were assigned to give him a tour of the prison before taking him to his cell. The officers wore dark blue uniforms and toted batons and stun devices. Bret carried a canvas sack that contained a change of clothes, bed linen, a blanket, towels, and toiletries. He was wearing the prison regulation two-piece light gray uniform, but had been told one of the perks for good conduct was the ability to wear civilian clothes.

The male, whose nameplate said Officer Grayson, was slight and had a narrow face like a rodent. The stocky, muscled and meaner looking female with skin the color of ebony was Corporal Murkum. She would be considered hot to someone attracted to female wrestlers. When the two came for him, Murkum told him that most corrections officers hated inmates with life without parole sentences. They were referred to as non-paroles and were potential discipline problems because they had nothing to lose.

On the other hand, she and a few of the corrections officers preferred a wait and see attitude. If a non-parole followed the rules, they tended to cut him slack. Not much, but some. Enough to make it worthwhile. They were going to be together a long time, and cooperation was good for everyone.

The officers took turns reviewing prison amenities. There were medical and dental clinics, a large gymnasium used during bad weather, and vocational opportunities. The latter included cabinet making, automotive repair, and culinary arts.

Grayson said, "We'll let you take classes, but it's mainly to keep you occupied. With your sentence it's really a waste of your time and ours. You'll never be able to put what you learn to use." The sarcastic tone revealed he wasn't one of the slack cutters.

As they walked a lengthy cellblock, Grayson said, this time with ominous implication, "Your cellmate is Sammy Tompkins. The con he was bunked with got discharged." He tapped Bret's shoulder with his baton causing Bret to turn. His wide smile allowed a whiff of untreated gum disease to escape from his mouth. "You're going to just love him," he said, placing emphasis on love.

Murkum chimed, "Stop messing with him, Charlie. He's going to find out about Sammy soon enough.

Bret sensed the officers didn't like each other, and he knew Grayson was taunting him about life in prison. He tried to resist asking, but couldn't, "How so?"

"Well," Grayson was eager to answer, "How should I put it? Sammy's a horny guy. Always on the prowl. Outside it's women, but when they ain't around, it's men. Get my meaning? Lot's of the inmates are like that. Normal in the streets. In here, they're queer." He snickered at the rhyme. "I think I heard someone call it . . . let's see if I can remember . . . ah, something like incarceration homosexuals. Yeah, something like that." The rodent face continued, "He's in his seventh year of a fifteen-year sentence with earliest possible parole at ten. That means you'll probably get to live with him for at least the next three years." He uttered a laugh more irritating than fingers scratching a blackboard.

Murkum interrupted, "He was part of the gang that pulled off the big bank heist in Hartford several years back. Maybe you heard of it? Got away with three-and-a-half million in cash. Most people figure they had inside help, but they couldn't prove it. At least that's what my old man says."

Grayson said, "Your old man always says that. Everything's a conspiracy with him."

Murkum stopped and turned a nasty eye to Grayson who bumped into Bret who had stopped with Murkum. "Watch what you say about my man."

Grayson flinched as if expecting a punch or slap. "Sorr-ry," he said.

Satisfied, Murkum continued walking. Soft wheezing noises began to emanate from her chest. She coughed, cleared her throat, and inhaled. "Got to stop smoking before it kills me."

"Me, too," rodent face agreed.

Murkum continued the conversation about Bret's cellmate, "Anyway, Sammy was the only one they caught. Rumor is they're holding his cut of the money for him for not ratting. More than half a million. If he gets out of here after serving only ten years . . . which I hope he doesn't, but you never know with Parole Boards and prison overcrowding . . . it comes to a cool fifty thousand a year just for hanging around in this place. Not bad for a scumbag who didn't make it beyond the sixth grade."

Listening to the story of Sammy Tompkins was unsettling. Bret had expected to encounter difficult and dangerous situations in prison but hadn't considered the first might be the man he was assigned to bunk with.

Grayson continued the tale. "When Sammy came here, he was a skinny punk. You know, the type you meet on the outside, you automatically beat the shit outta." He said it as if he could do it. "After a while, he began to pump iron. You won't believe what he's done with his body. Could enter a Mr. America contest."

Murkum again, "He also hooked up with the Skinheads. Nobody messes with them." She took a moment to catch her cigarette smoke-tinged breath. "That was a good thing for Sammy. He was always forcing himself on the younger inmates . . . you know . . . like you. And he was always getting his ass kicked. Now, with his new and stronger body and his pals, no one picks on him. He usually gets what he wants sooner or later."

"Unless he decides to try his charms on the wrong Hispanic kid. They're likely to cut him," added Grayson.

"Normally," Murkum said, "The Skinheads want nothin to do with Sammy's type, but I'm thinking he promised them some of the money he's expecting when he gets out. Worth every penny, seeing what they do for him."

Wondering what danger he was being placed in, Bret asked, "Think he'll bother me in, you know, that way?"

Both officers had to stop walking as their guffaws and bellows filled the corridor. When he regained his composure, Grayson said, "After what we told you, what do you think?"

The group arrived at the assigned cell. It was mid-afternoon and doors were open to allow inmates access to the recreation room, library, and snack-bar at the end of the block. Lights were off, hiding the back of the cell in shadow. At first glance it appeared empty. Bret's eyes adjusted, and he saw someone leaning against a wall.

Sammy Tompkins was wearing skimpy briefs, the kind worn in bodybuilding contests. The man took two steps forward and remained immobile with his massive arms folded across his chest. The move caused him to be fully viewed, and by the beads of sweat on his forehead and arms, he had a recent workout. His sneer warned, *fuck with me at your peril.*

Murkum and Grayson had not exaggerated. Sammy Tompkins had a world-class bodybuilder's physique. The informative custodial pair had neglected to mention Sammy had shaved all his hair, and, with the exceptions of his face, neck, and hands, his five foot nine inch frame was covered with tattoos.

If he lets the hair on his head grow, the man can walk around in a shirt and tie and look normal until he wants you to see what he's hiding, Bret thought.

On Sammy's body were devil's horns, hearts with knives piercing them, dragons, and fierce birds. *Love* in large font was visible on the inner aspect of one wrist, and its twin, *Hate,* was on the other. The expected *Death Before Dishonor* was emblazoned on his right forearm with each word a different color. The most significant tattoo was the Nazi SS double lightning symbols on the left side of his neck above his collarbone. It meant he was a member of the Aryan Brotherhood, referred to as Skinheads at MacDougal-Walker.

Murkum turned to Bret and said, "Inmates who claim to be artists do the tattoos. They get paid a few packs of cigarettes for each one. Your admission sheet said you don't have any. My guess is you'll have a few before long. Everyone gets them."

Don't bet on it.

Sammy had a large, hawk nose and deep lines around his mouth that gave him a look of perpetual anger. Like those of a bird of prey, his dark eyes darted from one to the other of the three standing before him. They fixed upon Bret, and the sneer became a leer. Sensing danger, Bret knew Sammy Tompkins was going to make his life wretched.

Pointing to his briefs, Murkum ordered, "All right Sammy, put something over that. You know the rules."

Sammy looked at Murkum and appeared about to hiss before he reached to his cot and grabbed a pair of white boxer shorts with a yellow stain in front. He put them over the workout briefs and as he did, let out a thunderous fart.

"Good one," mocked an unfazed Murkum, "What do you do for an encore, crap in your skivvies?" She gave a short chuckle and said in a low voice to Bret, "I'm no prude. You been here long as I have, you seen everything. I gotta let him know I'm the boss, or he'll try to walk all over me."

Bret had been surprised by Murkum's non-confrontational demeanor toward him, as if she wanted them to be friends. In spite of her talk about taking a wait and see attitude, he wondered why. He understood when, as she was leaving, she said in the same low voice, "Don't forget what I said about following the rules. So far, I been nice to you. You be nice to me, and we get along. Otherwise, you won't see my good side no more."

Grayson gave the new tenant a rough shove into the cell.

As he stood a few feet in the small room, Sammy approached and eyed him from head to foot. "What'd the cunt say to you?"

Not wanting to begin their relationship on bad footing, Bret told the truth, "Just said to make sure I obey the rules and not get into trouble."

Sammy gave a "Huh. With menace in his eyes, he said, "You'll do." He went to his bed and sat, "Yeah, you'll do."

The cell was smaller than expected. Rectangular in shape, it was designed to house two men without cramping the occupants. A stainless steel uncovered toilet and adjacent stainless steel sink were located in the back. A metal partition jutted from the wall between the toilet and sink. If you were sitting on the john, the partition came to shoulder height and covered half your leg. Bret concluded architects who design prisons have a lot to learn about privacy. Other than the plumbing fixtures, everything was painted battleship gray.

Extending from the longer walls on both sides were two rectangular metal bed-slabs. Judging by their size they were installed when inmates were shorter than the current batch. Fastened to the walls, they stood a few feet above the floor. Metal legs supported the outer corners, and each held a thin mattress and pillow.

Murkum and Grayson had said there were two architectural layouts of cells. One had bunk beds, and the other, the design assigned to Bret, had separate cots on each side. Some inmates were afraid of heights and couldn't sleep in an upper bunk which resulted in the different arrangements.

At the head of each bed was a fixed metal dresser. Folding chairs allowed the dressers to double as desks. Because of space requirements, the dresser on the right, the side with the toilet and sink, was smaller than the one on the left. Sammy was using the larger dresser, so Bret emptied his sack on the cot with the smaller dresser.

If his appeal wasn't successful, the small space with its utilitarian atmosphere was the latest substitute for his lovely country home on Lover's Lane, a name not the good omen it portended.

That afternoon, he visited the recreation area and struck a conversation with an old non-parole who went by Tommy Boy. Judging by his appearance, Bret figured Tommy Boy was nearing the end of his sentence. When Bret asked about Sammy, the old con shook his head and said, "Reason I even talkin to you is we in the same boat. Otherwise, I don't give you the motherfuckin time of day."

Bret turned to leave.

"Hold on," said Tommy Boy. "Said we in the same boat. We go'in to be here after Sammy gone. Don't hurt to get to know each other."

Bret faced him.

The lifer said, "He a fuckin nasty one, that one. Glad you, not me in a cell with him. Ice pick he carry, stick you with it as look at you. What I see, he be wantin' to put somethin else in you. Ain't talkin bout his pick." Tommy Boy's cackles revealed his few remaining teeth.

Bret scrunched his face in disgust.

"You got a wom'n?" Tommy Boy asked.

"Yes . . . I mean, no . . . I don't."

"Well, what is it? Eitha you got one or not."

"Had one once. No more."

"Same here. Didn't work out." Tommy Boy said. "Means no con-gell visits 'less you strike it up with a pin pal. Some wom'n willin to come in for them. Not many. Eitha can't find a man or think they helping society."

Tommy Boy looked at one of the TVs in the corner. A sit-com was beginning. "Gotta go," he said. "Don't forget what I say bout Sammy." Bret didn't see a connection, but the man added, "Rumor is, he go'in to be rollin in green when he outta here." Sputum from Tommy Boy's cough sprayed as Bret moved to avoid the droplets.

While he assumed Hubie Santos worked pro bono in his efforts to clear Dr. Manley's name, Bob Dillon, P.I., received his usual hefty fee. He and Hubie Santos were sitting in the attorney's private office at 51 Russ Street in Hartford. Hubie at his desk and Bob across from him.

Surveying Hubie's office caused the P.I. to smile. In addition to his laptop, the desk held piles of case folders that had to be swept to the side in order for the men to see each other without standing. One of the legal secretaries had joked the hardest job was clearing the boss's desk at the end of the day and replacing the scattered files in their secure cabinets.

Hubie was a collector of presidential campaign memorabilia and antique clocks. Banners and pins of various campaigns were strewn about, and two valuable antique timepieces sat on tables in separate corners of the room. Many of the campaign mementos were souvenirs of the Connecticut campaign of a presidential hopeful that Hubie ran. No matter the clutter of the office, Bob Dillon knew Hubie's mind was organized and brilliant, befitting one of the top lawyers in the country.

"I appreciate all you did to help us, Bob."

"Thanks. Just sorry we didn't get a better result. I haven't given up on the case. With your permission, I'd like to keep digging. See if I can come up with something to help the appeal. There's got to be undiscovered evidence out there for me to find."

"You took the words out of my mouth. We're down but not out. I want you to continue your investigation. Take all the time you need. I'm not concerned about cost. You'll be compensated at your usual rate."

"Hubie, you've made my day twice."

The P.I. left the attorney's office determined to see justice done in the Frankie Grimaldi murder. Although the woman had died in Dr. Manley's surgical chair, Bob Dillon was certain Dr. Manley hadn't killed her. It couldn't be proven, but he believed Dr. Warden and his lover, the former Mrs. Manley, were the murderers. He was sure they enlisted Warden's assistant, Corrie Hunter, to help them. In addition to other information he had uncovered in his investigation, it explained why the testimony given by the three was similar, and in instances, word for word. It couldn't be coincidence.

The weakest link in their three-linked chain was Corrie Hunter. Jake Warden and Mai Faca had each other, but Corrie had no one. He had spent a good deal of time investigating the two lovers without results. It was time to concentrate his investigative efforts on Corrie. Exposing her lies and uncovering her role in the murder would give him the other two. She was bound to screw up. Everyone in her situation did. He'd be there when it happened.

The July Fourth holiday was around the corner. It had been six months since Corrie had testified against Dr. Manley, and every day took forever to pass. She continued working as Dr. Warden's office manager, but their relationship had changed. Although he continued to supply her with drugs, he became distant. Most of the time he didn't say a word unless it related to business and patients.

As for Mai Faca, Corrie had not heard from her since the trial ended. Was the bitch avoiding her? She hadn't agreed to be a part of their scheme because of Mai. It was for the narcotics and the money . . . and Jake Warden. The money would allow her to atone for a wrong she had done.

Corrie was guilt-ridden for having stolen her dying mother's diamond ring and pawning it for a tenth of its value. She had been fired from the convalescent home and needed the money to support her uncontrollable drug habit. Her intention was to repurchase it when she found another job. That became impossible when the pawn shop owner sold it and wouldn't tell her the name of the buyer. The drugs bought with the ring were gone within a short time, but the guilt remained.

It galled her that a commoner like Pearlie kept the stupid necklace her father made. Had changed her name because of it. Every time she saw the pearl, it reminded her of the terrible thing she had done. She hoped to make amends by replacing the ring with a comparable piece of jewelry worn in her mother's memory.

Corrie told Dr. Warden about Mai's emotional collapse in the office. Said it was fortunate she was there to rush her home. To make matters worse, she had to tolerate Mai's screaming insults on the way. The women in the office asked questions about Mai's strange behavior in the waiting room before Mai could have known what was happening to Frankie. Brittney wondered if she had a premonition. It was tricky, Corrie said, but she was able to cover for Mai before anyone became suspicious.

Prior to the trial, Dr. Warden had coached them on what to say when in the witness chair. Several facts had to be memorized. He had authored their separate stories ensuring each meshed with the testimony of the others. If all went as planned, Dr. Manley would appear guilty of the murder, and they'd have cemented the case for the prosecution. Each had an important role in the frame. Because her role was to be the eyewitness who saw the drug switch, the prosecution lawyers said her testimony was the most crucial for a guilty verdict.

Dr. Warden had asked her to visit him at his condo where he turned over a key to a lock box. "At the end of this month and every month from now on until you have all your money, two thousand dollars will be placed in a box at the main Hartford train station that this key opens."

Angered by the unexpected restrictions on the money she felt was hers, Corrie vented her displeasure, "Bad enough I've had to wait six months. You never said I wouldn't receive it all at once. If you had, I'm not sure I would have helped you."

Corrie was upset. She could tell Jake's mental wheels were spinning trying to think of something to placate her.

"It's the safe way, Corrie. I've had to borrow the money to pay you, and I'm not talking from a bank. These are the restrictions placed on me. The thinking is that giving you two thousand a month won't raise suspicions on where it's coming from."

"But ... but, I wanted to do things with it. Like buy a nice piece of jewelry or something." Making a quick calculation, "Besides, it'll take more than two years to get the money. What if, God forbid, something happens to you in the meantime?"

Jake answered, "Nothing is going to happen, but if something does, I've made arrangements for you to continue receiving payments until you get everything you're owed. And you can still do something nice with the payments. Just on a smaller scale."

Continuing his effort to placate her, he said, "Think how it would look if you suddenly took a trip to, say, France. People might wonder where the money came from. There'd be no problem with going to a place like Williamsburg or Disney World. As far as jewelry is concerned, there are many inexpensive but quite beautiful pieces."

Corrie acquiesced, "Okay, exactly how do I get the money? With a sigh, "What do you want me to do?"

Jake reviewed the arrangements that had been made and ended with, "You have to collect the money at Union Station in downtown Hartford during the first few days of the month. The collection has to be done at a time when activity is high. Like early morning or late afternoon when a lot of buses and trains are arriving and departing. You're the only one allowed to make the pickup." He warned, "If you don't do it without an excuse that's deemed legitimate, payments will stop. If we find you've made a big-ticket item purchase, payments will stop. Your actions will be monitored to insure compliance with our instructions." Jake's final admonition was, "And, don't doubt we can do it."

Jake knew there was no real mechanism to monitor Corrie's actions. If Corrie failed to make a pickup, it would be a month before Carlton's man discovered it. He was sure that if she made a fuss, the money drops wouldn't be terminated. It would be dangerous to anger her. Intimidation and lies were his weapons.

Corrie was fuming and determined to bypass the odious restrictions. She could collect and save monthly allotments until there was enough to buy an expensive piece of jewelry. She'd make the purchase in another state and in cash. To honor her mother and to justify the risk taken by helping Dr. Warden and his mistress, it had to be of great value. Something to be proud of. She had put her life on the line and deserved to do what she wanted with the money.

The weekend after her meeting with Jake Warden, Corrie discovered Sparkling Ice, a jewelry store in Newport, Rhode Island. It carried gems of exceptional quality and required a high level of security. The entrance consisted of bulletproof glass double doors that were never unlocked at the same time. A buzzer opened the outer door after a visual inspection by a security guard.

Cabinets were stocked with beautiful and expensive jewelry, including precious stones in every imaginable setting. In one of the cabinets she spied a multi-stoned sapphire bracelet. It was the most gorgeous piece of jewelry she had seen. Corrie was determined to have it. Sparkling Ice was a candy shop, and Corrie was the proverbial kid in it. As a child craves a piece of candy, she craved the bracelet.

The French speaking proprietor, Mr. Joseph . . . Jos-*ceff*, accent on the second syllable . . . was short and rotund with classic male pattern baldness and a pencil mustache. Corrie visited the store several times and found he possessed a wealth of information about the items in the display cases. She insisted upon dealing with no one but him.

Listening to the history of the piece intensified her desire to have it. Mr. Joseph held it in the palm of his hand and became animated, "This bracelet, ooh, la, la, she contains an extremely rare assortment of pastel colored sapphires. Oui, it took many years to collect zee stones before they can be incorporated into zee lovely piece you have 'ere. Putting them in a bracelet has resulted in, how you say, creation of a true masterpiece. There is no other like it."

"I can see it's really a work of art," Corrie agreed. *Pearlie's pearl is less than insignificant compared to it. Mother would be proud.*

"If you are to be considering its purchase, I am most happy in encouraging you to do so."

Corrie responded, "Like how?"

"Umm," thinking, "I sell it to you for thirteen thousand dollars, although its value, as anyone can see, is considerably more. You are to be made aware such a price is for you alone, as it is obvious you appreciate and desire it very much."

"Why so cheap?"

The proprietor gestured with his hands. "Zee economy, what else?"

"Can I put it on layaway with a deposit of five hundred dollars and pay the rest six months from now?"

Mr. Joseph shook his head, "For one thousand dollars, I will hold it for six months, no longer. Of course," he informed her, "You must have full payment at that time, if you are not to forfeit zee deposit."

"I understand," Corrie said, and without hesitation said, "It's a deal. I'll return tomorrow with the deposit."

It would be another insufferable wait, but in six months she'd have collected enough money. Purchasing with cash would minimize the chance that Dr. Warden and whoever he was working with, would learn what she had done. Corrie could feel goose bumps. Jewelry of its quality had been an unattainable fantasy.

As she walked to her car, she imagined the reaction of her friends. *They'll be terribly impressed and so envious. When they ask where I got it, I might be evasive and let them think a mysterious lover gave it to me. Seeing their reactions will make it worth having put my freedom on the line for Dr. Warden.*

She would have loved to show the bracelet to the women in her office. They'd be ravenously jealous. No, someone would mention it to the doctor. He'd get angry and stop her payments. Overcome by a fit of temper and knowing she had blackmail power, she thought, *Let him try.*

An advantage a modern private detective has over those of past eras is the ability to utilize electronic and wireless surveillance monitoring equipment. In Bob Dillon's business it was essential to know what the latest surveillance techniques were, and he had acquaintances who supplied the information. If the general public were aware of the devices employed by those in his profession, people would demand the equipment be removed from the investigator's tool kit. They'd be correct in thinking rights of privacy were violated.

Using a secure cell, Bob Dillon was making his weekly report to Hubie Santos. "I'm using two of my gadgets on Hunter. The same ones I'm using on Faca and Warden, but getting nothing. No doubt they assume they're under surveillance and don't say or do anything that would incriminate them in the Grimaldi murder. Hunter may be different."

"You're the expert, do what you feel is appropriate," Hubie replied. "I'm curious, though, what are they?"

"One is a Sony listening device I'll stick on her living room window. Maybe tomorrow night while she's sleeping. There's no dog around to alert anybody so it'll be safe to snoop around. It's no bigger than a flyspeck, but it turns the entire window into a voice activated audio receiver. It'll pick up sound from almost anywhere in the house. It's especially helpful when she's on the phone."

"How do you record and retrieve what it picks up?"

"The listening dot transmits everything to a wireless remote receiver that I'll fasten to a tree or a utility pole about a hundred yards away. A utility pole is best because the receiver looks like it belongs there. It's a three by five by one inch black box that has "Official Use Only" and "Penalty for Removing" stamped on it. It's always left alone. Inside is a long playing mini CD. I can retrieve it whenever I want."

He detailed the other piece of high tech equipment. "It's a Garmin GPS recorder designed to be attached to the underside of an automobile. Super-sticky pads fasten it securely in place, and its battery lasts up to a year. If someone tries to remove it or the battery nears the end of its life, it sends out a burst of energy that fries the electronics in the unit. After that, any information recorded can't be recovered. The device is made of a material designed to disintegrate and, in time, begins to fall off the car in unrecognizable pieces. You never have to remove it."

"Impressive," was Hubie's response.

"That's not all," Bob said enthusiastically, "It's movement

sensitive and turns on when it detects a fifty foot change in position of the car. Once activated, every thirty seconds it records its GPS position in longitude and latitude until five minutes after it no longer senses changes. In other words, it turns on when the car moves and off soon after it stops."

Bob explained the automobile's position was known at all times. When desired, the cumulative information gathered by the GPS was wirelessly transmitted and downloaded onto a Garmin laptop dedicated to the transmitter. He had to be within half a mile of the transmitter when he wanted to receive the data.

The computer displayed the positions and times in a 24 hour clock format. In another window of the Microsoft Windows program, the coordinates were plotted as points and connected into lines on a map of the northeast United States. The scale was adjustable allowing for in-depth viewing of any route a car took. The coordinates were synchronized into a Google Earth-like picture resulting in comprehensive displays of roads and their associated structures.

Repetitive routes appeared as dark lines on the map. The more use, the darker the line. In the Google Earth setting, adjusting the scale revealed details such as turning in a driveway. The information garnered gave a complete picture of a person's travels.

"I've used the device several times and am always impressed by the confirmation that people spend most of their lives within a relatively small geographic area." Bob lowered his voice, "Your ears only. Next generation of devices includes drones. They're working out the bugs, but should be ready in a year or two. Can't wait."

Ten days after the equipment was installed, Bob phoned the first report of his Hunter findings to Hubie. "Other than a few embarrassing details concerning her personal life I picked up from telephone conversations, I don't have anything to link Corrie to the Grimaldi murder. The GPS confirms her routine of going back and forth to work and staying home evenings. Last weekend she went into Willimantic to shop."

"Continue what you're doing, and keep me posted. Get in touch immediately if you uncover something interesting."

"You'll be the second to know."

"Good luck," Hubie said ending the conversation.

It was the detective's routine to retrieve and analyze the information gathered by the audio device and GPS recorder every week. He became familiar with the patterns of Corrie's existence. The first break came when he discovered she had made four trips to a parking lot in Newport, Rhode Island in a three week period. During that period his listening device recorded a phone call to a jewelry store and a discussion about the purchase of a bracelet. Bob assumed the Newport trips were to the jewelry store. Knowing the location of the parking lot would make it easy to find the establishment. There was nothing incriminating in her activities, but intuition told him his investigation was about to yield dividends.

It was approaching a year and a half since the death of Frankie and the beginning of Bret's tragic ordeal. The heat of summer persisted into autumn, and temperatures in the non-air conditioned areas of the prison soared into the nineties. Bret was conferring with his uncle in the prison's lawyer-client meeting room. The room was one of the areas not cooled.

"Our automatic appeals haven't been answered, but we're still pursuing all our legal options. No court seems to be in a hurry to reopen our case." As he spoke, Hubie wiped sweat from his forehead with a handkerchief. His open collared shirt was wet and stuck to his skin. "It's a good thing I brought one of these," he said, indicating the handkerchief, "It's obvious they keep this room too hot in summer and too cold in winter on purpose."

Bret responded, "You said it, they want to make it as uncomfortable as possible for us. The corrections officer who escorted me here joked you were waiting for me in the hot-box."

Referring to the lack of progress on his appeals, "Every day for me in this place is a copy of the day before but with slightly different horrors. My most pressing problems stem from my perverted and crazy cellmate. To put it bluntly, he's after me, if you know what I mean."

Hubie said, "I've spoken to the warden about him, but he's unwilling to do anything. Says unless something overt happens . . . like he tries to kill you . . . his hands are tied. Otherwise, he would be constantly changing cellmates as if it was a game of musical cells."

"Good luck on finding evidence against anyone in here," Bret said. "Everything is covered up by the inmates and a lot of the guards who don't want to create extra work for themselves."

Hubie shook his head in disgust over the conditions in which his nephew had to live. "Don't give up hope. I'm not. You're going to get out of this place."

Heartened by his uncle's words, "I appreciate everything you're doing. I'm just blowing off steam."

"I know," Hubie said, "By the way, I see you got a tattoo."

Bret, who was wearing a cut-off t-shirt, looked at his right upper arm, and said, "Yeah, never thought I would, but some of the guys talked me into it. Didn't hurt. The artists use homemade tools and dyes, but they're real experts."

"Why'd you pick a pair of dice?"

"I don't know. I guess they represent luck or events you have no control over. Like, if you're careful when you cross the street, but a car swerves and hits you. You were simply in the wrong place at the wrong time. Your bad luck."

Hubie saw a deeper meaning in his nephew's words.

"Know what I'm talking about?" Bret said.

"I do, and the tat looks good on you. Just don't try to outdo Sammy."

Bret rolled his eyes.

"Have you made any friends in here?" Hubie asked.

Bret thought a moment, "Maybe one. Lifer like me. Name's Tommy Boy. Cantankerous old fart. Got an opinion on everything. We get into heated discussions about the silliest things. Always making me laugh." Bret looked at his uncle, "Yeah, I'd say he was my friend though he'd never admit it."

As if Bret were a child, Sammy Tompkins tried to tempt him with offers of candy or fruit. When the ploy didn't work, Sammy changed tack and offered protection saying he and his pals could insure no one harmed Bret. He claimed his friends overheard some of the Black inmates refer to him saying they were going to "bleed the White motherfucker." No specific reason for the threat was given. Sammy said, "They're like that, you know. They'll cut you just to make sure Whitey knows his place." It was what Bret had dreaded the first night in the Brooklyn jail with Roman Hernandez.

"All we have to do is let everyone know me and my boys are protecting you. No one would put a fucking hand on you." As if an afterthought, he added, "Of course, we help you, you owe us."

"What do you mean?"

"We'd think of a way you could pay us back." Sammy didn't supply details.

Bret knew how he'd have to repay Sammy, and no telling what the members of his gang would want. "No thanks," he said, "I'll take my chances."

Sammy was unable to control himself. "Shit!" he said as he slammed his open hand on the wall of the cell.

For a while Bret gave Blacks hanging out in groups a wide berth in case this was the one time Sammy wasn't lying. None of the Black inmates tried to harm him.

Sammy made overt amorous advances that Bret rejected. The result was increased anger and escalating violence. If he displeased Sammy in any way, such as not giving him what he considered enough room to pass in the cell, Sammy would punch him in the arm or shoulder with enough force to cause bruising. They escalated to punches to the diaphragm that knocked the wind from him. He'd fall to the floor in pain trying to catch his breath. At times, as Bret lay there, Sammy urinated on him like an animal marking his territory.

Defending himself or informing the guards were not options.

Sammy would beat him to a pulp, or one of the Skinheads would put a shank in his heart during an unguarded moment. Violation by Sammy was inevitable.

The GPS attached to Corrie Hunter's car revealed her trips to Newport stopped. Bob Dillon discovered the jewelry store she visited was Sparkling Ice. When he produced his credentials, he found the proprietor willing to be helpful in order to prevent a police investigation of his business.

"Why did Ms. Hunter come to your place?"

Mr. Joseph was nervous, and lost his French accent. He spoke like a native of Brooklyn, New York. "She's looking to buy a bracelet." Unlocking a cabinet, he produced it, "This one here," he said as he held the bracelet in one hand and pointed with the index finger of the other. "She came by several times. I don't remember how many, maybe three, four. Wanted to do a deal, so I gave her a break and discounted the bracelet to thirteen grand. The jewelry business ain't so great right now. She agreed to put down a G. I'm supposed to hold the piece for six months. Said she'd have the dough by then." Replacing the bracelet, "She's making out good. It's definitely worth it."

Bob Dillon pressed for more information. "Did Ms. Hunter say where she'd get the money?"

"Naw, just that she'd have it. She's going to lose her deposit if she doesn't come up with the rest. That's for sure. I assumed she worked, and it'd come from her salary." Wiping sweat from his forehead with the sleeve of his suit jacket, "Did I do something wrong? Am I in trouble?"

"Only if you tell anyone about our conversation. If Ms. Hunter calls or stops by the store, don't say a word about my being here." The final touch was, "Otherwise, we may have to consider you an accomplice."

Placing both hands on his face, Mr. Joseph looked like he was about to have a stroke. "I won't say a thing."

As he walked to his car, Bob Dillon reflected upon what he'd learned. He felt good about the interview with the phony Frenchman and was confident the jeweler was too frightened to defy his warning not to let anyone know of their conversation.

While he didn't have all the pieces in place and couldn't legally prove her guilt, he was certain Corrie was involved in the Grimaldi murder. The bracelet was going to be purchased with money earned for her part in the frame-up.

His decision to place the dot listening device on Corrie's window and the GPS recorder on her car was vindicated. They led to the discovery of her Newport trips and her intended purchase of an expensive bracelet with a lump sum of cash. He had access to her financial records, and someone of Corrie's means wouldn't do business in a high-end establishment like Sparkling Ice. It was the foolish move on her part he predicted. If she had arranged to make small periodic payments over a long period, he might not have questioned the purchase. Anyone can do that. It was the first sour note in what had been Warden, Faca, and Hunter's perfect symphony. Bob considered presenting what he had found to Attorney Santos, but decided to wait until he had more evidence.

Well past the institutionally prescribed bedtime, Bret Manley was lying on his cot engrossed in a paperback book of fiction, the type of reading tolerable to him. Nonfiction dealt with reality, and life had provided enough reality to suit him. The main lights in the cellblock had been extinguished, and although there was scattered light from nightlights throughout the facility, it wasn't sufficient for reading. He was using a small reading light attached to a stretchy band wrapped about his head.

He put the book down, removed the band from his head, and turned toward the wall to sleep. Sammy had been watching him, but Bret pretended not to notice. Several days had passed since Sammy punched or peed on him, and as the predicted Yellowstone supervolcano, the next one was past due.

Sleep was fraught with nightmares. Bret was more tired in the morning than when he went to bed. He alleviated perpetual drowsiness with short catnaps stolen during the day.

The nightmares were a progression of his pre-sleep thoughts begun in the Brooklyn Jail. Thoughts of punishing Jake Warden and Mai Faca for what they did to him. In his mind the two miscreants suffered unimaginable pain. Instead of leaving when he fell asleep, the thoughts morphed into nightmares.

Within this nighttime ritual, Bret felt a crushing weight on his back and bone breaking pressure on his neck. Saliva filled words poured into his right ear. "Don't move or make no noise or I'll puncture you."

Sammy was on top of Bret pressing his homemade ice pick to the back of his neck. Terrified and unable to move, he shouted, "Get the fuck off me. Now." It was hard to get air into his lungs. Breathing and speaking were difficult.

"Ain't I good enough for you? You been avoiding me long enough."

Sucking in a quick gulp of air, "I said, get off me!" Bret's mind was racing, trying to think of how to get the maniac to stop. His situation was desperate.

"You ain't getting away this time, pal." Sammy's free hand was tearing at his victim's clothes.

Bret turned his head from Sammy's heated breath. "No. Please. Don't," he begged.

Sammy used his heavier muscular body to keep Bret pinned to his cot. Twisting and squirming only caused the pressure to become greater. It was cutting the circulation in the blood vessels of his neck. He was lightheaded from the force placed on him and from the knowledge of what was about to happen. In spite of his resistance, Sammy managed to get Bret's pants and underwear below his knees. "Don't worry, you'll get used to it," he said, "They always do." His words dripped with malice.

As in the courtroom when his verdict was read, Bret passed out. When he came to, he was lying on the floor, and Sammy was sitting on his cot watching him.

The fog in his brain began to clear. Bret wanted to wipe the sneer from Sammy's face. He pulled his clothes from his ankles and attempted to get off the floor. "You bastard, I'll kill you," he shouted. The words echoed within the cell. He wanted to pummel with furious punches the man who had violated him in such a terrible manner. Bret lunged and managed to get to one knee before being hit with a sledgehammer of a fist.

When Bret awoke from the evening's second bout of unconsciousness, he was on his back on the floor, and Sammy Tompkins was sitting on him. The man was straddling Bret's chest with his legs, and the point of the pick was at his throat. Bret twisted his upper body in an attempt to dislodge Sammy.

"I can kill you now, or one of my people can kill you later." Sammy's eyes confirmed he meant what he said. "All's I have to do is say you was out of your mind and attacked me. You couldn't stand it no more." His smile was that of a ghoul who had taken a bite of a cadaver.

Bret considered trying to kick him in the back, but thought better of it.

"The screws would believe me," Sammy continued, "They know how sensitive you are. So, calm down and don't make no trouble."

Bret knew to fight Sammy would prove futile. He stopped resisting.

Sammy stood and returned to his cot. As if it justified what he had done, he hurled a final insult at his victim. "It wasn't that bad a thing I done to you. You been here a few years, you'll probably ask for it."

Bret couldn't begin to describe his feeling of revulsion from being violated. Bile filled his throat causing him to retch. He wanted to wash Sammy's filth from his body, but all the soap in the world wouldn't be enough. He vowed revenge upon Sammy Tompkins for what he did. The man joined Jake Warden and Mai Faca in his murderous nightmares.

What's this? Bob Dillon was studying the GPS locations he had downloaded. *Why is the woman making trips to Hartford's Union Station?*

The station was Hartford's main train and bus terminal. According to the GPS map plot, she had parked in the Spruce Street parking lot on the first day of three consecutive months. The visits lasted for about a half hour and were made during busy morning or afternoon times.

The first trip or two, she could have been picking up or leaving someone off. But, three times? All at the beginning of the month during peak activity and lasting about the same amount of time. Has to mean something.

Aware of her pending acquisition of money to pay for the sapphire bracelet, his instinct told him uncovering Corrie Hunter's reasons for making trips to Union Station would be critical to finding the source of the money and who murdered Frankie Grimaldi. If she continued to follow her schedule, Corrie's next trip to Hartford would be on Wednesday, the first day of the next month.

Come November, I'll be there waiting for you, Corrie Hunter.

Sammy and his skinhead buddies had access to cocaine. Bret noticed that on Fridays, a supply of drugs arrived. Sammy placed his cocaine in a plastic bag and hid it between the cardboard and paper of the current roll of toilet paper. He had seen Sammy hiding it.

On Saturday and Wednesday nights, after lights in the cellblock were dimmed, Sammy retrieved his stash, divided the coke into lines on a small plate, and got high. Since he remained in his cot and faced the wall, sniffing noises were all that betrayed what he was doing.

Bret didn't object to his cellmate's use of drugs. When wasted,

Sammy ignored him. On occasion, Sammy was bold and sniffed the white powder without turning from Bret. He'd warn, "Don't say nothing to nobody, and keep your hands off my shit, or else."

It was critical to discover the source of the cocaine. Bret would use the knowledge to get his revenge on Sammy. He noticed that in the outside recreation area referred to as the yard, Sammy would bump shoulders with a guard the inmates nicknamed Skunky because he reeked of stale beer. The contact was meant to appear accidental. Bret watched Sammy and Skunky until he was certain drugs and money were exchanged when they collided.

In the prison library Bret did an internet search of poisonous mushrooms. *A. phalloides* or Death Cap Mushroom intrigued him. Eating a small amount caused stomach irritation followed by severe damage to major organs such as the liver. Serious illness or death resulted. The Death Cap Mushroom satisfied his needs. He was careful to erase evidence of his internet explorations.

Bret had his mother call his friend Giovanni Rossi to ask him to visit. Within a short time, the elderly man was sitting on the other side of the thick glass that separated inmates from visitors in the visitation ward. Age was getting the better of his friend, and Bret hoped, as Dylan Thomas advised, he was not going gentle into that good night. They were happy to see each other and talked of old times. Giovanni apologized for not visiting, but health problems made travel difficult.

Because of the sensitivity of what he intended to ask, Bret had to be circumspect in making his request. "Do you still visit your favorite mushroom picking grounds?"

Using his hands for emphasis, Giovanni answered, "No much. Somma times."

"Are there ones called Death Cap Mushrooms where you go?"

With a questioning look, Giovanni said, "No many. Some." He looked about before speaking, "Why you aska me these things?"

Taking the chance Giovanni wouldn't betray his confidence, Bret said in a low voice, "Because I want you to get me one."

Giovanni said, "I no aska why, but I get for you. Wen you wan me to bring?"

Thinking of his other potential helper, Bret replied, "You won't have to bring it. Too difficult for you. Someone will pick it up at your house."

"I hava end of next week. After, they canna pick up wen they wan."

"Thanks, Giovanni, you don't know what this means to me."

"No tella me more. I know you hava good reason."

The old man was smart, and Bret was certain he surmised what he was planning to do with the mushroom. "Oh, one more thing, I want you to dry it and grate it into a powder. Like grated parmesan."

Giovanni shrugged his shoulders and gave a puzzled look, "If that'sa how you wan."

Bret nodded, "Yes, that's how I want it.

Business concluded, they chatted about anything and everything as they had in Bret's office. When it was time for his friend to leave, Bret was overcome with sadness. Considering the old man's health and his incarceration, there was an excellent chance it was their last meeting. Giovanni kissed the tips of his fingers and placed them on the window. Bret did likewise. They said their goodbyes.

Intimidating Skunky to pick up the mushroom at Giovanni's was the next challenge. Since one of Skunky's duties was patrolling the yard, it was a matter of time before Bret would have a chance for a private talk.

Bret and other inmates were pumping iron at one of the weight piles. He had begun working out in the forlorn hope of being able to defend himself against Sammy. Truth was, Bret enjoyed being with the motley group, although he had to endure the taunts and jibes of men with handles like Snake-Eyes and Crocodile. The crusty old con, Tommy Boy, watched from a bench. His taunts and jibes were second to none.

Corrections officers patrolled the yard or in teams of two or three. Batons in hand, they walked among the inmates prepared to stop the numerous potential altercations that threatened. If a serious problem occurred, backup was the prison equivalent of a

SWAT team. In addition, heavily armed wall and tower guards helped maintain tranquility. Intergroup fist fighting between individuals of the Brotherhood, Blacks, and Hispanics was the worse that happened. Fighting was controlled by the officers and resulted in the combatants having privileges taken. The loss of prized privileges kept yard conflicts to a minimum. Inmates relegated serious disagreements to private areas. It was not unusual for such encounters to result in hospitalization or death.

When Bret saw Skunky leave his three-person group and wander to a deserted area to smoke, he left his fellow weightlifters and made a roundabout walk to him. The corrections officer was in the shade of two intersecting walls. The convergence of the walls afforded shelter from wind and a modicum of privacy.

Skunky held his cigarette at his side and rocked on his heels between drags. Bret approached as he was blowing smoke from his nose.

He leaned and looked into the officer's eyes, "I need to get my hands on some coke. I hear you can help me."

Skunky reacted as if Bret had smacked him on the head with his own baton. He dropped his cigarette and quick-walked to his group.

He's shitting a brick worrying that someone might notice we talked privately. Just what I wanted. Make him think his cocaine selling business has been compromised.

Skunky was not seen for the remainder of the yard time.

That afternoon while Bret was reading in his cell and Sammy was in the recreation room watching a soap opera, Skunky appeared at the open cell door. "Manley, follow me."

When a guard summoned an inmate as Skunky had, it meant the inmate was going to be given skutwork. Being assigned to a cleaning detail was typical. In this case, Bret knew there was another reason. Without complaint, he followed the officer into an empty supply room from which on a weekly basis clean sheets and pillow cases were distributed.

Skunky turned to Bret and spewed, "What the fuck did you think you were doing out there?"

"You get Sammy and the boys their coke," Bret said as if it was common knowledge.

"Goddammit," he shouted before catching himself and lowering his voice. "That's none of your business, and you better keep it quiet." In a whisper, he said, "If Sammy finds out, you know … well, there's no telling what he'd do."

He fears Sammy as much as I. "Don't worry. Neither of us is going to tell him. Know what I mean."

Skunky was relieved, but Bret wasn't going to take the hook out of him. "You have to return the favor."

Caution antennas seemed to spring from Skunky's head, and he began to sweat. "I know what you want. No way. You'll have to find another source."

Ignoring the man's words, Bret said, "Stop getting all hot and bothered. It's not what you think. I want you to do something else for me, and I'll pay."

Pay grabbed Skunky's interest. "What do you want me to do?"

I've got him, the mercenary scumbag. "You have to pick up a package for me. On the outside."

"A package? What kind of package? I don't want to get in no trouble because of you."

Bret said, "Don't worry. It's small, and all you have to do is bring it to me without anyone knowing. That's all the information you need for now."

Considering the proposition, Skunky asked, "How much?"

"A hundred."

"Make it two bills, one now, and the other when I deliver."

"Two hundred when you deliver it."

As if he were doing Bret a favor by agreeing to the terms, Skunky said, "Alright, but don't fuck me, or I'll make your life miserable."

As if it isn't now. "You bring me the package, and you'll get paid. I'll give you the address when it's time for the pickup."

Bret had four hundred dollars in the prison bank. Hubie and others in the family made periodic deposits into the account. He would use the money for the purchase of magazines, soda, and candy in the commissary. He had been willing to use the entire amount to entice Skunky to bring him his powdered mushroom.

Skunky delivered a small sealed envelope, the type that jewelers put rings in when they're taken for repair. Giovanni had placed duct tape over it to insure Skunky wouldn't' know what it held.

When able to open the envelope in private, Bret was pleased. It contained the Death Cap Mushroom ground into a dull white powder the consistency of flour. Except for a slight difference in color, the powder was indistinguishable from cocaine. Mixed with his drug, Sammy wouldn't detect the difference.

It wasn't going to be difficult to add the powder to the coke. Sammy's snoring would signal when it could be done. Bret had done a dry run of the procedure. One night as Sammy's snoring filled the cell with its familiar discordant chainsaw in need of a tune-up sound, Bret removed the stash from the toilet paper roll, pretended to remove half the cocaine and replace it with mushroom powder, and returned the stash to the roll. It took less than a minute.

Because the cocaine would be diluted, Sammy might think he received a bad delivery or was becoming immune to the drug. The solution would be to take more hits, increasing the amount of mushroom in his body.

Bret had acquired the power of life and death over Sammy and was savoring the feeling. By virtue of his training, he was an expert in the anatomy of the head and neck, and he fantasized what would happen when the cocaine-mushroom mixture was snorted. The cocaine would anesthetize the nasal membranes as it was absorbed. Beginning to get high, Sammy wouldn't notice the mushroom powder mixing with his secretions in his nasal passages and throat. He would swallow it. In a week, his liver and other vital organs would fail. Be it death or severe and permanent injury, Sammy Tompkins was going to be destroyed for what he did to him.

Bret carried the packet of poisonous powder with him for days deciding when to make the transfer. He had no fear of being caught. Everyone would assume Sammy had overdosed. His death would be blamed on the coke. No one would think to test for mushroom poisoning. Bret blocked thoughts of the similarity of what he was doing and what had been done to Frankie Grimaldi from his mind.

Bret came to a decision. He would make the switch the coming Friday.

At five a.m. Bob Dillon drove into the Spruce Street parking lot. A beehive of activity, no one would think it unusual if he waited in his vehicle, an eleven-year-old Toyota Landcruiser as tough, used, and nondescript as he. If Corrie proved to be a no-show, he'd return the next day and, if necessary, the day after. If she didn't appear that month, he was prepared to return in December unless his surveillance information dictated otherwise. It was fortunate Hubie Santos allowed him to clear his schedule in order to concentrate on the Manley case.

If Corrie intends to come to the station today, she'll be here early morning or after one this afternoon. I'll wait all day if necessary.

The morning passed without a sighting of his quarry. Not wanting to leave his car for any reason, Bob brought a thermos of coffee and his favorite ham sandwiches. A plastic bleach container would come in handy when he had to relieve himself.

"Where are you?" he said, as he drummed on the Toyota's steering wheel with the palms of his hands. The weather, unpredictable in November in New England, cooperated. A warm breeze was blowing, and Bob took advantage by opening the driver and passenger windows. After several false sightings, at one-forty-five in the afternoon, Corrie's blue Taurus drove into the parking lot.

Bob Dillon, following twenty feet behind Corrie, walked into Union Station hidden among a crowd. He wasn't concerned about being recognized, as he had taken pains not to be seen by any of the prosecution witnesses. It was part of his standard investigation technique.

When witnesses were testifying, Bob sat in the rear of the courtroom and leaned in a fashion that shielded him from the view of those in the witness chair. By proper positioning of his hands and head, anyone sitting next to him would have difficulty describing him. In spite of the precautions, he took pains to keep Corrie from discovering she was being followed.

The great hall of the station was teeming with people using the train and bus services. Because of its cavernous halls, there was a constant low roar of noise that filled the building. Corrie diverged from the main body of commuters and went toward a door marked *Staff Only*. Insuring that at all times there was someone between him and his quarry, the P.I. followed. The door was unlocked, and she opened it as if aware it would be. Corrie glanced over her shoulder before entering. Bob Dillon followed. He entered into a wide hallway with doors to four administrative offices, two on each side. Although it was early afternoon, the offices were unoccupied.

Probably not used every day, or only mornings.

Mounted on the right side beyond the main door were twenty numbered lockboxes arranged in rows of five. Corrie stopped in front of them as Bob Dillon walked by. He appeared to be on his way to one of the administrative offices.

"Good afternoon," he said in passing.

Corrie nodded, although her expression said she didn't want to be bothered with pleasantries. She reached into her bag and produced a key. Bob stopped at the first office on the left. An embossed sign to the right of the door said, *Unclaimed Baggage.* Watching her in the mirror formed by the glassed upper half of the office door, he fumbled with his pockets so Corrie would think he was searching for a key. At the same time Corrie opened lockbox number eleven, third row on the left, and removed a thick envelope.

At that instant Bob Dillon turned and with all the speed he could muster blocked her from leaving by placing his body between Corrie and the hall door. He grabbed her wrist, removed the envelope, and held it in one hand behind his back.

"Ahhh!" emanated from the surprised woman. Corrie tried to retrieve the envelope but Bob discouraged her with a smack on her arm.

"Let's see what we have here," Bob said as he brought the envelope from his back and checked for markings before opening it. He adjusted his position to pin Corrie against the wall with his body. When several of what was a large amount of twenty dollar bills fell to the floor, Bob's suspicion of Corrie being involved in the Grimaldi murder was vindicated. She attempted to escape, but a strike to her shoulder stopped her.

"Ouch," she cried, "Who are you, and what the hell do you think you're doing?"

"If you don't want to spend the rest of your life in prison, you better cooperate," Bob ordered.

Corrie turned her head to the door and hollered, "Help me. Please, someone help me." The closed door and the cacophonous noise in the main hall made it impossible for anyone to hear.

Quick firm slaps to her face got her attention. With iron in his voice, he said, "Cooperate. I won't say it again."

Corrie brought both hands to her reddening cheeks. Tears came to her eyes, and her body slumped.

Bob Dillon was breaking the rules and violating the oath and principles of his profession, but he was willing to sacrifice his license to get to the truth behind the Grimaldi murder. Of greater concern was his actions could jeopardize the case against Corrie and anyone involved with her. *Screw the consequences, I'm going to make this bitch crack.*

To maintain situational advantage, he grabbed the front of her jacket and lifted her several inches from the floor. "I know you were involved in the Grimaldi murder. I've had you under surveillance for some time. Come clean and I may go easy. If you don't, I'll beat the truth out of you." He didn't intend to get physical. It was a ploy to frighten the woman into revealing her role in the crime. He released pressure and her feet returned to the floor.

Sobbing, and shaking, she took a breath and asked, "How did you find out about this arrangement? Everything was so well planned."

Bob ignored her question. He wanted a full confession. "Don't try to deny that the envelope holds payoff money for your part in the murder of Frankie Grimaldi and for testifying against Dr. Manley."

Corrie grimaced at the accusation. "Are you a police detective? Before I say anything, what did you mean by going easy on me? Can we make a deal if I tell you what you want to know? I watch a lot of crime shows. Deals are made all the time."

Bob was pleased she assumed he was with the police and continued the deception, "If you tell me everything about your involvement and that of your accomplices, there's a good chance we'll be lenient on you." With emphasis, he added, "And I want you to understand I'm serious when I say you're to leave nothing out."

Cringing, Corrie said, "Don't worry, I'll tell you the whole story."

She was shaking to the point that Bob thought she might fall to the floor. He held her arms to steady her. He was in control, but experience taught he had a few minutes to get what he wanted. Corrie would realize there was no hard evidence linking her to the Grimaldi murder. There were a number of reasons she might be receiving money, some legal, some not, but not for committing murder.

Drawing from information gathered in his investigation of the Grimaldi case, and what he discovered at Union Station, Bob was certain of who murdered Frankie Grimaldi. His goal was to intimidate Corrie and force the truth from her. Bypassing preliminary questions, he went to the heart of the matter.

"Why did you, Dr. Warden, and Mai Manley murder Frankie Grimaldi?"

Corrie became hysterical, "No. It wasn't me, it was them. It was them." Her head rocked from side to side.

As he suspected. "So, you didn't want to murder Ms. Grimaldi?

It was all Dr. Warden's and Mai Faca's idea?" In court such questions would be challenged as leading to a conclusion, but in the transportation center there was no one to stop him.

"Yes, yes, that's it. You've got to believe me. That's just how it was."

Bob realized she was desperate and on the verge of a meltdown.

Corrie began to sob, and fluid dripped from her nose.

He said, "I'm going to advise you of your rights, and then I want to hear your side of the story. All of it."

Bob advised her although not sure of the exact legal wording. It didn't matter. Anyone could advise a person of their rights. The police would do it in the proper manner.

In the confines of the hallway off the main lobby of the train station, Corrie Hunter took deep breaths before relating the events surrounding the murder of Frankie Grimaldi. Her delivery was slow and calm. Listening to her story, Bob Dillon, who thought he had heard and seen the worst of what people do to hurt others, was appalled. When Corrie finished, Bob called the Hartford police and explained who he was and what had transpired. Officers were dispatched to Union Station.

Corrie was taken to the North Meadows police station in Hartford's North End. She agreed to submit to an interrogation without a lawyer present. The questions were to determine if there was enough evidence to hold her.

"If I cooperate, will the authorities go easy on me? Mr. Dillon said it was a good possibility," she asked.

Not surprising, upon repeating her story, the police and a judge found evidence to hold her as a material witness and an accomplice to murder. She was booked and placed in a cell.

During the interrogation she became aware of who Bob Dillon was. Although upset at allowing herself to be duped by him, her major concern was the seriousness of her situation and its potential consequences. Her hope was the method by which she had been caught would lead to a technicality her lawyer could pounce upon. In the interim, she decided to let the police have their way.

Although her cell phone had been confiscated, she was allowed use of a police phone. Insisting upon having legal representation present during further questioning, she made a call to Saul Cantor, her Willimantic attorney who agreed to come to her aid.

Corrie made a call to Jake at his Storrs condo. When he answered, a frantic voice said, "Dr. Warden, it's me, Corrie."

Planning on going to Mai's for a late dinner, he was spending the afternoon watching television. Since Bret had left the office, he didn't have the luxury of an entire day off on Wednesday. He worked in the morning and took the afternoon off. In order to lessen his workload, he was interviewing candidates to replace Bret.

He heard the anxiety in Corrie's voice. Whether working in the office or helping to plot murder, she was cold and calculating in her actions. On rare occasions having to do with her drug habit, she could become emotionally unstable. He suspected she had finished her last supply of drugs and needed more.

Making an effort to sound cheerful, he said, "Hi Corrie, how are you doing?"

Corrie said, "You've got to forgive me, Dr. Warden. You've got to know that I care for you and didn't want to do it. It's only that I have to think about myself."

God. Please not make it have anything to do with Frankie's murder. "Now, take it easy. What are you talking about?"

"I had to tell them, Dr. Warden."

"Tell who? What?"

"A private investigator and the Hartford police. They've locked me up. I'm not sure where I am, just in a Hartford police station somewhere in what they call the North Meadows." Taking a moment to swallow, "I told them what we did. Had no other choice. They knew about us."

It was Jake's turn to swallow. He and Mai were going to be charged with the crime they had pinned on Bret. He couldn't believe what he was hearing. There was ringing in his ears, and he felt lightheaded, but pressed for more information. "What did you tell them?"

Corrie began to relate what had happened beginning with the money pickup at Union Station. It wasn't long before Jake stopped listening. He hit *End Call* on his phone and left Corrie talking into dead air. He had to be with Mai. Not chancing a phone call that might make her panic, he left for Lover's Lane and the home slated to be his after they married.

As soon as the decision to book Corrie was made, Bob Dillon called Hubie Santos, "I've got important news."

"I'm guessing something big has come up concerning my nephew's case. Go ahead, let me have it."

"I've broken the Grimaldi murder. It happened pretty much like we thought."

"Give me a second," Hubie said, "I've got to sit."

The P.I. heard the sniffle and understood. He gave Hubie the moment he wanted before filling him in on the day's events.

When Bob finished, Hubie said, "Stay there. I'll be right down."

By the time Attorney Cantor arrived at the North Meadows station, Hubie had developed a plan to get Bret released from prison. The Willimantic lawyer was informed of Corrie's plight and recognized the best option for his client was to attempt to cut a deal with the State.

The two attorneys had faced each other in court and had an amicable working relationship. There was mutual respect on both sides. By working together, they had the best chance of freeing Bret and of lessening the life without parole sentence Corrie faced. The problem was to get the State to accept a plea deal in exchange for Corrie's testimony against her co-conspirators.

Getting word of the events at the station, Hartford's Chief of Police, Ty Adams, arrived and met with the attorneys.

"I want the team that prosecuted the case notified immediately and summoned here," Hubie demanded of Chief Adams.

Saul Cantor indicated his agreement.

Hubie Santos was determined to convince the prosecutors to make the deal with Corrie Hunter that he and Attorney Cantor had discussed among themselves. He would demand Judge Clarke, the Superior Court judge who had presided over the State of Connecticut v Manley case, be contacted. Hubie would ask her to begin the process of freeing Bret from his hellhole at the MacDougal-Walker Correctional Institute.

Chief Adams turned to Captain Sweeney, his second in command, "See to it," he ordered. "And call the Willimantic police. Have them issue arrest warrants for Warden and Faca."

Within the hour, three members of the prosecuting team were at the station. A tentative agreement between the State and Corrie Hunter was made. For testifying against Dr. Jake Warden and Mai Faca the State would recommend she be given a sentence of seventeen years in prison with eligibility for parole in ten years. If Corrie reneged on her commitment to testify and give a complete accounting of the crimes against Frankie Grimaldi and Dr. Bret Manley, the State would seek a sentence of life without parole. In spite of the irregularities in obtaining her confession, the prosecutors were confident they would get it.

Jumping at the deal, Corrie agreed to testify and signed a statement chronicling the events of Frankie Grimaldi's death. In her statement Bret Manley was exonerated of wrongdoing.

After the signing, Hubie said to her, "If you're fortunate enough to get out of prison in ten years, you'll be in your early fifties and should have many years of quality living ahead of you in a place far, far, from Connecticut.

Mai peered out the picture window and wondered why Jake had arrived before expected. When he walked into the kitchen, she saw by the look on his face that something terrible had happened. She ran to him. Grabbed both his arms and shook them. "What's wrong?" she cried, "What's the problem?"

Jake wiped sweat from his forehead with his sleeve although there was a chill in the air. He sat in one of the chairs placed around the table. She followed, took a chair opposite him, and waited for bad news.

"They've caught us," he said. "Corrie told them everything." He shook his head, "My guess is that they're looking for us. It won't be long before they show up here."

Mai blurted, "I was afraid this would happen. That bitch." Forcing herself to maintain control, she asked, "What about us?"

"We both know the answer. They'll make us pay for what we did."

Standing and staring at Jake who remained seated, "I couldn't handle it. What we will have to go through." She put her face in her hands and sobbed, "They'll take you from me. There is no way I could live without you."

"I couldn't live without you either . . . wouldn't want to," he responded.

In a halting voice she said, "I've prepared for this moment, but I need your help."

He understood. "I know . . . I've been thinking the same thing."

"It's just that I can't live without you," she repeated.

Jake stood. Went to her and held her.

Mai said, "So you know what we have to do. There's no other choice. Are you willing to die with me?"

"Yes," he replied.

They kissed their last kisses.

Mai went to the medicine cabinet in the bathroom and removed a jar filled with tablets. Handing it to Jake, she said, "Be sure to give me enough. Make sure I don't wake up."

The label said Valium, ten milligram capsules. It held enough for both to enter the dreamless sleep of death. He counted out ten tablets. "Take these," he said. "It won't be painful. Not like cyanide."

She filled a glass with water from the tap. Her back was to him, "Don't watch me do this. It shouldn't be among your last few memories of me." She took two swallows, faced him, and said as she handed him the glass, "Your turn to be strong."

Jake's voice cracked. "I will be, darling. I'll hold you until they begin to take effect, then, follow you."

"The sooner you do it, the sooner we'll be together," Mai said.

She went to the living room couch to lie down. "It's always been comfortable, a secure and good place to sleep, and now to die," she said. Jake sat so she could place her head on his lap. They held hands and waited. Mai yawned, and said, "Remember, be strong."

Jake nodded. It might be an hour or more before the Valium overwhelmed Mai, and Jake was prepared to wait. As promised, he would follow her. Since there was no one to insure he was successful, he planned to take twenty tablets of the tranquillizer. It would be enough to do the job.

A half hour passed and Mai was in a deep sleep and her breathing was shallow. Evening had arrived and light came from a small living room lamp Jake turned on. A shadow on Mai's chest showed slight movement with each breath. In the dim light he noted a bluish hue to her skin. It wouldn't be long before it was his turn to take the Valium. There was no doubt he would be as strong as she.

The noise of automobiles entering the driveway could be heard. Red and blue flashing lights reflected on the living room window. Laying Mai's head on the couch, Jake went to the window to confirm what he knew would be there. Police cars were parked on the front lawn. He went to Mai. She didn't appear to be breathing and had a look of serenity on her face. Even in death her beauty was exquisite.

Confident he had accomplished what Mai wanted, the

moment had come for him to end his life. There was little time. Not for Valium to work. They'd pump his stomach before it did its job. Jake looked about the kitchen. There was urgent knocking at the front door. Loud staccato voices emanated from the other side.

Hastening to a kitchen drawer, he opened it and found what he knew it held. He pulled out the largest of several knives, a chef's knife with an eight inch blade. It was a fitting weapon. He and Mai used cooking classes as a shield for their clandestine encounters.

The knocking on the door turned to pounding. Jake heard someone shout to break it. He had to act. He placed the tip of the blade below his sternum. The knife pointed at his heart. Like a samurai warrior committing hari-kari, he held the handle with two hands. Before he could think about what he was doing, he dropped to the floor and onto the knife. The force of the fall caused the blade to penetrate his upper abdomen and slice into his heart. As a surgeon, he would have appreciated the clean and efficient manner with which he did it. A hint of a smile on his face seemed to confirm in his last thoughts he knew he and Mai achieved what they had wanted since falling in love. They were together. In death.

As two Willimantic police officers were breaking the front door and others were waiting to swarm into the house, Mai arose from the couch and looked at Jake with tears in her eyes. Turning, she said, "Uncles," and grabbed her phone and purse from the counter and hurried out the back door. As she reached the path between her house and the Grimaldi house, she thought, Sorry Jake, I just couldn't do it. Entering the pathway, Mai's hand brushed the bulge of the Valium tablets in her pocket.

The scene the police burst upon was not to be forgotten. Turning on lights revealed the kitchen floor covered in blood. Care had to be taken not to slip. They recognized the man lying on his side in the center of the darkening puddle with a large knife protruding from his chest was Dr. Jacob Warden. His open eyes saw nothing.

"Search the place for the Faca woman," the officer in charge said.

It was nine p.m. when a conference call was initiated between Judge Clarke, the prosecutors—all seven had arrived at the station—and the defense lawyers. The judge was at her Manchester home. She had been faxed Corrie Hunter's confessional statement implicating Jacob Warden and Mai Faca as the murderers of Frankie Grimaldi and exonerating Bret Manley.

"I want to meet with Attorneys Shields and Santos at my home." Alice Shields was the head prosecutor. "I don't want the whole prosecuting team here. She can speak for them. We'll discuss the new findings and decide what to do. I'll authorize Chief Adams to have you brought here in a police vehicle."

The judge lived on a tree-lined suburban street in the city across the Connecticut River from Hartford. The three principals in the case were assembled in the study of her Tudor style home. Judge Clarke was at her desk. Hubie Santos and Alice Shields were sitting at each corner. They had presented the new evidence.

Looking from one to the other of her visitors, she asked, "Do you believe Dr. Manley is innocent of all wrongdoing in the Grimaldi murder?"

"Most definitely, your honor," Hubie replied. "There's no doubt of it."

As if reluctant to admit her numerous hours of work in the case had been for naught, Alice Shields answered, "It seems to appear that way, your honor."

"My duty is clear," the judge said, "I'm going to contact the Attorney General and recommend Dr. Manley be released from prison." The judge shook her head as she remarked, "We've done a grave injustice to an innocent man."

Pulling from one of the desk drawers a list of telephone numbers of State officials, Judge Clarke contacted Attorney General Rabin and informed him of what had transpired in the Manley case. It was approaching midnight when the Attorney General woke Governor Lyman.

After the AG informed her of the evening's events, the

Governor said, "The new evidence speaks for itself. Dr. Manley is innocent. Considering the media thrashing the State is about to take for imprisoning an innocent man, I'm issuing an immediate pardon for him."

In one of the fastest bureaucratic movements in Connecticut history, the Governor awoke Warden Connor of MacDougal-Walker and ordered him to prepare for the release of Bret as soon as practicable. "That," she said, "will be no later than tomorrow morning." She added, "Dr. Manley is to have all the State's resources at his disposal. If he has nowhere to go to, you are to arrange lodging for him at a Connecticut hotel at the State's expense for up to two weeks. In addition, I'm authorizing you to give him one thousand dollars in cash from the prison safe for his immediate personal needs. The money will be reimbursed from the State's slush fund.

As the governor spoke, Warden Connor repeated a series of, "Yes, Your Excellency" and, "As you wish, Ma'am," during verbal lulls.

"I'm sending a State trooper with the official pardon and a letter confirming all I've said." A final admonition was, "Keep in mind Dr. Manley has been wrongly imprisoned and deserves every courtesy the State can offer."

As soon as his discussion with the governor was over, Warden Connor called Lieutenant Spaulding, the head security officer of the overnight shift at the correctional institute. After reiterating the evening's events, he ordered, "Arrange for Manley to be discharged this morning." Shouting into the phone, "Do it personally."

Early Thursday morning Lieutenant Spaulding approached Bret's cell and rapped on the door with a flashlight. He shined its beam in Bret's face. "Manley, get up and come to the door."

Now what? Did Skunky rat on me? Tell his superiors I brought in contraband? If they found out about his cocaine business, he would try to make a deal with them and willingly sacrifice me to save his ass.

Sammy had been awakened and was sitting on the edge of his bunk feeling the effects of his Wednesday evening hit of cocaine.

Bret approached the cell door. "Yeah."

"I was sent to tell you, ahh, the Governor has pardoned you. You're going to be discharged this morning."

Bret did a double take. The unexpected news, unlike what he had become accustomed to, was beyond belief. He half expected Spaulding to laugh and say, "Only kidding, just wanted to see your reaction. You're needed in the kitchen to peel potatoes for the breakfast hash browns." When it didn't happen and the officer's expression indicated he was serious, Bret was overwhelmed with joy. He thought his smile might split the corners of his mouth.

Sammy approached the cell door and gripped the bars.

In unison, they uttered, "Why?"

Spaulding answered, "All I can say is something big developed in your case. In the morning, the warden plans to see you and fill you in on what happened. After that, I understand you can go whenever you want providing you have a place to stay. We'll even help with that." Spaulding extinguished his flashlight and walked toward the guard station beyond the metal door at the end of the hall. His heels clicked and echoed. The cellmates pressed their heads against the bars and strained to watch.

Bret noted Spaulding didn't have the decency to congratulate him.

Neither man moved nor spoke. From three cells to the left, an inmate began a rhythmic banging on the bars of his door with something hard. Other inmates followed, hitting their doors in sync with the first sounds. The cellblock filled with the cadence of objects banging against metal doors creating a rhythmic and deafening din of sound. Word of Bret's leaving had spread from one cell to the next until everyone was aware of what happened. The banging was the inmate's way of saluting. Even those who had no hope of leaving prison were striking the bars of their cells in honor of Bret. They celebrated because one of them had beaten the system. If one beat the system, they all had. In MacDougal-Walker's closed society, no man was an island.

Except Sammy. Seething with anger, he couldn't mask his jealousy of Bret's unexpected news. He returned to his cot and in a nasty voice said, "Get back to bed. I need my sleep."

Before going to sleep, he snorted another line and didn't hide it. When he replaced the coke in the toilet paper roll, Bret saw there was a quarter of the drug remaining from the previous delivery. Bret sensed that given an excuse Sammy would have slit his throat. His worst fear was the cocaine would stimulate the natural violence in the man and cause him to do something bad. He wasn't thinking sexual.

That night would be Bret's last chance to slip the mushroom powder into Sammy's cocaine. If he did, there would be two things to celebrate. It was a matter of waiting for Sammy to fall asleep. Proof of sleep came from the bone rattling noise emanating from Sammy's throat.

The packet of the poison mushroom powder was under Bret's mattress. He removed and opened it taking care not to spill anything. Packet in hand, he slid among the light and shadows created by the nightlights and made his way to the toilet. As practiced, within moments he opened the plastic bag of cocaine. All that remained was to add and mix his flour-like powder into the contents in the bag. He tilted the packet of mushroom powder and in the soft light saw it begin its slide toward the opening of the plastic bag.

As with the prostitute in Las Vegas, Bret stopped doing what he had intended to do. Although Sammy had done unspeakable things to him, he was unable to extract an eye for an eye. *Am I a better person than I pretend to be? Have I been all bravado without substance?* He had no answer.

Sammy's bag of cocaine was resealed and put into the toilet paper roll. The death cap powder and the torn remnants of its packaging went in the toilet and were flushed. Returning to his bed, he stared at the ceiling.

It might take a lifetime to understand or justify his actions. Why he completed ninety-nine percent of the plan to hurt Sammy and not the one percent. His confused mind ran in all directions.

During the course of that restless night . . . one that should have been among his happiest if he lived for a hundred years . . . he attempted to find an answer.

By morning, Bret had concluded that every person has demons. His were Mai Faca, Jake Warden, and Sammy Tompkins. The pain they caused was devastating. To avoid a mental breakdown, he had to believe he would make them pay for what they did. He'd "settle all the family business" as Michael Corleone did in The Godfather. That night proved he wasn't able to settle the family business. He was not Michael Corleone. He couldn't hurt Sammy and there was no reason to think it would have been different with Mai and Jake. *As a poet said, "I am that I am."*

How heavy do I journey on the way...

———

On the road: At eight that morning dressed in civilian clothes, Bret was led to Warden Connor's office. The happiness that engulfed him when given the news of his release had evaporated and been replaced by the uncertainty of his future.

When Bret entered the office, Warden Connor stood and greeted him, "Welcome, my dear boy. It was such good news we received last night, wasn't it?"

Bret said without emotion, "Yes, I was pleased to get it, but why have I been pardoned? I assume there was new evidence exonerating me."

The warden looked surprised, "You mean to tell me you haven't heard. It's been on television all morning. By now, almost everybody in the state and, indeed, the nation has heard about what happened."

"I purposely didn't watch TV or listen to the radio. I wanted to hear it from you. I've learned the media exaggerates or reports things wrong. They only want a story. The more sensational the better."

The warden smiled and nodded, "Yes, yes, I couldn't agree more." He arranged papers on his desk before beginning a rehearsed statement about the pardon. Warden Connor iterated what had taken place the day before that led to the conclusion Bret was innocent. He spoke of the suicide of Jake, and of the nationwide manhunt for Mai. "Shouldn't be long before we catch her."

Bret displayed no visible emotion upon hearing the news of the two people who had a profound effect on his life. Justice had been served in Jake's case. Although Mai had caused him unimaginable hurt, wedged in a small corner of his heart was a nugget of love for her. It would always be there. It was why he answered "yes" when Tommy Boy asked if he had a woman.

The warden said the framing of Bret for the death of Frankie Grimaldi wasn't the State's fault. "A jury convicted you on evidence that seemed valid at the time. Now we know better, and we're doing the right thing by freeing you without delay."

My reprieve has come a little late. A great deal has happened in prison that will scar me for the rest of my life. I won't sue, but I'm not about to say all is forgiven. His voice cracked as he said to the warden, "My regret is that the injustice Frankie Grimaldi endured can't be as easily undone."

Ignoring the comment, the warden continued, "I have more good news. Connecticut is ready to help you. I've made arrangements for you to be released to your mother's home, but if that isn't satisfactory, we'll house you for a time at a hotel of your choice."

"My mother's home is fine," Bret lied.

Removing an envelope from his top desk drawer, the warden handed it to Bret saying, "Take this. It's for you. It holds a thousand dollars the State wants you to have as well as the hundred and seventy-five dollars that was left in your prison account."

Accepting but not opening the envelope, Bret placed it in his front pants pocket. One of the lessons he learned in prison was other than a body cavity, a front pocket was the place to keep money or valuables.

Business taken care of, Warden Connor and a corrections officer escorted Bret on his return to the world.

The gray morning clouds over Suffield mimicked Bret's mood. Although glad to be free, more than a year and a half of his life had been wasted. The past couldn't be erased. As for the future, he had no aspirations. He wanted to be alone . . . to think . . . to be homeless . . . a hermit.

His mother and Uncle Hubie were parked in the administrative lot in front of the warden's office. When Bret and his escorts exited, Hubie, who was standing by the car, ran to him and gave a hug with backslaps, "Good to finally have you out of this place. We missed you," he said.

Bret spoke from his heart, "Words can't express how much I appreciate all you've done for me, Uncle Hubie."

Hubie turned to dry an eye.

They walked to the car. Bret leaned into the open car door and hugged and kissed his mother who was sitting in the back seat.

Choked with emotion, she said, "I love you, son. I'm so happy you're free and your name is cleared."

Hubie said, "Get in. We're going to take you home where you can recuperate." Looking toward the front gate, "And we'll keep the media away. Right now, they're staking out the front entrance. We should be able to get past them quickly."

Bret looked at his uncle and said, "No, I'm not going with you."

"What are you saying?" his mother reacted, "You've got to come home with us." Her hand reached out to him.

Hubie reinforced her words, "Yes, we'll help you with whatever you need. Now please, get in the car."

"I'm not going," Bret repeated. "I want to be alone and travel a bit. Clear my mind."

"Please," his mother implored.

"I've got to do this. I've decided. Don't worry, I'll be okay."

"Not going to try to find the Faca woman, are you?" Hubie said.

"No," Bret shook his head, "Believe me, she's the farthest thing from my mind." It wasn't the truth.

When Hubie and Rose couldn't dissuade Bret, Rose reached into her purse and Hubie produced his wallet.

Bret raised a palm toward them and took the cash envelope from his pocket. Waving it, he said, "This trip is going to be on the State."

He watched as the limousine pulled away and headed toward the front gate. In order to avoid the mass of reporters, the warden allowed Bret to leave by a side gate. The one undertakers used when picking up deceased inmates. It fit with the empty feeling in his gut. As he walked the narrow driveway leading to the gate, he thought about Sammy's next cellmate and what was in store for him. He hoped that man could handle Sammy better than he did.

With nothing but the clothes he was wearing and the cash in his pocket, Bret made the first decisions of his new life. He'd enjoy the long walk into downtown Suffield where he would purchase extra clothes, a good pair of sneakers, and a backpack. He planned to hitch rides and go wherever the driver was going. Y's and cheap hotels would be his home, and no-frills food would sustain him. By the time his money ran out, he should have discovered good soup kitchens and church groups that provided food and a place to sleep.

He didn't know when or where his travels would end. He'd keep going until he found within himself a new Bret Manley. Wiser and stronger than the one who began the journey. The old Bret Manley, he hoped, would be as dead as the man who betrayed him.

As the gate closed behind, a familiar song played in his head. About a man boarding a midnight train to Georgia, trying to rediscover his roots. He was that man.

He said he's going back to find
Ooh, what's left of his world,
The world he left behind
Not so long ago …

www.ingramcontent.com/pod-product-compliance
Lightning Source LLC
Chambersburg PA
CBHW071856220626
47052CB00002B/145